The Pallampur Predicament

A Superintendent Le Fanu Mystery

Brian Stoddart

CRIME WAVE PRESS

The Pallampur Predicament

This paperback edition first published in 2014 by

Crime Wave Press
Flat D, 11th Fl. Liberty Mansion
26E Jordan Road
Yau Ma Tei, Hong Kong
http://www.crimewavepress.com

ISBN 978 988 13510 4 3

Cover Design by Hans Kemp

One

Le Fanu wondered how this Madras day could be any worse. The weather was its only saving grace. This close to Christmas (an odd celebration in India, he thought) it was bearable, seventy-five degrees Fahrenheit with little humidity, by local standards anyway. Just as well, wearing full dress uniform on parade like this was torture. He had arrived in Madras seventeen years earlier, in 1905, to begin his Indian Police Service career. In the hottest weather back then, recruits "called" on the martinet wives of senior officers to be received into "society." It was laughable, but serious. A "calling" faux pas blighted several careers because some of those women were far more frightening than their husbands. Most recruits fainted at some point, dressed in full morning suit and top hat while waiting outside a suburban gate to be received as the temperature climbed well past one hundred.

"Parade, Atten-SHUN!"

The command snapped him back. This display of police force along the Marina Beach front near Fort St. George was more about reminding the populace who was in control than honouring the troops being inspected by the Governor. The war years aside, 1922 was the most difficult Le Fanu had experienced since that first one. Indian National Congress leaders in the Madras Presidency followed Mahatma Gandhi's Non Co-Operation campaign to the letter. Police, military and civil service personnel faced boycotts, demonstrations and withdrawal of services for months. Le Fanu's barber of fifteen years refused to cut his hair, until a local Congress leader's slight prompted the resumption of normal service.

Even now, corralled behind a military cordon but not bored let alone cowed after months of demonstrations, thousands of Madrasis and countryside recruits chanted slogans and waved placards at the police parade, and especially at the Governor:

"LEAVE INDIA!"

"INDIA FOR THE INDIANS"

"LONG LIVE MAHATMAJI"

"GO HOME!"

Dressed mostly in the simple, homespun cotton cloth Gandhi made the symbol of India's struggle, they had arrived at the ground from all over the city and surrounding towns hours before the police. Wandering snack vendors kept up a steady supply for those needing food. Here and there, speakers addressed smaller groups, stirring opposition to the British presence. Street musicians boosted their meagre incomes. The assembled throng, growing by the minute, produced constant noise so that parade members could scarcely follow their commander's shouted instructions. Le Fanu knew this crowd would remain for a long time. British rule in India faced its toughest challenge yet as demands grew for independence and self-rule.

Superintendent Christian Jolyon Brenton Le Fanu, MC, stood reluctantly in the parade's front rank alongside Deputy Inspectors-General, the Commissioner and Assistant Commissioners. Trim enough; he was sturdy and six feet tall, fit from playing a lot of golf in the past two years because his empty house was especially unwelcoming at weekends. Under the police cap the hair remained fair if sporadically grey-flecked. His skin had not yet worn from the Indian climate. The grey eyes remained curious. As head of the innovative Crime

Unit he was tolerated by most police officers, but despised by several, particularly the rotund, sweating figure accompanying the Governor around the ranks.

Inspector-General Arthur Jepson had once been Le Fanu's district boss, and that had ended badly. A couple of years ago he was then the surprise, compromise choice as Commissioner of Police for the city. He clashed again with Le Fanu, himself appointed by the previous I-G, Sir Maurice Wilson, to head the Crime Unit that used investigation methods created by the Austrian criminologist, Hans Gross. Jepson hated the idea, the unit, the methods and Le Fanu, not necessarily in that order. However, the unit's continuing success blunted Jepson's attack. He tolerated Le Fanu's team, but with ill will and constant threats of closure. Adding to Le Fanu's pain, Jepson somehow became I-G. Wilson was forced to retire, taking blame for shooting deaths caused by Jepson's incompetence at a demonstration. Le Fanu and Jepson had sparred regularly since.

Jepson and the Governor walked slowly along the first rank as crowd noise escalated further. When the pair reached Le Fanu, the Governor stopped.

"Morning, Le Fanu. All well?"

"Your Excellency. Yes, thank you, sir."

"Good man, your unit's doing excellent work. Pity Special Branch wasn't doing likewise. We'd have less of that racket if it was." He gestured towards the demonstrators now straining to breach the cordon of police and military personnel holding them back.

Le Fanu watched Jepson's legendary temper rise to the imagined personal cut. The Governor spoke his mind. Since arriving in Madras four years earlier, Willingdon had constantly derided the Presidency's conservative civil service and its opposition to political reform.

"Jepson," continued the Governor, peering from underneath the curved black velvet hat topped with ostrich plumes that crowned the ostentatious uniform, “please spare Le Fanu immediately after this little display. I need his advice. Le Fanu, could you come to Government House at, say, eleven this morning?”

They all knew it was command rather than request, Jepson livid at being excluded. He held back as the Governor moved on.

“Le Fanu, as soon as you leave that meeting, you report to me. That clear?”

As Humpty Dumpty already fallen stomped away, fuming, Le Fanu sensed the arrival of a case complicated more by internal dispute and suspicion than by external villainy. If the Governor was involved, that was inevitable.

After another half hour of preening, the parade was dismissed. The Governor was driven off in a recently purchased Rolls Royce. That, thought Le Fanu, summed up the British image problem. The Government announced serious economic woes for the Presidency and prospective cuts to services at exactly the time the car turned up. Its cost would keep several villages, perhaps even a district or two going for a decade or more. It gave the local Congress yet another opportunity to castigate British rule as insensitive, uncaring and unwelcome.

Crowds streamed along the road and the sands, reinforcing the unwelcome message to departing police. Placards were waved vigorously, noise levels raised even further. Looking on nervously, armed guards awaited their own orders to retire, alert to any sign of a surge among the demonstrators. The human wall was holding, just. Tension rose, nerves were tested. Several recent demonstrations had ended in gunfire, and deaths. One untimely move and the same could happen here.

Le Fanu ran his fingers inside the stiff collar, trying to ease chafing caused by the sweat worked up even on this mild day. He removed his officer’s cap, clamped it under his arm and used his free hand to brush back the still-thick hair. At his fortieth birthday three months ago, he found himself staring into the mirror, wondering how he looked and what he was doing with his life.

That introspection passed, but some reflections remained. A parade started any day poorly, let alone one when a messy problem had already thumped on to his desk. Was this what he wanted to do for the next ten or fifteen years, even if the politics allowed? He was still considering that and other options when up rolled a squat, dark, beaming uniformed man with a flourishing beard and short, black, brushed back hair.

"Good morning, sir. Did you enjoy the parade?"

Le Fanu laughed. "Good morning Habi. Of course not. Did you?"

"Not at all, sir. We might've been off catching criminals."

Sergeant Mohammad Habibullah had joined Le Fanu at the Crime Unit when it had started and he, too, was despised by Jepson and other conservatives. Not only was Habi Indian but Muslim to boot, and in Jepson's narrow view unfit for positions best held by British personnel. To make it worse, Habi was a brilliant and therefore untouchable detective. He had spent two years at a minor English public school before the war and had developed perfect, idiomatic English to match his fluent Hindi, Telugu and Tamil. By rights, thought Le Fanu, Habi should be an officer already but that would not happen while Jepson was I-G, even though the sergeant had solved several difficult cases.

"I see you had an audience with the Governor, sir." The smile widened.

"Very observant, Habi. I'm bidden to see him at GH shortly."

"And I'm assuming the I-G stayed just that little bit longer to instruct you to report to him immediately at the conclusion of said audience?"

Le Fanu appreciated shrewdness, it made Habi an excellent policeman. When India gained independence, people like Habi would make it work. Le Fanu was in a Madras minority, of one he sometimes thought: Europeans who thought India should gain autonomy soon and full independence eventually. Its people were ready and the British bereft of ideas. That view ensured his unpopularity. Too many Europeans considered his support for Indian colleagues as a betrayal of the British cause, whatever that was now. His unpopularity was greater still within the small European civil community clinging doggedly to a rapidly fading way of life. Indians no longer obeyed the British unquestionably. More and more asked questions the British rarely had answers for. That added numbers and momentum to Gandhi's movement and prompted further political debate.

"Right again, Habi. He's angry about not being invited to the meeting, of course."

"Any idea what it's about?"

"None at all. So far as I know, His Excellency has no direct interest in any of our cases. Do you know of anything?"

"Not really, sir. There's that up-country embezzlement matter, but it's so low level I doubt it would interest him."

One current investigation involved a European merchant living in one of the northern districts. Financially pressed because of poor trading in wake of a crop failure, he siphoned drought relief funds away from local peasants. District officials uncovered the story, the nationalist press found out and published it as further evidence of British perfidy. But it was a small storm in a tiny teacup, and the Governor rarely touched that sort of crockery.

"I agree, Habi. There must be something else we don't know about. He did mention in Jepson's presence he was unhappy about Special Branch's poor performance, but I doubt he'd discuss that with me."

"He might want you to take over SB, sir."

These moments often made Le Fanu think he was being

made fun of. Habi's sense of humour was wicked.

"He may think a pro-Indian would make a better fist of it, sir," Habi continued, straight-faced.

Yes, he was being teased. "Quite so, Habi, the force and the European Association would be thrilled if I ran Special Branch."

They laughed, knowing European and service conservatism was growing rather than shrinking, a dangerous turn.

Le Fanu's driver bowled them south along the Marina towards police headquarters opposite the beach at the Elliot's Road corner. Le Fanu never tired of the sea view. It reinforced him against the daily pressures. Solving crimes was tough enough without doing it amidst internal dissent, bickering and enmity from above and below.

The distinctive white, two storied headquarters building came into view. Madras had its first policeman in 1659, and this had been headquarters since 1865. It was overcrowded because business had grown, dramatically so in recent years. Le Fanu thought it symbolic that the building was originally a Masonic Lodge. They still ran the city, and he was not a member.

Two

Looking into his office he thought, not for the first time, he should tidy up. Papers and files elided off over-packed shelves into tottering columns of other papers and files. The desk was lost under a paper avalanche. He was not sure how things had reached this point. Jepson increased the caseload at a ridiculous rate to try and break his bete noire. Maintaining the bookwork was impossible but, even so, the chaos was not Le Fanu's style. Jepson's pressure might have created a psychological reaction, but Le Fanu knew he must change this look because it denied the ordered, logical police work mandated by Hans Gross. Any gap between illusion and reality would only advantage Jepson.

Le Fanu spied the latest addition to his desk mountain, this morning's arrivant file. Its first few pages suggested that if any of this was proved and became public knowledge, the Government would look bad at an especially inopportune moment. And now having responsibility for the matter, Le Fanu would-be the convenient scapegoat in any Jepson blame deflection game.

Superficially, it looked simple. Ramsheed was a Telugu-speaking district in the Presidency's north. Its Collector, the district's principal Indian Civil Service officer responsible for about two million people, was charged with taking a substantial bribe from a local landowner. The landowner was a supporter of the Indian National Congress whose leaders had organised this morning's demonstration. If the story was correct, chaos wasn't far off.

The ICS was the "Steel Frame" around which India's administration had rebuilt after the 1857 Mutiny shock. In south India, Collectors gained huge powers over districts like Ramsheed, which was amongst India's largest. The Collector was well-titled. He collected land and other taxes that allowed Britain to run the country. In the years following the Mutiny, senior Madras administrators had rooted out district deal-making. No ICS man had been charged for corruption since the 1870s. If the Collector of Ramsheed was guilty, Congress had gained another propaganda tool.

Then there was the alleged bribe-giver, the Rajah of Pallampur. South India had fewer wealthy landlord princes than other Indian regions. The nearest was the Nizam of Hyderabad, one of the richest people in the world. Le Fanu thought immediately of Roisin McPhedren, now in Hyderabad running the household for an English general serving the Nizam. Two years ago she was Le Fanu's lover and housekeeper. Ro had left Madras, thinking her Anglo-Indian heritage would wreck his career if their affair became public. Conservative Europeans despised mixed race people more than they despised Indians. She now sent him a weekly letter. Each one reinforced his guilty thought that he should have been stronger and kept her in Madras. For that reason, he replied rarely. Gutless, he knew.

However, the Presidency had substantial landlords, none more important than the Rajah of Pallampur. He ruled over some three hundred square miles and 400,000 people north-west of Madras. The Rajah had attended school in England, followed by one year's Sandhurst military training before inheriting the fiefdom from his father who promptly retired to the Riviera without his consort whom he replaced with a younger French model. That sequence of events saw the-then

Governor of Madras castigated by London's India Office bureaucrats who feared anything remotely radical. The Governor devolved as much criticism as possible to his underlings, and Le Fanu remembered highly qualified and capable people banished to dry, barren station districts.

The new Rajah was an odd mixture, able but quixotic so far as Members of the Board of Revenue and senior Secretariat officers were concerned. These days he was the only subject on which those two perennial rivals agreed. One wag had suggested the Rajah had achieved something unique in three hundred years of British rule in Madras; he had created Government unity. The only problem was that the unity was entirely against him. Neither camp trusted him. Despite his British training and upbringing, he now entertained senior Congress leaders, and a Special Branch report detailed his secret meetings with M.K. Gandhi, the Mahatma. That enraged Government leaders for whom Gandhi was unfathomable. One board man memorably had described the Mahatma as a "disgraceful, snivelling, ungrateful little turd." That was diplomatically unsound, but it did indicate the level of fear Gandhi raised in the administration.

The Rajah upset the establishment even more by marrying a foreigner. And it was not even an Englishwoman who might have been just barely acceptable. While in Australia buying horses, he had spied another filly whom he had married within a year. Charlotte Lacey was a Sydney lawyer's daughter, and a Roman Catholic. There was scarcely one of those in senior Madras ranks, or junior ones for that matter. The Rajah was pilloried. New Delhi and London barraged Madras with ideas on how to manage the maverick, but he proved unmanageable.

Le Fanu anticipated a publicity nightmare. If the file was correct, an ICS officer was corruptly in the pay of a local noble supporting Indian independence. Newspapers across India and around the world would relish that. The Madras

Government would look like it had lost control of its service and leading supporters. That would bring untold wrath from London and New Delhi. Carnage would cascade through the Madras ranks.

This rats' nest was delivered personally from the office of the Chief Secretary, Sir Charles Whitney. He was the archetypal ICS man who had smoothly risen to the top. Essentially a law and order man, he was not fond of political reform. But, oddly, he was also one of Le Fanu's few local supporters. His support had followed Le Fanu's successful handling of an earlier case, the murder of a visiting Englishwoman. The Crime Unit had identified the murderer and had uncovered a local drug ring led by the city's leading businessman. Whitney had been grateful that Le Fanu kept the investigation at a discreet level amidst the drama of Gandhi's passive resistance campaign. They had kept in touch ever since.

The envelope also contained a personal note asking Le Fanu to telephone and make arrangements to meet at Whitney's Nungambakkam home. That meant Whitney was worried. By meeting there instead of the Secretariat, this would be "off the books." That troubled Le Fanu because with the Chief Secretary keeping matters confidential, Le Fanu would have to advise the I-G selectively. That would feed Jepson's paranoia. Originally, Le Fanu reported directly to the Commissioner of Police for Madras. But when Jepson became I-G he changed that report line, so anxious was he to control Le Fanu. Their relationship was poisonous.

Le Fanu dialled Whitney's private number. "Good morning, Sir Charles, I've looked over that file. I see why you want to meet."

"Thanks for looking at it so quickly, L.F., I know you had other matters to deal with today. The parade go well?" A chuckle came down the line. Le Fanu imagined the dapper little man sitting behind his desk, large cigar alight.

"Hardly, Sir Charles. It was so bad it makes even this file

look simple. That should tell you something."

The chuckle continued. "I hear you're to meet the Governor later this morning."

"Is it about this file?"

"That'll be part of it, I imagine, but there'll be other things of interest as well."

"Any clues?"

"Could well be some other confidential matters the Governor's bothered about." Le Fanu knew he would get no more over the telephone. They would meet at six that evening.

He looked over the file more carefully. A "secret source" suggested the Rajah of Pallampur bribed the Collector, James Westshire, to overlook legal indiscretions committed by the Rajah's principal administrator. Thugs in the administrator's pay had handed out beatings to rival crooks in what seemed a dispute over protection money. The source suggested Westshire overlooked the beatings in exchange for a substantial payment to relieve debts he'd racked up in a private business selling mineral deposits. If this was correct, Westshire was in double trouble. Since the nineteenth century scandals, ICS rules banned officers from running private businesses.

The reliability of the secret source was an immediate issue. It could be someone trying to discredit the Collector, the Government of Madras, or the Rajah of Pallampur, or all of the above. That was the first question to put to Whitney. Who was the source and what was known about the person?

He looked at his watch, nearly time to set off for the Willingdon meeting. Le Fanu left his second floor office at the back of the building, descended the outside stairs and entered what were once the stables. He kept his motorbike there now, something else that stood him out from his colleagues. The 1,000 cc Indian Powerplus had come back from the war with him, and most Madras Europeans looked at it sideways. It was "too American," and too individualist.

He wheeled it out, kicked it into life and roared out the

gate, up onto the Marina and turned right, heading eventually for Luz Church Road that led towards his Mylapore home, but only after enjoying the cool breeze and salt air drifting off the Bay of Bengal. He would reach home, park the bike and have his driver take him to Government House, no sense drawing undue attention to himself with the bike there.

Three

He reached the Governor's outer office just before eleven, still wondering what was in store. When Willingdon had first arrived in Madras he had preferred the Governor's residence out at Adyar, so given the travel distance, meetings were time-consuming. As political strife had grown, he'd decamped to the Government complex residence on the lower reaches of the Cooum River, opposite the island with its Gymkhana Club golf course. It was easier to meet quickly at the main Government House. Major roads leading into the complex were now sealed off by police and army contingents so the Governor was not hemmed in by demonstrators. Madras clearly was not its pre-war relaxed self.

Willingdon's office door opened, the Principal Secretary showed Le Fanu into the cavernous room having taken his order for tea. The Governor advanced, hand out in greeting.

"Good morning again, LF, and thanks for coming over." He steered the superintendent towards a small table with two chairs set against a window looking over an expansive lawn. "Good show this morning but it won't produce any benefits for us. And no need to be on your guard, nothing'll be reported back. Getting on any better with Jepson?"

Willingdon was tall, angular, a military man with a presence, and he was well-informed.

"I think you know the answer, sir. You'll also know I think we're not handling this Gandhi campaign to our best advantage. The repression is losing us public support."

"Yes, I know your views, LF, and see some sense in them. Not sure I agree totally, though one or two people in Delhi do. The real point, I think, is that we've never faced anything like this so the brain's trust is stretched."

The tea arrived along with snacks. Willingdon looked tired, Le Fanu thought. Dealing with this at local level while trying to keep Delhi happy would test any leader.

"But I didn't get you here to talk about this, well, at least not directly," the Governor continued.

Le Fanu wondered if the Special Branch offer was about to arrive.

"You'll have seen the Pallampur file Whitney sent you this morning?"

"I have, sir, Sir Charles and I will discuss that this afternoon."

"Good, I know we'll get a sensible view out of you, and the Chief Secretary will ask you to do some digging. Even if he's innocent, Westshire's been a bloody fool, and we know the Rajah of Pallampur for an even bigger one."

Le Fanu said nothing, wondering where this was going.

"There's another dimension, though," Willingdon continued. "We have information suggesting that the Rajah or his employees are running an extortion racket. The funds raised are used to buy arms and ammunition. If that's so, the Rajah's dalliance with Gandhi makes some of us even more nervous. Gandhi's bad enough, but if some of these chaps get armed it'll be even worse."

"But, sir, all Gandhi's messages stress non-violence. He's appalled when things get out of hand."

Willingdon thought for a moment. "That's true, LF, but he can't control everybody. And we know some of the northern radicals want an armed movement. Nothing like that down here so far as we know, and I want it kept that way." He took some more tea.

"Indeed, sir, I agree, the situation's bad enough without a flood of arms reaching the wrong places."

"And one of those wrong places is not far from the Rajah's home turf."

Le Fanu got the reference immediately. A few months earlier, tribal communities in the north around Rampa had begun protesting their restricted access to forests. Rampa was on the edge of Pallampur's territory. The rebels had killed several officials, policemen and soldiers. Affronted, Willingdon had appointed a tough New Zealander to stop the uprising, but that had proven difficult. If more arms reached this gang then the rebellion could spread.

"The problem, LF," Willingdon continued, "is that Special Branch is more useless than ever. I've spoken with Jepson and mentioned your name. No secrets here, you know, he hates your guts. So I don't want you to take over Special Branch, but I've insisted this matter gets switched to your unit. Hope you don't mind."

There was no choice, of course. "Not at all, sir, we'll do our best. When will the files get transferred?"

"They're on their way now. Unfortunately, though, that's not all. What do you know about this merchant corruption case up in Changarore?"

Now Le Fanu was surprised. Like Habi, he doubted the Governor would know or care about that case. Perhaps he had missed something.

"Pretty low level matter, sir. Gerald Taylor runs a grain trading business there. The crop returns were low this year, and he was already under financial pressure following some poor commercial decisions. When drought relief measures began, local traders got preference to help spread funds around. Taylor had the bright idea of short weighting his sacks, so received about thirty per cent more funds than he warranted. A smart local clerk weighed a couple of sacks on impulse, found the shortage. The local police were called in, there was a leak so the news got to the press, and we know what happened then."

Willingdon nodded. "Yes, that's all so. But what do you know about Taylor?

"Not much, sir. The matter's petty theft, really, so we haven't dug too deeply. He's been in Changarore about five years, has his family with him, doesn't come to Madras much, and has nothing else on his record."

"Could you do some more checking, please, LF? I know this seems a minor issue and an odd request, but Taylor might not be all that he seems."

"Of course, sir, but it might help if you gave me some more clues."

"I'm told he's well connected back in England, and that the political strand might become an issue. That's all I have, but given the present situation I don't need any more surprises."

"Does London have anything more on him, sir?"

"Oddly enough, no, and I don't want to push too much in case his connections are as good as I'm told they are."

Le Fanu left, concerned. The Pallampur issue was dangerous and significant, yet Willingdon was more bothered by the Changarore case. And he had not revealed his source on Taylor. The murk was mounting and they had scarcely started.

When he reached the office, Le Fanu and Habi set up their investigation blackboards for the two separate cases, Pallampur (with separate boards for the Rajah and James Westshire) and Changarore, chalking up the currently minimal information.

Habi was sceptical. "This Changarore matter will fizzle out. Taylor's a petty thief who ran short of funds and saw the Government as an easy solution. We'll throw the book at him, he'll get a short prison term, then be told to leave India, unofficially of course."

"You're probably right, Habi, but the Governor's interest gives it an edge I don't like. We'll need to keep alert. Pallampur will be the difficult one, but we'll run the two concurrently for now. Have the Pallampur files reached us from Special Branch yet?"

"Yes, came in shortly before you arrived back from the Governor's. He didn't waste any time there, did he? The Special Branch delivery man looked most unhappy."

"I can imagine. We won't have any friends there now, if we had any before. Special Branch being Jepson's favourite outfit makes it worse. Anyway, you look through those files and I'll go back over the Taylor details to see if there's anything we've missed. Then I'll draw up some additional questions. Also, we'd better make sure those SB files are secure. Put them in the safe, and we'll sign them in and out. That way we're covered."

Habi left for his office, Le Fanu sat down to the Changarore file. Thinking the matter closed, he had ignored the papers for several days. There was little to read, really. Looking over the file and remembering Willingdon's comments, Le Fanu realised they knew precious little about Taylor's life, background, connections or business affairs. Perhaps they had assumed too much. If so, he and Habi had better reread Hans Gross' Criminal Investigation as well as the file. Sir Maurice Wilson had read the Indian edition of Gross when it had first appeared and established the Crime Unit to follow its principles. So far they had been successful, despite the opposition to modern investigative approaches raised by many force members, led by Jepson. At any time, the smallest mistake could see the unit terminated. So if they had assumed too much in the Taylor case, they must fix that.

Le Fanu constructed some questions he thought they should now ask about Taylor, and reached for the current edition of the Asylum Press Almanack. Though less detailed than in the old days, the Almanack remained the starting point for assembling any biography because it listed all Europeans and "leading" Indians in the Presidency.

Taylor's entry was brief, conveying little about his United Kingdom background and education. That was unusual. Le Fanu was surprised he had not realised that earlier. Taylor had arrived in 1915. He did not serve in the war. Interesting. Neither age nor birth date was listed, but he had two school age children so must have been technically eligible for service. That produced another question, or two: why had Taylor not served, and why had he come to Madras while the war was on? Taylor had gone on to Changarore almost immediately he had reached Madras. Two more questions: why Madras, then why Changarore? Taylor had started his trading business as soon as he had arrived in Changarore. Further questions: how had that been financed and where was the paperwork?

Le Fanu enjoyed the analytical work, and drew heavily on the Gross principles. It was a pity others in the force were not as curious and open to new ideas, he thought. If anything, as political demonstrations grew police minds shut ever more tightly. That promised an unhappy future.

So did a meeting with Jepson but he could not delay it. Doing so in the past had produced considerable grief. Le Fanu called his driver who steered the car between, around and sometimes almost over pedestrians, cyclists, bullock carts, noisy trucks and the few pony carts still in the city as they crossed towards Egmore. Le Fanu wondered if all the new cars and trucks helped India. Probably not but it was inevitable, like Jepson's foul mood in every meeting with his least favourite person. After the usual long and deliberate wait, Le Fanu was shown in. The Commissioner was pacing up and down, thrashing his polished boots with a riding crop. As the man grew more portly, the force's "Jockey" nickname became more ironic.

"Well, Le Fanu, what d'you have to say for your bloody self?"

Yet another good start.

"About what, sir?" Le Fanu could not help himself, a fault,

he knew.

"That fucking meeting with the Governor, of course."

"Yes sir, of course, sir. His Excellency wanted to discuss the Pallampur case, and the Changarore matter."

"What in particular?"

"His Excellency wants me to do more checking into both matters, sir"

"Why?"

"Not sure, sir, probably just wants to keep on top of things."

"Is that all? He asked you over there for that?"

"Yes, sir."

"You know, Le Fanu, if you're concealing things I'll have your balls cut off and made into earrings for my wife. Be warned."

Le Fanu thought it an odd gift idea, but realised Jepson was on another ill-tempered and vituperative campaign. He must be even more on guard than normal.

"Very good, sir, I'll keep that in mind, sir."

He escaped under a fusillade of insults from the Commissioner, found the car and headed back to police HQ.

Four

During mid-afternoon, he and Habi updated the investigation boards and reviewed available information. Not nearly enough, as usual. Le Fanu suggested they had assumed too much about the Changarore case, and chalked up his new questions about Gerald Taylor.

Habi recounted the Pallampur story. There was little beyond what they knew already, but Habi had details on some points mentioned by the Governor. The Rajah's thugs were thought to have set up an arms smuggling operation, coming into the Presidency on small ships that landed at unpatrolled fishing villages up and down the coast north and south of Madras. Given the extensive coastline, smuggling was a regular activity the authorities could not stem. Goods came in from around India and further afield like the Straits Settlements on the other side of the Bay of Bengal. That trade was mainly in food, liquor, cigarettes and, occasionally, people needing to enter India unofficially. They were usually Indians with criminal records or European vagrants likely to be turned back at immigration. Arms and ammunition were not normally part of the trade so the Pallampur initiative, coinciding with the Rampa rebellion, alarmed the senior officials in the know.

The source of the arms was unclear, and there were no confirmed destinations even if the suspicion was Rampa. Special Branch reports suggested rifles, revolvers, ammunition and even grenades were being stockpiled. Again, the reasons were unclear, but the unstated assumption was that the arms would aggravate an already agitated political situation. Le Fanu confronted that new assumption. They were mounting up.

"Habi, does that make any sense to you?"

"Not really, sir. The Mahatma doesn't want violence and neither does the Congress. A violent movement's too hard to control. It would damage the nationalist cause here and abroad. There's sympathy for Congress in countries like America, but if the movement turned to guns and violence that support would decline."

"That's what makes me wonder why this suggestion has arisen. There's no direct evidence the arms are here, just suggestions they've been smuggled in. The Governor 's worried about Special Branch, and I understand why if this is the best it can do. There's more rumour than fact. It almost looks like the idea's been planted deliberately for some reason. Who wrote the report, Habi?"

"There's no name on it, but I'll find out."

"Good. Let's list this on the Pallampur board as a rumour until we get firmer evidence. You spend the rest of the day on this, then later we'll decide whether to concentrate more on Pallampur or Changarore."

Le Fanu worried about the obscure nature of this report coinciding with a similarly obscure one about Westshire. It could be coincidence, or not. Then there was the so-far secret nature of Willingdon's source on Gerald Taylor. It seemed unlikely, but these disparate developments had a similar feel to them.

Habi went off in search of more information. Le Fanu prepared for Nungambakkam and his private audience with the Chief Secretary. He understood Whitney's concern about the Collector of Ramsheed but was bothered by the prospect of this meeting. Too much was left unstated in the files.

He filled in time feebly attempting to reduce his paper mountains, gathered the files for his meeting, put them in a battered briefcase, and called for the car.

Le Fanu had the driver take a circuitous route, partly to time his arrival but mainly to cover his tracks. Secrecy seemed paramount, and that put him on another collision course with Jepson. The usual direct route to Whitney's would register his presence there around official circles within minutes. So they left headquarters by the back gate onto Elliott's Road, turned left and wended their way through the maze of streets leading into Triplicane before crossing over Mount Road near the Thousand Lights mosque. That led into the meandering, dusty wide streets of Nungambakkam with its large houses, spacious grounds and quiet prosperity. These were the mansions of senior administrators, wealthy landowners, business magnates (especially old money ones), and local legal luminaries.

They arrived at Whitney's ten minutes before six so Le Fanu had the driver continue through the area to check they were not being observed. Finally, they drove through a high gate adjoined by an even higher hedge towards a large house set behind wide lawns on which several servants squatted, removing weeds and clipping errant grass strands. Le Fanu had been here before, but was still struck by how most senior administrators cut themselves off from the India they governed. Whitney was good at his job, but it was a long time and a big mental distance from when he last experienced the hurley-burley of ordinary daily life and people. This oasis kept the Chief Secretary away from what was happening on the streets of Madras. His neighbours shared that rarefied world. Whitney was no drone, though.

Le Fanu was met at the front steps by a uniformed servant who showed him into a waiting room inside the front door. It was small, lined with pictures of the King and Queen and the previous Viceroy, Lord Chelmsford, who initiated the Indianisation so loathed by the Madras ranks. Whitney and his wife appeared in other photographs with Willingdon and earlier Madras Governors. There was a picture of the Chief Secretary with the Duke of Connaught who visited Madras the year before in an unsuccessful attempt to boost Raj morale and impress the locals. The furniture was simple but Le Fanu noticed three tables bearing medieval bronzes of Hindu deities notably Ganesh, the remover of obstacles. Whitney was not all he appeared to be, Le Fanu knew that, but this was new. And Ganesh might well come in handy.

Sir Charles Whitney walked in, still dressed crisply after a full day at the office. His suit was dark and double-breasted. Le Fanu wondered if by dressing that way Whitney was defiantly drawing attention to his short stature. The wing collared white shirt was immaculate, as was the knotted dark silk tie that could nearly be seen reflected in the black shoes. They were as highly polished as a Horse Guards officer's boots. The pince nez dangled off the right lapel at the end of a dark silk ribbon, and Whitney gripped a newly-lit large cigar in his right hand. Le Fanu had never seen the Chief Secretary without one.

"Hello there, LF, thanks for coming. I lit a new one knowing it was no use waiting for you."

He waved the cigar about. The voice was warm but controlled. Whitney had run the Presidency for seven years, a long time for a Chief Secretary yet he was still comparatively young. Gossip had him soon being lifted into a senior position in Delhi. That was rare for someone from Madras whose administration was reputed elsewhere in India to be conservative, negative, incompetent and truculent. Whitney had none of those attributes.

"Thank you, sir, quite right." Le Fanu was a non-smoker, almost the only virtue he brought back from the war, he sometimes thought.

"Let's go outside, I've had a table set. That way we won't be disturbed."

Whitney walked into the corridor then through a door onto a verandah, down some steps and off to a secluded small garden under old trees with shading branches. A small table, a bottle of Glenmorangie, two glasses and a water jug awaited, along with a plate of vadas and mint flavoured yoghurt. Le Fanu had been astonished a couple of years earlier to find that Whitney preferred local food to the grim English fare clung to in most official houses. The man was a paradox.

"Sorry if this seems mysterious, LF, but we've a problem you might help sort out." He sat, poured two whiskeys and handed one to Le Fanu. Neither man used the water jug.

"Quite alright, sir. You'll know I met the Governor earlier and he has us looking into the arms issue, but we don't think the report makes any sense. I have Habi checking on who wrote it and whatever evidence the claims might be based on."

"Good, I don't like that bit myself. The Rajah of Pallampur's an idiot, but not that much of one. I'm more bothered by the Westshire thing."

Le Fanu felt disadvantaged, there was obviously something else he did not know. "We've had a look at the file already, Sir Charles, and will report back as soon as possible. It shouldn't be too difficult to establish the real facts."

Whitney did not look reassured. "Oh, I'm sure you will, LF, but that isn't the real problem. What do you know about Westshire?"

"I've read his personnel file, and the entry for him in the Almanack. Heard a few things around the Club, mostly good. Seems a good man, more a district type than a Headquarters one, and has done a good job in tough posts."

"Seen his Personal Conduct Register?"

In Madras a small, secretive office kept a personal dossier on each ICS officer. The file recorded performance issues, career histories, difficulties encountered with other officers or superiors, and family details as well as other information the powers that be thought relevant. That register was a millstone for colourful and outspoken officers, marking them out for non-promotion. The PCR often condemned them to punishment postings as they creaked towards retirement. The existence of the registers was not well-known and their location (a secret safe in Whitney's office) advised to only a few.

"Well, no, sir, I'd need your permission for that, and this early in the case I hadn't thought it necessary."

"Well, you have my permission now."

Whitney reached under his chair, retrieving a thick file in a brown folder tied up with scarlet ribbon top to bottom and across. He handed it to Le Fanu. "Hold onto it for the moment but no-one else is to know, apart from Habi. I know you trust him. So do I."

Given Le Fanu's earlier recitation on what he knew of Westshire, the file was thicker than anticipated. This was the file of a renegade, a troublemaker who irritated senior people.

Whitney smiled. "That's surprised you, LF, eh?"

"Ah, yes, sir, not what I anticipated. Can you give me an outline?"

"You'll read it and get the full flavour, but Westshire's been a standout from the start. For one thing, he's even more pro-Indian than you are." Whitney paused, eyes sparkling, a smile lurking. Le Fanu said nothing.

"Sorry, LF, I'm being provocative, a little." Le Fanu's more crass enemies in the police and civil service painted him as a radical, a deserter of his own kind who championed Indians and independence. Smart seniors like Whitney knew the story was more complicated, but the crass version prevailed.

"As soon as he arrived in Madras in 1900," Whitney continued, "Westshire favoured transferring some power to Indians, and seemed to oppose all aspects of the Raj and the Empire generally. Made people wonder why he bothered joining the ICS at all. In one spectacular piece of stupidity, he wrote a piece anonymously for the Madras Mail supporting the Boers during the war in South Africa. The editor published it but got so many negative comments he confided the author's identity to the government. Westshire was hauled up before the Governor and the Chief Secretary, read the riot act and threatened with the sack."

Le Fanu had heard the story but never the culprit's identity. The Madras Mail was the perennial mouthpiece for the conservative European community, so Westshire would have been a marked man since. He became more interesting to Le Fanu by the minute.

"Has he improved at all since, sir?"

"He's been more circumspect," Whitney replied, blowing a perfect smoke ring up towards the overhanging branches. "But we've had Special Branch watching him constantly, which is why the file is so large. He has chipped away at our credibility wherever and whenever possible, and recently we intercepted a letter from him to Gandhi."

That stunned Le Fanu. For a district Collector to write directly to Gandhi at this point was career madness. "Why would he do that?"

"Oh, he rambled on about the state of animal health in India. He reads Gandhi's newspaper. That makes some people distrust him immediately, although you and I might think that knowing what Gandhi is saying would be good for our side. Anyway, Gandhi wrote something on cows and Westshire felt compelled to respond. The real issue is that he wrote to the leader of the forces opposing us. If that got into the Madras Mail there'd be hell to pay."

"So there's more substance here than I thought, Sir Charles, but where do I fit in?"

"The file will tell you that, eventually, but I'll give you the shortcut. Do you know Westshire's wife, Marjorie?"

"No sir, we've not checked his family ties as yet." Le Fanu remembered he had to do the same checks on Gerald Taylor. Even more assumptions were coming under scrutiny.

"Well you'll get the connection when I tell you she's the daughter of the Secretary of State for India. They've kept it quiet, but she has a direct line to London."

Le Fanu understood immediately why he was here. If Westshire was corrupt, then the British Government faced a political crisis. The Secretary of State was responsible for overall British policy towards India. Any hint that his son-in-law was both corrupt and a supporter of the Indian cause would produce torrents of criticism from political opposition and press alike. It would be infinitely worse if he was connected to gun running. The Government of Madras had to keep this quiet, but its senior leaders could not trust Special Branch to do that or to establish the truth. Le Fanu had to do both. He felt vulnerable.

"I see you get the implications, LF, I knew you would. Better have another Glenmorangie." Whitney looked sympathetic, and tipped a generous whiskey into Le Fanu's empty glass.

They sat for another hour as the light faded and the night sounds rose, discussing the best ways to resolve the issue, how to keep it quiet, what to do with Westshire, and Special Branch. By the time Le Fanu left for home around eight, he was as drained as the bottle.

Five

And home was no longer the sanctuary of earlier times. It was never the same after he saw Ro off to the train two years before. He loved the house when he first bought it at the end of the war. When she arrived as chatelaine he loved it even more. That changed when she left, for the worse.

He had bought the old, rambling place in Mylapore with his military demob pay, a physical recompense for being psychologically drained. He bought it despite all the markers that initiated his alienation from the European community. Mylapore was the bastion of the Brahmin lawyers, many of whom who ran the local Indian National Congress. Brahmins were the top ranked caste in India's complex social chain, dominating the priestly and educated ranks. Towards the end of the war, senior British officials elevated a non-Brahmin group to power in local politics, trying to break that Brahmin power. Le Fanu buying a house amongst the out of favour lawyers was automatically considered an act of defiance against the Raj, a declaration of choice for Indians. He was barred from several European houses, and still remained unwelcome in a few. That isolated him from the prime European areas in the city like Kilpauk, Nungambakkam and, these days, Adyar along the river on the city's southern boundary.

Before and during Ro's time, the house provided solace from work and an escape from increasingly belligerent, bellicose and bombastic colleagues who now mostly hated India and its people. When he had first arrived, Madras had been different. His colleagues then had hope for India and had liked the people, even if they had not always understood them. They frequently puzzled him, he admitted to himself. Now it was all conspiracy theory, suspicion and enmity. For that reason alone, puddling around with a few golf balls on the large lawn converted to a practice area provided pleasure and escape. Neither condition was as complete once Ro left.

He had not seen her since, by choice. He wanted to, but feared the consequences. Either he would decide he really did want her and she would decline his offer, or vice versa, or a mixture of both. He could not face those possibilities. At the time Sir Maurice Wilson had told him to ditch Ro, but she had beat him to the decision. Le Fanu felt guilty. Interestingly, Wilson was now in Hyderabad and reported on Ro frequently. Maybe he had changed his mind, too.

Ro dominated Le Fanu's thoughts, and he had been with just one other woman since, despite some candid offers. The once had been a year ago when he, like other Madras senior officials, had been in retreat from the lowlands summer heat up in Ootacamund, the Nilgiris hill station known forever as "Snooty Ooty". He had stayed in the hotel there. So had an army widow from Delhi. He had answered a knock on his door one night to find her there, wearing an elegant coat. When he had helped her out of it, the only other garment on display had been the string of pearls at her throat. For the next week he had done little work and gotten even less sleep before she had returned to Delhi on her way back to England, having retrieved her widow's pension and lost her grief.

Ro's latest letter sat with the other mail on the side table inside his front door. That could wait. After today he needed a break. He went up to his room, soaked under the shower, dressed simply and took dinner on the verandah. He opened a bottle of Sancerre shipped out by a friend, stuck it in a bucket of ice by the table and drank slowly as he ate his cook's vegetarian curry speciality. The latest edition of The Telegraph brought little cheer. Britain was still in its post-war malaise, policy on India more incoherent than ever.

A letter from his brother made him even gloomier. Their parents were failing, the money available to keep them in the surroundings to which they were accustomed dwindling. He hated this. His favoured older brother had gone into the Foreign Office but had somehow wrecked his career. Le Fanu was labelled the family failure for joining the IPS, even though it had been his goal all along. He could never explain that. Serving in India as a policeman rather than as a civil servant offered more impact, more satisfaction. His not being able to articulate that had alienated his father. They had not seen each other now for nine years, but the gulf between them predated that.

The war years helped. His father was proud of the Military Cross Le Fanu had won at Shaiba in the Mesopotamian campaign, but had no idea how much those events had changed his son. To be fair, Le Fanu had never told him. He would, sometime, but not yet. He would probably tell his mother first, rather than a father who offered little warmth and less encouragement.

Le Fanu poured another glass. The bottle had about a third left. Given he was adding wine to several whiskeys taken with Whitney, Le Fanu was pleased to feel as good as he did. The rest of the mail brought more bills, notably for repairs to the bike and his subscription to the Cosmopolitan Club, another conundrum. He had joined mainly to play on the golf course, but in British Madras that was not the done thing. The Cosmo was established to foster cross-racial relationships. It did not matter that only the "best" Indians were admitted. For the whites-only, male-only, class-conscious denizens of the Madras Club, joining the Cosmo was another act of betrayal. Given the current politics, he wondered whether he should continue his membership. Of course he should. He wrote a cheque, stuck it in an envelope, which he sealed, addressed and put in the "send" box.

The Westshire PCR lay next to the box so he picked it up, found a chair with a decent light, sat down, pulled off the ribbons and opened it up.

Westshire was standard ICS, at first glance. His Anglican clergyman father had ended his career as a Dean in Durham. Westshire had attended Winchester then All Souls at Oxford where he had taken a First in Classics before surviving the dreaded ICS entrance examination in the Burlington in Piccadilly. He had done better than survive, finishing in the top ten of his year and so having the pick of the provinces. He had chosen Madras, the first surprise. Given his choice, leading candidates invariably made for Bombay or the United Provinces or, at a pinch, Bengal. To go south was a consciously contrarian choice. It would be interesting to know why Westshire had done it.

As Whitney had suggested, Westshire had made a career out of wrong footing and upsetting superior officers. Le Fanu smiled. Given his own problems with Jepson, he could scarcely criticise Westshire. The renegade had followed up on the Boer War episode by defending freedom of the press when the Government of India imposed censorship. Then the war had come, and Westshire had looked like a pacifist. Le Fanu had mixed feelings about that, having endured five years surrounded by death, disfigurement and despair. He thought that was for all the right reasons at the time, but later decided he had been mistaken. Perhaps Westshire was right.

Westshire had remained in Madras during the war. Given his pronounced views, his bosses had thought him less troublesome there than on the frontline. He had been promoted to Collector, while a lot of other officers had been absent, but had been suddenly transferred out of a district during Gandhi's first Non-Co-Operation campaign. He had defied instructions from Fort St George on how to deal with protestors.

Le Fanu was conflicted as he began another Sancerre. He

himself rarely agreed with official policy and that landed him in difficult spots. This made him no different from Westshire who would have his own versions of Jepson to deal with. Le Fanu wondered again whether he should tell Jepson about the meeting with Whitney. But Whitney did not want the meeting revealed, so the decision was easy. Le Fanu knew that was rationalisation.

Westshire's wife, Marjorie, was scarcely mentioned and her father only by name rather than title or position, which was odd. She was a well-educated lawyer, unusual for a woman, and worked in London chambers before marrying Westshire while he was back in England on leave in 1907. She had come to India, travelled with him and joined women's organisations, most notably the Indian Women's Association, which she had helped, establish. Now married for fifteen years and in their early forties, they had no children. Le Fanu was forty, single with no children that he knew of, and unbothered, but he knew married couples who were.

He read on. There was speculation rather than demonstration about what Westshire was supposed to have done with and for the Rajah of Pallampur. It was shadowy. The Collector was accused of protecting the Rajah's goondas when they appeared on assault charges. Significantly, the court files were not in the dossier so he had to find them, quietly. Westshire ruled there was insufficient evidence to convict the men, so reading those files was vital.

By the time Le Fanu finished reading he was reflective. Westshire had principles, but made poor career choices. Le Fanu recognised that pattern. Westshire achieved good things in his districts but got pilloried by deskbound Madras bureaucrats over minor matters. Le Fanu recognised that, too. Westshire had married well and happily, apart from the children. Le Fanu envied him that. The file depicted a man of ability and good intent belted by superiors possessing neither.

No direct evidence connected Westshire to whatever it was

the Rajah of Pallampur was said to be doing. For an official record and report it was flimsy, at best. It looked like an attempt to smear Westshire. But there was no clear objective, no clear culprit, and no clear reason for that. Deciding there was now more fog than light, and not only because of the Glenmorangie and Sancerre, Le Fanu fell into bed.

He dreamed about Ro's last night in the house before leaving for Hyderabad, another night when he had gotten no sleep. The dream recalled her opening the door, slipping off her clothes and under the sheets, and what followed. Le Fanu was not sleeping well now, either, caught half in the past with Ro and half in the present with this mess assigned to him because other agencies could not do their work effectively. He and Habi would be in the limelight, and in the sights as potential Jepson victims if things went wrong. The woman in Ooty had also slipped into the dream. Wrong, but pleasurable and definitely memorable. But he cared more for Ro than the army widow.

Somewhere towards dawn he became aware of four things. First, he had a huge thirst even though he had drunk the entire contents of the refilled water jar. He had not had that much alcohol for a while. Second, he had the worst headache in several years, and put it down to worries about the new cases rather than the drink. Third, he was dreaming again about Ro. Fourth, the telephone was ringing.

He thought the last an illusion. The telephone had reached Madras a few years earlier but was still a novelty. In truth, he hated the thing because he had no idea what to say. Even so, he thought the ringing was part of the dream about Ro he was willing to finality.

The ringing persisted. He awoke regretfully, Ro slipping away. He surfaced drearily, regretting the decision to have the extension put through to his bedroom. He needed to go to the lavatory. Leaning over, he grabbed the receiver.

"Yes. Le Fanu."

"Good morning, LF. Sorry to call so early." It was the Chief Secretary.

"That's alright, sir."

"I know it's not, LF. I had a few more snorts after you left and assume you did the same, so apologies again."

The man was human, after all.

"Thank you, sir. What's the time, and what's happened?"

"Well, it's five in the morning and I'm afraid I have to rouse you out."

"Right," Le Fanu replied, struggling to focus.

"Bad news, I'm afraid. The Rajah of Pallampur has been murdered at his residence here in Madras. Well, to be strictly accurate he's died violently, assumed murdered. I'm at his house now. Would you join me, as soon as possible? I have a car on the way to you."

Six

Fifteen minutes later Le Fanu was in the back of the car, shivering in the cool despite wearing his suit jacket. Madras was stirring as the light rose. Hindu men headed for their temples, bare-chested above lunghis and chappals. Many wore the sacred thread looped across one shoulder and upper body, foreheads marked with either the trident sign for Vishnu or the horizontal lines for Siva, copper ablution bowls in hand. Street sellers were urging their wares on passers-by, and food stall sellers were beginning their day's business. Stray dogs and cattle searched for food. A couple of enterprising mendicants were at their posts, hoping early temple devotees might be generous. Smoke drifted up from dung fires used to cook breakfast, adding to the shadows cast by the first glinting sunlight. Devotional bells echoed faintly in the thin, clear air about to be swamped by the sounds of a workaday city.

He was headed for Kilpauk where the Pallampur rajahs had maintained a substantial city house since the mid-nineteenth century. The present but now seemingly deceased scion spent more time in the city than his predecessors, prompted more by activist politics than commitment to business. His father had branched into general trading, but the family still relied on rural tax revenue and crops for its substantial wealth. That included a large London house in Knightsbridge, and another just completed in the emerging Edwin Lutyens-designed New

Delhi. The usual trappings were on show: new motorcars, plenty of horses, even the odd elephant (in New Delhi), along with art and archaeological treasures.

If this was murder, India's princes and leading landlords would join the ranks of the alarmed that already included most Europeans. As protected elite, they were all concerned about their personal safety, and the sanctity of their property. Le Fanu observed grimly that his Crime Unit landed all the spectacular cases along with the concomitant publicity and criticism. The only advantage was that he and Habi experienced the challenge and satisfaction of unravelling these crimes, even if this one would spring a wider range of critics than ever.

As the car turned into the Pallampur House driveway, he spotted Habi in the pale headlight beams. Given Habi had no telephone at home, Le Fanu had dispatched a duty constable to awake him. His sergeant looked remarkably alert.

"Good morning, sir, I got here as fast as possible."

"Well done, Habi, sorry about this, but the Rajah of Pallampur's been murdered, apparently, and we're in the firing line. The Chief Secretary's waiting for us."

"The constable who brought me over says it's gruesome in there, he was one of the first to arrive." Habi was readying himself for what would follow.

"Any other details?" Le Fanu was not looking forward to the next hour or so.

"Not really, sir, but he assured me the scene of offence is undisturbed."

Le Fanu hoped that was true. The Crime Unit being unpopular, many officers ignored pleas for no one to enter a crime site before Le Fanu and Habi arrived. Because some scenes were contaminated before they arrived, applying the Gross principles became difficult. On a case this important, they would need the best possible information from the outset.

Every lamp in the house was alight. The lawns looked like they had their own dawn. The house was an ostentatious pile in the Madras Indo-Saracenic style begun in the later nineteenth century. Vast quantities of local granite and sandstone were shipped in from Presidency quarries, matched up with red bricks then topped with Mughal domes. The high cost meant few private homes were built this way, Pallampur House a spectacular exception. Le Fanu was ambivalent. It was garish, really, but similar buildings like the Senate House at the University of Madras along from headquarters were impressive.

Servants rushed in, out and about, presumably hoping any activity would make them look busy as well as distract their thoughts. A row of police cars blocked the front steps and Le Fanu noticed Jepson's among them. The boastful "I-G1" number plate he had initiated stood out. He was inside, no doubt lining up a scapegoat in case publicity turned sour. Two constables guarded the front door but without obvious effect on anyone entering or leaving. Le Fanu wondered if the scene of offence really was secure. They entered a huge reception area, marble floored with an atrium soaring to the roof three levels up. On either side of this expanse, wide marble staircases led to the upper levels. Le Fanu was relieved to see the stairs guarded keenly by two sergeants. The body must be upstairs. He felt more confident about the scene of offence.

The elephant, deer, and tiger head-studded walls created a violent undertone. Having scarcely touched a gun since the end of the war, Le Fanu was mystified by colleagues who still thought shooting an animal a great achievement. Elegant tables stood around the walls, displaying eclectic treasures ranging from medieval statues to Sevres glass. There were even two suits of armour on show. They were never used in India.

The Chief Secretary, Jepson, the Commissioner and two of his deputies huddled around a table loaded with papers. Looked like his desk, Le Fanu thought. He must clear that backlog. Sir Charles Whitney looked around.

"Ah, LF, Habi, thanks for getting here so quickly. Just to let you know, I've asked the I-G to put you in charge of the investigation."

Le Fanu looked at Jepson who looked away as if he had seen something putrid. Would this ever change? The Unit achieved so much but Jepson still ran a personal vendetta, ignoring the quality police work. He would have abhorred that instruction from Whitney.

"Thank you, sir, I-G, we'll get on it immediately. We'll need some extra hands, though."

"Quite so, LF. Anyone in mind?"

Habi and Le Fanu had discussed this already. "Assistant Superintendent Caldicott, sir, if he's available."

Jackson Caldicott was another force oddity, so their choice would further anger Jepson. Having arrived in Madras at the end of the war as a trading company executive, Caldicott had become known as the Presidency's best cricketer. He had served with military intelligence during the war, and had spent the last eighteen months of it behind enemy lines in France. He had come to Madras for a quieter life but had gotten drawn into Le Fanu's 1920 murder and drugs case. Caldicott had enjoyed the work so much he had forfeited his business career for a police one and had been seconded quickly as a detective. The plodders hated that rapid rise.

"Are you sure, LF?"

"Yes, sir."

Jepson looked like an incendiary about to go off.

"Very well, he'll be made available. I-G, can you have Caldicott summonsed, immediately?"

Jepson, displeasure on full display, barked orders at a passing officer. Whitney looked disapproving but said nothing.

"Where's the body, sir?" Habi asked, changing the subject.

"Upstairs on the second floor, in the library," Whitney replied. "Mad place for a library. Some poor sod had to lug all the books and furniture upstairs. A servant found the Rajah there about ninety minutes ago, and called us. The room's been under guard since, thankfully."

That meant Le Fanu could not follow his normal procedure, which was to survey the scene of offence alone for several minutes. That helped him establish some initial views, and determine his immediate actions. Not this time, though, so he already felt at a disadvantage, and that was aggravated by Jepson's presence.

His anxiety about encountering the body grew.

They climbed the stairs, turned into a corridor along the wall and then immediately right into one of the biggest private libraries Le Fanu had seen. He had visited Sir Walter Scott's at Abbotsford in the Scottish Borders once, and thought this a reproduction. Floor to ceiling bookcases lined the walls, while smaller stand-alone cases scattered around the floor held particularly treasured items. A large desk, before a window looking out to a garden, was covered in volumes. Two other tables displayed more rarities. Le Fanu noticed a first edition of Francis Buchanan's A Journey From Madras Through the Countries of Mysore, Canara and Malabar published after Britain's 1799 defeat of Tipu Sultan at Seringapatam. He thought again of Sir Maurice Wilson whose grandfather had fought in and gathered mementos from that battle. Wilson had inherited them and added many others. Le Fanu wished Wilson was overseeing this rather than Jepson, who must have read his mind.

"I hope you don't give us your usual lily-livered squeamishness here, Le Fanu. Bloody useless in a policeman."

Le Fanu flushed. Most people in the force knew he had a phobia about blood and bodies. In his early days he was fine but the war had had an odd impact. Having seen so much blood, he developed an acute aversion. Whenever he saw a body and blood since, he could barely avoid vomiting. His condition was more controlled now but remained, and Jepson was trying to bring it on. Le Fanu readied for the waves of nausea. The library treasures were forgotten as soon as he spotted the body. He swallowed hard, wishing he had some water. Surreptitiously, Habi slipped a small bottle into his hand.

The Rajah of Pallampur lay face up on a carpet in front of the desk. He had been stabbed repeatedly. More accurately, he had been slashed in a frenzy, the vertical wounds starting at his forehead and running the full length of his body. His face was carved rather than cut, almost unrecognisable given the smashed cheekbones and layers of skin and bone dangling loose, barely attached. Blood oozed from gaping wounds all over the body. The carpet on which he lay and a couple of others nearby were soaked thick, and other pools had gathered on the tiles. He must scarcely have any blood left, Le Fanu thought as he removed the bottle cap and swigged some water. He saw Jepson's self-satisfied smirk.

The Rajah was dressed in a regal military outfit complete with turban, and all the garments were slashed. The murder weapon was evidently the sword missing from the scabbard tied at his belt. This was so vicious, Le Fanu imagined the assailant wanted the Rajah of Pallampur humiliated as well as dead.

"Do we know where he was last night?" Le Fanu asked no one in particular, more thinking aloud and, he admitted inwardly, taking the chance to not look at the body. "He was clearly at some gathering somewhere, given the uniform."

"He was at a Government House reception, with the Governor and other dignitaries," replied Whitney. "Ironic, I know, given his recent dalliance with the Congress. His Excellency has been, ah, had been trying to get the Rajah back on side. That opportunity's gone, it seems."

That was a rare sardonic note from a Chief Secretary known for his clinical approach. He's worried this death will lend more sympathy to the nationalist cause, Le Fanu thought.

"Habi," Le Fanu said, "can you start fixing a timeline with the servants. Usual thing: time out, time in, who saw him last, what time, what sort of a mood was he in, any unusual visitors. If we get that done quickly we can start making sense of this."

"Bloody hell, Le Fanu," exploded Jepson, "for once can you get off your arse and just get people searching the house and grounds for the murder weapon? Fucking obvious what's happened. Some disgruntled servant snapped and carved up the Rajah over an imagined insult. Happens all the time. Bloody savages. Can't rely on any of them anymore."

Le Fanu thought it astonishing that such a crude and ill-equipped man had charge of the entire Presidency police force. Whitney looked unhappy.

"We'll do that as soon as we've laid out the baselines, sir" Le Fanu replied. "The timeline's important. We'll have other officers record the scene of offence as it was found, then we'll search it thoroughly. Gross tells us that knowing what was there at the scene helps explain why and how other things happened."

It was a gratuitous put-down, but Le Fanu could not resist. Jepson was a paid up member of the bull in a china shop school of detection, and the reference to Gross underlined that to those present. Habi turned away, snorted and went off to start work. Whitney fought a grin. Jepson turned scarlet, then hurried away, looking back over his shoulder.

"Baselines, my arse. Just fucking get on with it and report directly to me later this morning, and you'd better have some fucking results. You're a shit policeman, Le Fanu, but I'll get the best out of you if it kills me."

The blood pressure might do that first, thought Le Fanu, who immediately organised some constables to record the scene of offence before starting a systematic search.

"Sorry about that, LF," Whitney said, catching up with Le Fanu and steering him into a corner. "His Excellency wants me to tell you personally you have his full support, and full powers to act independently. Jepson knows that, and will toe the line despite all the spluttering. There's some talk about what we might do with Jepson, actually, but that's for another time. This is important, you know that. Let me know if you need anything, and report to me. It might be awkward cutting out Jepson but that's what Willingdon wants."

"Thank you, sir, I'll keep you up to date."

As the Chief Secretary left, Le Fanu rued the complexity that surrounded this death already, took a deep breath, and returned to the work.

Seven

He heard the Rani of Pallampur before he saw her. Rather, he recognised the Australian voice and knew it must be her. Le Fanu had worked with Australian officers during the war and admired their professionalism, but never accommodated accents that emanated from somewhere in between the eyes and the top of the nose. The sound was flat, strident and almost unintelligible. He heard it now in feminine version, but why was it coming from the front door? He had assumed she would be in the house but it seemed that assumption was wrong, too.

"Will some bugger tell me what's going on?" He'd heard that expression before. "Why are you buggers all here, and where's my bloody husband?"

He'd heard all that, too, but she obviously did not know what had happened.

"Some bastard had better tell me quick or there'll be a bloody scene."

He raced over to where she was blocked at the library by a knot of police. If she did not know what had happened, she must not discover that by looking into the library and seeing her husband's body.

Le Fanu realised why the Rajah had overlooked, perhaps never even registered the voice. She was one of the most beautiful woman he had ever encountered – more so than the

Delhi widow, and than Virginia Campbell who had turned out to be deadly two years earlier. She was almost the equal of Ro. He felt disloyal at that last reflection.

Charlotte Lacey, the Rani of Pallampur was tall but not thin. The legs, perched on black high-heeled shoes, were long and shapely up to the knee-high dress hem. Their continued form above that was obvious from the outlines against the tight dress. The narrow waist was accentuated by the full bust, the top half of which was on full display thanks to the low-cut black evening dress that was matched by gloves, bag and scarf. Her hair was black, too, cut short around the oval face that was dark in complexion but fresh and finely boned. Green eyes flashed out above the snub nose that sat above a full-lipped mouth lined with scarlet lipstick.

Le Fanu was entranced, but worried. "Your Highness?" he asked.

"Yes, of course, but who the hell are you and what are all these people doing in my house? And forget that Highness nonsense, Rani will do."

"Rani, I'm Superintendent Christian Le Fanu, head of the Crime Unit for the Madras police. Can we talk privately somewhere?"

"Crime Unit? What the bloody hell is that about? Oh alright, there's a room through here. Follow me."

She turned away from the library door and walked further down the corridor. He followed the dress. She turned into a small, elegant room where floor lamps cast shadowed light over Persian carpets and Kashmiri furniture. He was puzzled. She showed no alarm, seemingly unfazed by all the police officer in her house.

The Rani turned towards him, slowly, showing her profile off to advantage and indicating him to sit. "What did you say your name was?" The nasal voice seemed so odd coming from that remarkable face and body.

"Le Fanu, Superintendent Christian Le Fanu. I run the

Crime Unit that investigates serious incidents in the city."

"Serious incidents? So I ask again, what are all you bastards doing in my bloody house?" She reached to a drawer in a small table, opened it, extracted cigarettes and matches, and sat down. "Would you like one?"

"No thank you, Rani."

She lit up.

"Rani, have you just arrived back in the house?"

"Yes, I've been out in the country at a friend's house. Dinner ran very late."

It was six in the morning. Le Fanu had never been home later from dinner than three. Perhaps being a Rani was different.

"Rani, we'll need an account of your movements, I'm afraid."

She looked puzzled. "Why?"

"I'm afraid there's bad news." He hated this part of the job. "There's no easy way to say this, but your husband is dead, I'm sorry. We think he's been murdered. His body is still in the library, and we're beginning our checks."

Le Fanu normally tried to be gentle in these situations, but for some reason wanted to see her reaction to this blunt announcement.

The Rani stood, drew deeply on the cigarette, held the smoke in her lungs for what seemed like minutes, her impressive chest rising and falling. She exhaled, exaggeratedly.

"Dead? How?" She was not surprised, he thought.

"Rani, I can't say much because we're still investigating. However, we think he was attacked with his own sword by someone already in the house, or someone who returned with him from the Governor's reception."

She sat, drawing hard at the cigarette. "Silly bugger, I told him to be careful."

That caught him off guard. "Careful about what?"

"Anything. Some crank's been sending him hate mail and

death threats. He thought it was nothing but I told him it might be serious."

"Any reason you told him that?"

"Nothing concrete, it was just different from the other nut case messages he got, seemed a bit more real."

"You mean there were other threats?"

"Superintendent, people like Pally get threats all the time. Especially now that he'd cosied up to the Congress, silly bugger. I warned him about that, too, but he wouldn't listen. Wasn't enough to be a Rajah, he wanted to be important as well."

Le Fanu was nonplussed. She seemed unmoved by her husband's death. It could have been shock. She might have been more hard-bitten than she looked but he doubted that. This was odd.

"Can I see him?" she asked.

"Not yet I'm afraid, we'll have to finish our assessment and then, well, ah, we'll have to get a medical opinion." He hoped she would not see her husband until after Dr. Ramachandran tidied him up at the morgue.

"You mean an autopsy."

"Yes, unfortunately."

"Fair enough. Seems sensible in the circumstances. What do you want me to do?"

"If you could be here in case we need to talk to you, that would be excellent. Can you bear to stay here, though?"

"Oh yes, I'll have a couple of friends come in once you clean up. I'll be right as rain. No sense shifting out. I'd just have to transport clothes and things and let's face it, where else would I stay in this God-awful city? The Connemara? That's not up to much."

Le Fanu had stayed at the city's finest hotel just once, at someone else's vast expense. He'd thought it very good. The Rani's experience of leading hotels exceeded his, clearly.

"Of course. Here's my card with my direct telephone number. If you need to ask anything, just call me, I'll be ready to help."

She looked him up and down, slowly. "Yes," she said, "I'm sure you will."

Rising, she stubbed out the cigarette and left regally, calling for a servant who had hovered outside. They disappeared further down the corridor, through a door that closed behind them.

Le Fanu had never seen a victim's spouse act so coolly. He had no experience of dealing with the Australian wives of dead rajahs, and he knew there was no section in Gross' procedural book about that. He doubted the book on criminal psychology covered the subject, either. Had it done so, he thought, it would anticipate far more grief than was on display here.

He returned to the library where Habi and the team were finishing their preliminary work. The process took longer now because the photographic team was on hand. Madras police photographers had captured the likenesses of known criminals since the later nineteenth century, but photographing scenes of offence was new. By the time the photographers arrived, unpacked their equipment, set up shooting positions and lights, then completed the work, most investigating police officers were fuming that the criminals responsible might well have left the country already.

Le Fanu tolerated the delays, though. Photographs set a frame around the scene of offence, or crime scene as Le Fanu preferred, and picked up details missed by the eye. Besides, he knew the chief photographer, respected his work and integrity.

"Raja Rao. Nearly finished?"

"Yes sir, another ten minutes and we'll be out of your way."

Le Fanu turned to find Habi nearby, talking with some servants.

"Sir, these servants say the Rajah returned after midnight, perhaps towards one, but we know he left the Governor's about ten, so we have at least two and perhaps three hours to fill in on his timeline."

"That's significant."

"Yes, sir. We'll ask at the Governor's residence to see what else we can find there."

"What about the Rani?"

"More difficult, sir, they're not saying much so that tells me something. She was not home when the Rajah arrived, certainly."

"No, she tells me she was at a friend's in the country. We'll need to question her about that and other things. It won't be easy."

"A job for an experienced man like you, sir" Habi shot back. The tease was back.

"Perhaps I should send you, Sergeant, you seem to have all the answers."

"Not me, sir, when it comes to European women I don't even know the questions."

Great answer, thought Le Fanu. Join the club. "What else do we know?" he asked.

"Not much, sir, although one servant says the Rajah was receiving threats in the mail. No-one seems to know why, but their guess is that someone didn't like the Rajah supporting Congress."

"The Rani confirms the letters," Le Fanu said, "and says she warned him but that he took no notice."

"You think he was murdered for politics, sir?"

"I doubt it, Habi, but we're all in new territory here. Tempers are fraying everywhere. It would be unusual, though, not too many political killings in the Presidency over the past few years. Not since 1907 and Bipin Chandra Pal's tour, really."

That tour by a Bengali radical sparked political activism in Madras. That was the official view, anyway. It suggested

Bengali terrorism arrived in the south then and that things had never been the same since. Le Fanu did not believe that. There was no supporting evidence and Gross warned against accepting immediate, obvious answers to what were never simple questions. Even so, people like Jepson automatically assumed political terrorism was abroad.

"The I-G will expect us to have some obvious answers, sir."

"I know that, Habi, and I'll have to see him sometime today, no matter how little evidence we have."

"Sir, we have something else, I think, though we'll need to check. One servant says the Rajah kept a loaded gun in his desk because of the threats. We've looked there but found no gun and, it wasn't with the body, either. The killer might have taken it. We'll search the immediate area in case it was ditched, then check the pawn shops to see if the killer tried to cash it in. Long odds on either chance, but we can at least do that and report to the I-G."

"Excellent, Habi. Do we know the make of the gun?"

"Yes, sir. It's a Webley-Wilkinson revolver from 1912. The servants think the Rajah brought it back from England."

That was a high quality revolver to have in the house, thought Le Fanu, military officer material. Most Indian princes and nobles kept hunting rifles rather than revolvers, but the Rajah of Pallampur was different in most other respects so this came as no surprise.

"Pawnbrokers would love to see that, Habi, so start with them as soon as they open. We'll get troops searching the nearby area in case the weapon was ditched. I'll meet you back at the office. We'll need to find that sword, too."

"Yes, sir. One of the constables has information on that."

"Already?"

"Well, he knows the make. He's a fanatic on military swords, and identified it from the calf leather scabbard and its attachments."

"That's impressive. What is it?"

"You'll know it, sir, one of those flashy Highland Officer broadswords. The ones with the metal basket guards to protect the hand. They have white buckskin inside, with blue and white silk ribbons tied to the pommel and the basket."

"And it's one of those? That constable should be a detective."

"The servants have confirmed it, sir. Apparently the Rajah brought it back from Sandhurst."

"We'll pass that on to the I-G, as well. Habi, you'd better take off and see if you can find the thing. It sounds hard to miss!"

Habi disappeared, taking some constables and leaving Le Fanu to watch the photographers finish work. For the first time in several minutes he was forced to look at the body. The bile rose, he felt faint. He took another swig from the water bottle.

"Get the body over to the morgue so that our friend there has an early look." He turned away.

A pair of constables came in wearing rubber gloves and bearing a stretcher. They lifted the Rajah's body onto the stretcher, covered him with a sheet, and carried him out to a waiting, unmarked van. He would soon be at Government General Hospital for a handling no rajah should endure, even when dead.

Eight

It was eight by the time he reached the office to find Jackson Caldicott awaiting. Slim, athletic, brown haired and wearing his fashionable clothes easily, he did not look like an ex-spy.

"Good morning, sir, thanks for getting me into this."

"Call me LF when no-one else is around, and you might not thank me later. This could go very wrong, and we'll be the target for blame if it does."

"Sir, I'll call you sir here at work. Makes it easier all round. Away from work, LF it is, and thank you. And aren't we in this because we like things complicated?"

"Ha, I see why you left the business world, not enough excitement! There's an immediate task for you, though, using your London connections."

Le Fanu explained the possible interconnections between Gerald Taylor in Changarore, James Westshire and Marjorie in Ramsheed, the now-dead Rajah of Pallampur and his Australian wife, and alleged arms smuggling. He explained how he and Habi were retracing their steps because earlier assumptions might have missed vital points, especially personal ones. The more Le Fanu talked, the more he convinced himself the stories might be linked, even if the available evidence was unconvincing or possibly non-existent. He chalked up new ideas on the case boards as he went, creating ever more intricate networks.

"So, Caldicott, we need to learn much more and quickly about Gerald Taylor's UK background, Marjorie Westshire's family story and connections, and what the Rajah of Pallampur was doing in London. Habi's chasing the revolver angle and the arms smuggling story. Can you handle the London end for me?"

"Of course, sir. You know I've a couple of contacts in London who'll help. Get me direct access to a telegraph outlet I'll correspond in code, that'll be safest."

Le Fanu telephoned the police telegraph office on the other side of the city, arranged Caldicott a machine in a secure room, and a car to get him there.

"Let's meet back here later," he said, "after four. Habi should be back then. Hopefully we'll have a convincing story for our masters."

Caldicott left, and Le Fanu confronted the mess on his desk. Two hours later he had cleared files, reordered papers, boxed up records for the police archives and even a few older ones for the Government archives near Egmore station. By eleven he sat at an ordered desk that suggested he was in control. Inwardly, he was not so sure. He fiddled with the case boards that were already filled up, and ordered in more for the afternoon session.

He also thought about the Rani. She had appeared unaffected by her husband's violent death. Perhaps their relationship had soured. He needed to determine her whereabouts, and that could be awkward if she was uncooperative. The Government of Madras held the Rajah in low esteem but protocol niceties still prevailed. If she refused to reveal her mystery location, no one would pressure her. Even the Chief Secretary could not force her to speak. And she really was beautiful. Le Fanu found such women hard to handle and he knew they could manipulate him easily. He hoped this would not replay his difficulties with Virginia Campbell.

To put both women out of mind, Le Fanu re-read the

Westshire PCR. That reminded him of Taylor. Le Fanu telephoned records. They should send up everything available on the trader including immigration, taxation, commercial agreements and charge sheets. He knew there were no charge sheets but asked anyway. Cross-referencing might produce cases where Taylor was a litigant or witness rather than central figure. Those records would take a couple of hours to arrive so he opted for an early, solitary lunch away from the station, and time to think.

A few weeks ago he had happened into a small Acharappan Street hotel-restaurant in Georgetown and had met the young manager-chef. K. Krishna Rao hailed from Bangalore and specialised in the vegetarian Udipi cuisine that used no onions or garlic. The spiced rice, fried and curried vegetables were the best Le Fanu had tasted.

Half an hour later he sat in the restaurant, in front of a banana leaf onto which the food was dumped, and, to the surprise of other diners was eating happily with his fingers.

Krishna Rao came out from the kitchen. "Superintendent, welcome back to my humble place."

"Keep serving this food, Krishna Rao, and I'll be back a lot more if you'll have me," Le Fanu replied in Tamil. The other diners became more interested.

"You'll have me cooking for Lord Willingdon soon," Krishna Rao laughed. The diners joined in. There were about thirty other people there for lunch and Krishna Rao addressed them.

"You'd all better be on your best behaviour, because Superintendent Le Fanu here is chief of the Crime Unit. But he likes our food, so don't give him a hard time!"

They all clapped politely, Le Fanu nodded thanks, and Krishna Rao returned to the kitchen. Le Fanu ate slowly, washing the food down with a mango lassi, the buttermilk drink most Europeans found too rich. Before leaving he accepted business cards from half a dozen other diners including some lawyers and a journalist from Andhra Bazar Patrika, a pro-nationalist Telugu language newspaper based in Madras. Le Fanu wondered what Jepson would make of those contacts, but knew they would be useful. Le Fanu despaired that the distance between the Government and the locals was growing rather than diminishing. The more links he had, the better informed he felt.

The street was returning to life after the long lunch period. He stepped around cow dung, avoided deep potholes, looked out for the cyclists who took any route other than the legal one, and for a pony cart to carry him back to the office. There were none.

Some nearby shops dealt in cloth, one of the Presidency's main manufactures. A handful sold exquisite silks from towns like Conjeevaram. For some reason he thought of his brother's letter, and of his mother. He entered a shop, re-emerging an hour later with a sari his mother could use as a wall hanging in her Bath apartment. She would make it work in the incongruous Georgian setting. He bought at bargain price. The owner had been in the restaurant, and come away impressed by a Superintendent of Police who ate off a banana leaf and spoke Tamil. The lunch trip was beneficial in unexpected ways.

A now-available cart bumped him back towards headquarters, passing the imperious High Court buildings so irrelevant to ordinary Indians. He had the driver cut up Pycroft's Road, and they ambled along under the trees shading narrow dirt back streets. They turned into Edward Elliott's Road. Le Fanu had the driver stop around a corner, then walked to the office.

Habi was also returning from lunch. Whenever possible, he took it at home with his Indian Christian wife and their children. Habi was a great detective but an even greater person, Le Fanu always thought. A Muslim, he came back from school in England to marry across religions. That took courage.

"How was lunch, Habi?"

"Excellent as always, sir. What did you do?"

"Went to Krishna Rao's in Acharappan Street again. That fellow can cook."

"I want to see the I-G's face when someone tells him his Crime Unit head eats Udipi food off a banana leaf."

"Well, if you don't tell him I won't. Anything new?"

"None of the pawn brokers has a revolver in yet, but they'll let me know if one turns up. Constables are searching the streets around Pallampur House, but I doubt it will turn up there. The sword might, but we'll have to be lucky."

"I agree," Le Fanu said. "Follow search procedures for the next day or so and let's hope it pays off. Any breakthroughs will likely come from the analytical work. I have Caldicott working on the London end and he'll meet us after four."

"What about the Rani?"

"We'll need to see her again, but let's leave that until tomorrow morning."

"You're not putting that off, sir, are you?" Habi looked innocently serious.

"Am I that obvious, Habi? "

"Not at all, sir, I know how ruthlessly efficient you are interviewing attractive European women." They both laughed. "But this one's different, sir, isn't she? Can you understand what she's saying? Is she speaking English?"

"Australian English, Habi. You'll get used to it. What are you doing now?"

"I'll go and check on search party progress, sir, and be back here to meet you and Assistant Super Caldicott."

"Fair enough. See you then."

Le Fanu climbed the stairs to his office whose new neatness was still a shock. So was the waiting visitor.

Nine

Chester Barnes was the new Madras Mail editor whom Le Fanu had not yet met. By reputation he was less Neanderthal than his predecessors but in Le Fanu's opinion that meant little. The bar for excellence was set low in the Mail's case.

"Mr. Barnes. How can I help you?"

This editor was better dressed than the previous one, and younger. The cream linen suit was well cut. Cufflinks shone against the lemon coloured shirt that complemented the paisley silk tie. Tan brogues, well polished, completed the good looks. He handed his card to Le Fanu who was pleased to see the fingers were not nicotine-stained, a welcome change from the previous curmudgeon who masqueraded as an editor.

"Superintendent, I'm hoping this might begin a positive relationship, although I understand your previous experiences with the Mail might make you wary."

He was well spoken and educated, another unusual combination in Europeans working for the Mail.

Le Fanu thawed, a little. "You could say that. But you're an improvement on the last one. Better dressed, at least. Are you as much of a troglodyte politically as he was?"

"I hope not," Barnes replied, smiling, "but you'll be the judge. Have you read us lately?"

There was another assumption. This man had been editor

for four months and not once had Le Fanu read the paper. He assumed it was business as normal. That was not a good attitude for a policeman.

"Well, no. You have me there."

"At least you're honest. Have a look, see what you think and we can discuss a few things next time we meet, perhaps at the Club?"

That was another surprise. Editors were not automatically admitted to the Club, this one must be well connected.

"We could, though I don't go there that much," Le Fanu said. "Is there anything you want discussed now?"

"Yes, of course. We know about the Pallampur matter, it's all over town. I'm hoping you might update me so we can get something accurate in today's late edition."

Le Fanu would normally have said no, but realised that habitual response was because he loathed the earlier editors. This was an opportunity to cultivate a press friend.

"That's possible, but without going into too much detail. He was found this morning about four thirty or so, in his library. Death was not from natural causes, that I can say. He was attacked so we're treating it as a murder case, but will confirm that once we get the autopsy results. We're searching for possible murder weapons and some missing items. Will that do for a start?"

"Yes, thank you. Can you describe his injuries? I hear they were extensive."

"At this point, no, but I should be able to tell you more tomorrow. No promises, though."

"Thank you, Superintendent, I appreciate your help. What do you know of Pallampur's London activities?"

That odd question implied Barnes himself knew something.

"We're looking into all aspects of the Rajah's life, naturally, and that includes his London interests and interests elsewhere."

"Good answer, Superintendent, but a civil service one, if I may say so. You answered my question perfectly but without conveying any information whatsoever."

Le Fanu acknowledged him. "Quite right, I admit."

"As your inquiries deepen we might be able to help you on that London front, so if you don't mind can we keep in touch over the next few days?"

"As much as is possible, yes, and it has been good to meet you. Maybe there's hope for the Mail yet."

As Barnes left, Le Fanu reminded himself to get a copy of the Mail ordered home. Maybe there were other areas of his life where he was assuming too much. Some reflection was in order.

He had an hour before Caldicott and Habi were due in to discuss the day's developments. Le Fanu hesitated, left his room, turned left along the long corridor, left towards the front of the building, then left again towards the I-G's offices that looked out to the ocean. It was a wonderful view, wasted on Jepson he thought. The private secretary hurried in to Jepson's office, came out a minute or so later and ushered Le Fanu in. Normally he would have waited at least half an hour. This was progress.

"Good afternoon, Le Fanu. Thanks for coming around, I know you'll be busy."

The man had undergone a personality transformation since the morning.

"Not at all, sir, I know you need to be kept up to date. As yet we don't have a lot, but I can tell you what we do have."

He explained progress to Jepson who did not interrupt. Le Fanu kept strictly to the Pallampur case itself and did not reference the other matters.

"Very good, Le Fanu. Habibullah is leading the local search, then, and Caldicott dealing with other matters? Good arrangement, I think. Another matter, though – do you think this connects to Westshire in any way?"

Careful, Le Fanu.

"There's nothing yet to suggest that, sir, though it is a possibility. We're looking into everything we can about the Rajah, and something might come up but, as I say, no connection yet."

"Fair enough. Just keep me updated. Autopsy results in yet?"

"No sir. Caldicott, Habi and I are about to meet, and I'll go to the morgue after that. I've asked Ramachandran to give it priority."

"That's all to the good. Thanks for coming round. Perhaps drop back in tomorrow?"

"Yes, sir, thank you."

Le Fanu walked back to his office, dazed. Jepson's character and attitude had somersaulted since this morning. He had never been so reasonable and straightforward. Something must have happened. Whitney suggested senior officers were considering what to do with Jepson. Perhaps the I-G had heard that and decided he'd better repair relations given Le Fanu's support from the Chief Secretary and the Governor. Or perhaps he knew he was under scrutiny. Or maybe he was just up to something. Le Fanu realised he could no longer take Jepson's approach for granted, either.

Habi and Caldicott arrived soon after Le Fanu reached his office. Le Fanu reported his meeting with Jepson. Habi had nothing concrete: there was still no sign of either the sword or the revolver, the search parties were disbanded until early the following morning.

Caldicott had more. The Rajah had been watched by Special Branch in London, for reasons yet to be explained. Caldicott's contacts were sending information, but he might have to retrieve it from New Delhi. Apparently, senior officials in the Foreign and Political Department of the Government of India knew about the watch, and had the same information as London. Caldicott would know the procedure to be followed by next morning.

"Sir," Habi said, "that might raise problems for us."

"How so?" Le Fanu asked.

"Well, if Assistant Super Caldicott has to go to Delhi, we'll need approval from the I-G. To get that, we'll have to tell him why the visit's necessary. If we do that we'll have to tell him all we know, which is much more than you've just told him."

"Quite right, Habi, the usual little difficulty we have with the I-G."

"Sir," Caldicott interjected," I could take some leave. I've a little owing."

"Too risky, I think. If you met anyone up there it would go on the record and someone is bound to mention it to someone else down here. Delhi is not good at confidentiality when it counts. Let's wait until tomorrow. Maybe you won't have to go up there."

They all thought that unlikely. If the Rajah had been under watch, the situation was serious.

"If what I'm hearing is right," Caldicott said, "Delhi hasn't mentioned anything to anyone here, including the Chief Secretary and the Governor. If that's so, then we three are in the middle of a big jurisdictional fight."

"Right again," replied Le Fanu. "If I get a chance I'll raise it with the Chief Secretary because I trust him. Hopefully he knows and hasn't mentioned it because of the need for secrecy. Even so, it seems odd."

They finalised the information boards, adding to the growing list of unanswered questions. The next day would start with Le Fanu going back to the Rani, Caldicott following up with London, and Habi continuing local searches including for any new information on Gerald Taylor.

They talked for a while longer, but Le Fanu knew he was delaying the inevitable. Before he talked to the Rani he needed to know exactly what had happened to her husband. That required going to the morgue where, as usual, Dr. Ramachandran would have to accommodate his phobia.

Habi knew, too. "Ready for the morgue, sir?" the sergeant asked, full of bonhomie.

Le Fanu looked at him, wearily. "You know the answer to that, Habi. You want to go instead?"

"Oh no, sir, that's a job for a very senior officer."

"A sergeant could do it just as well."

"Not at all, sir, we defer to our seniors in all serious matters like this."

Caldicott was lost. "Sir, if I can help…"

Le Fanu laughed. "Sorry Caldicott, you're disadvantaged. I have a little difficulty dealing with the morgue, as Habi is reminding me none too kindly. I'll be off in a second. You both go home."

They packed up, Le Fanu shut the office door and mooched down to the back entrance where a car waited to carry him to the hospital, and the morgue.

Ten

Having done the work unofficially for several years, Dr. Ramachandran was now official pathologist at GGH. His devotion both touched and perplexed Le Fanu. Ramachandran wanted to serve victims and their families, a noble goal. To do that, he sacrificed the substantial income available to a man of his skill and English training. And he still worked in cramped, decrepit rooms at the back of the hospital, hidden away so his work did not remind people of the city's seedier side.

Le Fanu arrived bothered, as always. He looked forward to Ramachandran's positive views on life, the man found hope in everything. But Le Fanu also knew his phobia was never far off and, like Habi, Ramachandran would test him as part of the search for a cure. These days, at least, Le Fanu knew a quick way to the morgue so did not have to navigate the labyrinth of corridors and rooms filled with patients and, worse, jars of specimens and exhibit cabinets.

Ramachandran's office remained a trial. His desk was shoved into one corner of the small room. Papers and files proliferated over the remaining floor space. Le Fanu remembered that his office had looked like this until today, and was glad he had restored order. Ramachandran's walls were lined with steel shelves bearing all the jars and specimens Le Fanu hated, or feared.

The pathologist was exhausted. This work took a toll, and recent fatal shootings at demonstrations spawned a political strand to his work that he disliked. Ramachandran was a private man, but the shootings opened his work to public scrutiny and political slant. He wore that uneasily. His black hair was dishevelled, bags bulged under the now dull dark eyes, and he slumped behind the desk.

"Rama, you should go home and rest." The two men knew each other well now. They both lived alone, apart from servants, were dedicated to their work, and disliked the current political conditions.

"Great advice coming from you, Chris, you look as bad as I feel."

"That's not possible because you look dreadful. Pallampur too much for you?"

Ramachandran shouted to a passing chai-wallah and ordered two mugs of the steaming, milky sweet south Indian tea. Le Fanu preferred coffee but always allowed Ramachandran to order here.

"You'll need the tea, Chris, so that you can survive my room, as always. I've some new examples that might interest you."

Le Fanu threw his hands up in despair, jokingly, but his mouth and throat were beginning to dry, a bad sign.

"And then, of course," continued Ramachandran, "we must inspect the late Rajah of Pallampur."

The room started to swim, but the tea arrived and it did help. Ramachandran knew what he was doing.

"Before all that, Rama, how are you? We've not see each other for a couple of weeks." Le Fanu was buying time. Ramachandran played along.

"The usual. Too much work, not enough help, not enough money and not enough supplies. Government policies about firing on demonstrators are over-supplying me with clients who now come from all over the Presidency. The country hospitals are even worse off than I am here."

Le Fanu knew that. Reports on individual incidents meant the public got a disaggregated view of events. But people like Rama, senior Government officials, political organisers and Le Fanu alike knew the collective results of the shootings were far higher than the published ones. The Government kept quiet, knowing wider understanding of the real situation would produce more bad publicity.

"All the more reason for you to rest," Le Fanu said.

"I know, but you keep bringing me more business."

That was true, too. Heightened political tension spilled over into general crime. Another suppressed statistic indicated that general murders had risen in the past twelve months. Jepson put it down to low police numbers, but Le Fanu thought heightened animosity between rulers and ruled provided a better explanation. People took matters into their own hands now, rather than use a police force widely considered an instrument for repression rather than protection.

"My apologies, Rama, I'll put out the word and see if we can lower the murder rate."

"That would be much appreciated."

"Well, you'd better show me our latest victim." He could delay no longer.

Ramachandran rose, brushed past Le Fanu and punched him lightly on the arm. Le Fanu braced for his latest trial. Like the other wards, the autopsy room was made gloomier by the dark green paint on its walls and roof. That décor made the two examination tables look even more sinister. At least they were spotless, no signs of blood. Le Fanu knew that before he visited, Ramachandran's aides cleaned thoroughly to reduce the chances of their visitor becoming overwhelmed. Le Fanu appreciated that, and Rama's attempts to help him manage the phobia. They were not yet successful but he had improved, a touch.

Pallampur's body was laid out in a small and even more

antiseptic annexe. Ram had gone to great lengths this time, thought Le Fanu, so the Rajah must have been in bad shape. Ramachandran made ready to remove the covering sheet.

"What's the overall story first, Rama?" Le Fanu felt queasy.

"He bled to death, from multiple wounds as you saw on-site. Those wounds were cuts, slashes really, not stabs. As clear a distinction between cuts and stabs as Hans Gross himself could make. It was done with a large and very sharp blade, a sword at least three feet long I think, the usual double edge."

"That fits. There's a sword missing from a scabbard he was wearing. One of the constables says it's a Highland Officer's broadsword."

"That would do it. The thing certainly lived up to any manufacturer's claims. I have that scabbard among Pallampur's effects. Your people can pick them up tomorrow."

"How does it look to you, planned?"

"If it was planned, then the killer was either really angry or lost control once he or she started. I've counted seventy wounds and I'm not sure that's all of them. Whoever did it would have been exhausted by the end."

"He or she?"

"I say that to cover the options but, really, given the wounds and the scale of the attack, my bet's on a man, a big, strong one."

"Any signs Pallampur put up a fight?" Le Fanu was holding up, just.

"None at all. Probably because of the alcohol he'd consumed. He reeked, and his bloodstream shows high counts. Well, that was in what little blood he had left."

That hit Le Fanu. "Any idea what time he died?" He tried to concentrate on Ramachandran's answer.

"I'd say sometime between about 1.30 am and 3.30am."

They had to determine what time the Rajah had left the Governor's reception, how much he had to drink there, what time he had gotten home, whether he had received any visitors, and whether or not he had more to drink once home. If there was a gap between his leaving the Governor's and reaching home, where had he gone and, again, had he consumed more alcohol?

Also, Le Fanu thought, that meant asking the Rani some tighter questions, and he was as apprehensive about that meeting the following morning as surviving his current encounter.

"That gives us a good framework for building other questions, thanks, Rama. Anything else?"

"Hard to say if it's relevant or not, but he was seriously ill. He might not even have known, but he had a severe liver tumour. All that grog wouldn't have helped, but he would have felt weak most of the time. That might also have prevented him from putting up a defence. As I say, may not be relevant but you never know. I've a few more tests to do and I'll report those tomorrow, but apart from that, over to you."

He looked at Le Fanu, quizzically. Le Fanu nodded. Ramachandran peeled back the covering sheet. Le Fanu looked then immediately looked away, for a bucket. Nausea swamped him.

Rama's normal neat, respectful autopsy stitches were the only things holding the body together. Half a dozen vertical sword slashes had opened the rajah's face. Those were so deep that carves of flesh peeled out and sagged away. Two cross-stripes opened the base of the neck on both sides. An uncountable number of vertical cuts freed long strips of flesh that were now hanging askew across the torso. Those cuts stretched from chest to pubis, and severed ribs protruded at different angles. The legs were attacked crossways, one cut above the left knee almost severing the limb.

Le Fanu had seen nothing like this, not even during the war when he witnessed everything that he thought could possibly be inflicted on a human body. He squatted on the floor beside the table, head down, breathing hard, searching for control. Ramachandran handed him a standby glass of lemon juice with sugar syrup. Le Fanu swallowed that in one gulp and stood, slowly.

"You did say it was bad," he muttered, "but I hadn't imagined anything like that."

Wordlessly, Ramachandran showed Le Fanu back to the office. They said their goodbyes. In a couple of minutes Le Fanu was gulping in what passed for fresh air in the car park where his driver awaited, hastily stubbing out an acrid bidi that also offended Le Fanu's challenged senses. He walked around the car park for a couple of minutes, then climbed in and directed the driver to take him home.

It was eight and dark by the time he reached Mylapore. As they entered the driveway the car lights flickered across the trees and shrubs, disturbing birds already taken roost for the night. A couple of squirrels stood on the lawn, frozen in the lights and hoping they were not seen. The flagstick on his putting green looked forlorn. It would remain that way because he would not get out there tonight. He was too tired with too much to think about.

He went upstairs without checking his mail, had a shower, dressed in fresh casual clothes, came down, poured a Macallan 12 year old, then checked the mail. Another letter from his brother. He could not face that tonight. The latest letter from Ro still sat there. Not that either. Some newspapers sat ready, including the Madras Mail. A few small bills irked, some for things he could not remember having done. He hated those details. Ro handled them perfectly.

Downing the whisky and pouring another, he took the Mail over to a side table, sat down and flicked through the pages. Barnes was exemplary on the Pallampur story, keeping to Le Fanu's information and making no speculation. There were no snide references to police incompetence. This was refreshingly new for the Mail. Perhaps Barnes was making a difference.

Not completely, though. Another reporter took opinion

on the murder from European Association officials who ranted about the low levels of protection afforded important people, that is, themselves, during these troubled times. The Government was doing its best, they suggested, but the police were appallingly lax and unhelpful. Approached for a comment, Inspector-General Jepson actually defended his officers and the force. That was wildly different from his normal response - he usually laid blame on anyone in sight.

Le Fanu took another whisky. The Mail changing its spots a little was one thing. Jepson changing his entirely was highly unlikely. Le Fanu reminded himself to ask the Chief Secretary what was happening when he next met him, because if Jepson was being reasonable for a purpose, it would pay to know why.

Dinner was simple, a mutton curry, and lonely. He ate unenthusiastically, looked through the rest of the paper. Caldicott had made another century for the Madras Cricket Club against Bangalore at the weekend. Depressing news came from across India, especially concerning more police deaths in the north that was still shaken by the earlier Chauri Chaura incident. Police there had fired on a crowd, killing demonstrators. The crowd had set fire to the police station in turn, killing all the occupants. The Mahatma halted his Non- Co-Operation campaign after that, but it unleashed fear and hysteria within the European community. The current sporadic demonstrations aggravated already poor relationships between Indians and Europeans. It was a moot point how long the British could stay in India.

Le Fanu read a little more, paced the verandah for a while, then set off to bed for another solitary night.

Eleven

He arrived at Pallampur House at ten, following a quick visit to the office where Caldicott had nothing new and Habi was already out on the weapons search. He was tired, apprehensive and miserable. The last two conditions were caused by this imminent interview, the first by the sleep deprivation rapidly becoming his norm. He wore uniform, thinking that might cow the Rani. He was wrong.

"Superintendent Le Fanu, what on earth can I tell you? I wasn't here, you saw me come in!"

She was dressed in black. The dress was full in the sleeve, high in the neckline, long in the hem and flowing rather than tight. It looked like thick cotton. The shoes, low heeled, were sensible, and black. She had two black scarves, one at the throat and one over her hair. Black framed glasses made her face more angular and she was smoking, the cigarette carried in a long black holder. Charlotte Tracey looked sad but not in mourning.

They were in a ground floor annexe with gardens outside the full-length windows. A table, chairs and a sideboard were the only furniture. She had taken breakfast there because, as they entered, servants scurried about clearing dishes.

She sat on one side of the simple oak table, waved him into the facing chair. He removed and twiddled his cap, then set it on an adjoining chair before smoothing his hair anxiously.

"Yes, Your Highness, that's true…"

"Rani, remember, I can't stand that bloody Highness palaver."

"Yes, Rani, thank you, but forgive me if I lapse, force of habit."

"Well, try to remember. Smoke?"

"No thank you, Rani, I don't."

"Good God, how'd that happen? Someone told me you'd been in the army. Didn't you buggers all smoke there? Not that I think you're bugger, by the way, far from it."

He was at sea.

"I managed to avoid smoking," was all he could manage, and he tried to swing the conversation by describing her husband's body and the injuries that killed him. That quietened her.

"Rani, we have to gather all possible information about your husband's murder. I know you weren't here, but I don't know exactly where you were. Please enlighten me so I can move on with the investigation."

She looked startled, bothered, then angry. "Are you suggesting I'm a bloody suspect? You think I could have butchered my husband like that? I repeat, I wasn't even here! Do I have to call in our, my lawyer?"

He had predicted that. "Not at all, Rani, no need for the lawyer or for alarm. As I say, we simply need to know where people were at the time your husband died."

"But I wasn't here."

This was getting circular. She seemed reluctant to say where she was. "No you weren't, so it's highly unlikely you could be a suspect."

She calmed.

"But we do need to know where you were," he continued, "so we can rule out other people as well. It saves time later." He hoped he sounded convincing.

"I see that." She regained composure by drawing on the cigarette holder, striking a pose, blowing out smoke then tapping ash into a giant glass ashtray already half full of butts. She seemed nervous, which surprised him given the earlier bravado. "But you'll understand I'm not anxious to draw my friends into this, that would be unfair."

"I understand that," Le Fanu responded, "and I assure you, anything you tell me will be in the strictest confidence."

"Guaranteed?"

"Yes, unless the information links people directly to the death, of course, and that seems unlikely."

She stood, walked slowly to the sideboard and poured an orange juice that probably contained something stronger, the way she sipped at it before returning to the table, but still standing. Something was bothering her.

"This is embarrassing, Superintendent."

"It will be in confidence, Rani."

"I was with some friends, in the country, as I said. Well, a friend, at least, and it was not a she as I had suggested."

"Very well, I understand your concern. May I know his name?"

"Jason Palmer. He's a tea planter up in the Nilgiris, but also has a place outside Madras, at Saidapet in Chingleput district." That was just a few miles out of Madras. "We met in Ooty last year. There was nothing to it then but we met again recently here in town. I was fed up with Pally, so Jason and I started spending time together."

She was more relaxed, ready to talk, but it was not Palmer who interested Le Fanu. At least, not yet. "Why were you upset with your husband?"

"A couple of things. He'd become lazy, didn't want to do anything, wouldn't go anywhere, couldn't be bothered."

"Was he ill?" Le Fanu remembered Ramachandran's comments.

"Not that he mentioned to me. Well, he wasn't saying

much to me about anything, not lately."

"What do you mean?"

"He'd become quiet, almost secretive. It was unlike him. When I first met Pally, he was a real bloody livewire. He stood out even in Sydney, always in the middle of everything, especially parties. And he told me everything he was up to. But the last six months…"

"He changed?"

"Hugely, became a bloody dormouse. No bloody good to me. Madras isn't Sydney, you know, and I love that place. I told Pally if I was coming here he needed to keep me entertained, and the last few months he did not. That's how Jason came into the picture. He's highly competent, especially in a couple of departments." She looked directly at Le Fanu who understood immediately, and blushed. "Sorry, Superintendent, I didn't mean to embarrass you."

That made it worse. "Not at all, Rani, you're helping me get a picture. Do you have any ideas about why your husband changed so much?"

"No, but it began after he returned from a trip to London earlier this year. I didn't go because he spent only a few days there before coming back. All that sailing was too bloody boring for me."

What a terrible problem to have, Le Fanu thought, remembering tough days in the aftermath of the Non-Co-Operation campaign. Some long sailing days then would have been just fine.

"So he was not in London long, but was a different person when he returned?

"Yes."

"Did he sail from here or via Bombay?" Perhaps the problems were based in India rather than England.

"He sailed from here and connected to another ship in Colombo, and vice versa coming back."

So if something changed it was in England, probably London. "Do you have any thoughts on what the problems might have been?" Perhaps the Rajah had had a medical check, although she seemed not to know he had a problem.

"Money, I think." She placed a new cigarette in the holder, lit up. "When he came back he was more concerned about costs than before."

"Does, ah, did he keep any records, a diary, or anything like that?"

"To be honest, I've no idea. He kept me away from all the business things, which suited me fine. Couldn't be bloody bothered."

"We'll need to search the house, you understand? That will include his office and the library but also the other rooms, including bedrooms. If there are any records of what made him change, they could help us understand why he was killed."

"Of course, when would you like to start?"

"I'll get some people over straight away. And please ensure that your servants touch nothing in the meantime. There could be crucial evidence here."

"I'll make sure they stay away. And you'll keep quiet about Jason?"

"So long as his name doesn't arise in the investigation somehow, I'll do my best to keep that quiet."

"Thank you. I'm not ashamed, though I'm sad it happened because of the change in Pally. And now that Pally's dead, if Jason's name did appear you know what this bloody town's like."

He did, and thought of Ro, and how he let her go because of what "this bloody town" might think.

The Rani remained in the annexe while he telephoned Habi who answered immediately. Le Fanu arranged for another search party to come to Pallampur House. By day's end, they might know what had disturbed the Rajah. That could provide more clues on the London connection.

Le Fanu spoke with Caldicott, too, requesting a background check on Jason Palmer. The planters were a law unto themselves, so it would be useful to see where the man fitted into the picture.

As the car took him back towards headquarters, Le Fanu wondered how some of these people filled in their time. Charlotte Stacey was a social butterfly in constant need of entertainment. Her husband's violent death had not upset her. She was more concerned about gossip, and about how she could amuse herself in what she considered an inferior city. Oddly, her attitude towards Madras upset him. He did not admire the city's elite, but there were good people in the place who deserved her respect.

He was thinking too much. As they headed towards the Marina, he asked the driver on the spur of the moment to go towards the ancient, colourful Kapileswarar Temple. They stopped outside, he removed his shoes and socks and walked in, to remind himself of the real India. The towering gopuram with its multitude of gods and goddesses was as impressive as ever. This temple pre-dated the British presence in Madras, having stood here from around the eleventh century, about the time the Crusaders left for the Levant to eliminate Muslim rule. That turned out well. He was still fighting Muslims a few years ago, and the new Middle East boundaries looked set to continue the strife. Meanwhile, the British clutched onto their Empire. The Kapileswarar Temple had watched empires come and go.

Some devotees were puzzled to be joined by a European in police uniform, but others were pleased. Le Fanu walked around, reflecting. He liked escaping the shallowness that stalked the city's European elements.

Twelve

It was near lunch and Le Fanu knew he would not see Habi for a couple of hours. Back at the office, Caldicott was poring over papers, looking puzzled.

"Any problem, Jackson?"

"To be honest, I'm not sure. I may still have to go to Delhi, but suddenly this morning I'm visited by a London chap who just happens to be here in Madras for a few days but doesn't want anyone to know. He left these papers, obviously under instructions from my London contacts."

"Who is he?"

"Wouldn't give me his name. Came in, handed over the papers, swore me to secrecy apart from you and Habi – he named both of you, so he's well informed. Then he left."

"What did he look like?"

"Nondescript. I doubt I'd recognise him again easily."

"Secret service?"

"Undoubtedly. I know a few, but he's not among them. There've been some new branches opened, too, so he could be from any one of those."

"Hmm, I'll mention it to the Chief Secretary. If he doesn't know the fellow's here then no one else will. Which raises the question of why he is here. What's in the papers?"

Caldicott flicked through some pages he had flagged. "Background on the Rajah, especially on his English connections. I haven't digested it all yet, but he's been under surveillance for three or four years, since the end of the war."

So the Rajah of Pallampur was being watched by the British secret services. An agent here in Madras secretly, it seemed, meant the Rajah caused someone in London serious concern. An officer in Delhi doing similar things suggested London thought he was involved in something significant. If no-one senior knew about this secret service presence in Madras, the consequences could be catastrophic. The already maligned Special Branch would get unwanted attention again. This was becoming more complicated by the day.

"Do the papers indicate why London is so interested?" Le Fanu asked.

"There's a lot of financial records: bank accounts, transactions, funds tracking. Turns out friend the Rajah had an account at Coutts."

Even after all these years in India, Le Fanu was still surprised by the local elite's worldliness. Coutts was the secretive bank to the rich and famous, including the Royal family. It was discreet, but well enough known to feature in Gilbert and Sullivan lyrics and Robert Louis Stevenson's writings. Famous people entered its headquarters at 440 The Strand. That included Indian princes who found it more convenient to control their monies from there. If the Rajah had a Coutts account, then large sums were involved. Getting details would be nigh on impossible, unless the secret service sources helped. Le Fanu wondered if the Rani knew about the money. Probably not.

"Well, that's a surprise in one way, but not in another," he said.

Caldicott looked bemused. "Not sure what you mean, sir."

"Sorry for being muddled. If the Rajah spent a lot of time in London and Europe then Coutts is an obvious choice. It's just that I'm always surprised that someone from up-country knows how to find such a bank."

"His account's not at the Strand, though. It was transferred to the new Park Lane branch that opened last year. That's an interesting twist."

After almost three hundred and thirty years of trading, Coutts had opened its second branch in one of London's wealthiest suburbs. Either the Rajah was one of their most important clients, or this was some other kind of message.

"Do the papers mention property purchases?" Le Fanu asked.

"Not so far but I've still a lot left to read."

"Alright, keep going and we can meet later for an update. What about Gerald Taylor?"

Caldicott reached for a sheaf of papers and telegrams in another pile. "Curious," he said, "at this end so far there's not much beyond the basic outline you gave me. I'm still searching for the company registration papers, and that surprises me because those are usually easy to find. The registration people can't lay their hands on them yet. They're to get back to me this afternoon."

"And what's in those telegrams?" Le Fanu asked.

"I suppose that's why you're a Superintendent," Caldicott said, before looking more serious. "The telegrams are significant, because of what they don't say."

Now Le Fanu looked puzzled.

Caldicott grinned. "I believe the Chief Secretary or the Governor suggested there might be more to him than meets the eye?"

Le Fanu nodded.

"My contacts have produced almost nothing, apart from the fact that access to his files is limited to a few very senior people," Caldicott continued.

"Oh, no, not another spy," Le Fanu groaned.

"Not necessarily, but something like that. That makes it even more interesting that he's holed up in Changarore. Someone wants him out of the way."

Gerald Taylor was more interesting now than earlier, thought Le Fanu. The oddity was that the less they discovered the more interesting he became. "Any chance you might get more information from London?"

"I have one more person who might help," Caldicott replied, "and I've sent him a request in code so our telegraph people won't get interested. Hopefully he'll reply quickly."

"Alright, keep going on those fronts. When Habi returns, ask him to be available about five so we three can catch up on things. I'll seek an audience with the Chief Secretary, but you don't know that if anyone asks."

As he left, Le Fanu contemplated the escalating challenge. A leading Presidency notable is slashed to death in his own home early one morning. His flamboyant Australian wife arrives at the house a couple of hours later following an assignation with a European planter. The victim's main accounts are with England's leading private banker. Moreover, he was under on-going scrutiny by British security services. That included an undercover surveillance officer working in Madras at the time of the murder and, apparently, without local authorities being informed. New Delhi also had a watch on the victim at the time of his death. A senior ICS officer, the son-in-law of the Secretary of State for India, stands accused of being corrupted by the victim. And there is a possible connection between all this and an embezzlement case involving Gerald Taylor. Rather than being a simple Changarore merchant, his London files are available only to a privileged few, which suggests he is also involved with the intelligence services.

Le Fanu was convinced these elements were linked. After all, the Rajah's hired hands were suspected of gun running. If the investigation into Westshire's connections turned up something odd, then the links and the complexity were certain. Le Fanu longed for more information, if only to offer Jepson some scraps. But even Jepson was odd, Le Fanu remembered. Odd for Jepson, that is, because he was being reasonable.

The car took him towards Fort St George. It was a trip through history mixed with present day challenges. The Government tried hard to suppress nationalist sentiment in the university colleges, but as he passed Queen Mary's then Presidency he saw anti-British signs and posters plastered on walls everywhere, and workers scurrying to erase them. The signs would be back tomorrow. Congress had a strong following among the students who were the next generation of leaders, so the Government faced a longer struggle than it realised. The police knew that, but not the civil service. A daily stream of Secretariat memoranda offered advice about how to win back the students, but the students were not reading the memoranda.

Further along the Marina, the Board of Revenue basked in the splendour of the Chepauk Palace and generated its own memoranda. Those suggested that while crops were poor, living costs high, peasants restive and lawyers agitated, it was still time to raise taxes in politically sensitive districts. It was folly. District superintendents were hard pressed to maintain order even though the Non-Co-Operation campaign was suspended. The tax grab provoked more unrest. In Guntur district, the Government sacked the Collector, Arthur Galletti, who thought reasoned debate a better weapon than oppression. Le Fanu thought he, Westshire and Galletti were three against the tide. Galletti was replaced by a hardliner backed by a contingent of troops. More shootings, more deaths, and more trouble for local police resulted.

Le Fanu looked away from the buildings and out across the beach. Every couple of hundred yards or so small groups of people stood waving placards. They were defying Government orders that ruled meetings of more than three people to be unlawful assemblies. If the police or the army followed those instructions strictly, the courts and jails would be clogged and the administration grounded. Jepson wanted to follow that letter of the law but was held back by wiser counsel, for the moment. Even so, Le Fanu thought, it might be easier to deal with that political issue than with the tangle building around his cases.

Any visitor to Fort St George now passed through two checkpoints, such was the concern for security. English soldiers from the Dorsets checked him through the first one. They were returned from Malabar where they put down a Muslim uprising with great bloodshed. There was trouble all over the Presidency at present. The second group came from one of the Punjabi regiments posted south.

By the time he reached the Chief Secretary's door, Le Fanu had endured two further checks. But he was in luck. Whitney was free.

"Come in, LF. I know it's important because you usually avoid this place."

Le Fanu sat on the other side of the desk, wondering if he was really that transparent.

"Thank you, sir. I've come directly from a discussion with Caldicott who received information on the Rajah of Pallampur. We've yet to fully assess that information, but we're intrigued by its bearer."

Lighting another cigar, Whitney paused the match.

"Sir, are you aware of any London agent based here in Madras and checking into the Rajah?"

The match was extinguished, the cigar lowered. "What sort of an agent, LF?"

"Not sure, sir, but we think secret service or similar. Caldicott contacted his London pals. First we were told we might have to go to Delhi to talk to someone out from London checking on the Rajah. Then this person turns up unannounced in Caldicott's office, gives no name, but hands over a sheaf of papers saying he's instructed to do so by London."

"LF, I've absolutely no knowledge of this, so you'll know

I'm less than impressed. Thanks for coming straight over. I'll check with the Governor, but if he knew I'm sure he'd have told me. Very strange. You think this adds substance to the gun running issue?"

"Well, we wondered about that, but Caldicott's going through all the papers now so we'll have a better idea later. I'll let you know as soon as we know anything more. There's a further curiosity, however."

He told Whitney about the Gerald Taylor situation. The Chief Secretary looked even more puzzled, and as close to anger as Le Fanu had ever seen him.

"You know, LF, there's something really wrong here. Seems we have an ex-spy up in Changarore we know nothing about, as well as an unknown secret agent swanning about our city. That suggests something important is developing. If there is, I damn well need to know. And so does the Governor. You sure the police side knows nothing?"

"Sir, you'd best ask the I-G that. He's in a calmer frame of mind, but he'd not share that sort of information with me."

Whitney brightened. "Better behaved is he? Not completely daft, then."

Le Fanu said nothing.

"Sorry, LF, I'm being mysterious. You'll keep it to yourself, I know. The governor asked me to speak with the I-G, pointing out that his less than stellar performance and intemperate approach to command have been noticed. Perhaps he got the message."

"Perhaps, sir." Le Fanu wondered how long Jepson would remain calm.

"Be optimistic, LF. But I doubt Jepson knows any of this if I don't. At least I hope he doesn't."

Le Fanu wished he could be in on Whitney's next discussion with Jepson.

Whitney finally lit the cigar, and wandered over to take in the view from his top floor windows. "I'll have a chat to the

Governor," he said, "but I've a funny feeling he knows as much as I do, which is nothing. See what you can find out, and I'll give you a call tonight. Better still, meet me for dinner at the Club. Make it about eight."

Le Fanu could not refuse, but the political obstinacy of the Club held even less attraction than his lonely house. The car took him back to his office. The workers at Presidency and Queen Mary's were still taking down posters.

Thirteen

It was mid-afternoon by the time he got back. Habi and Caldicott were both there.

According to Habi, a pawnbroker heard someone was offering the private sale of a revolver similar to the one they were after. The pawnbroker specialised in unique firearms. He had an established UK market, working through a cousin who went there as a student but never returned. Apparently, the person selling the revolver came from the country where he was the servant of a European.

"Habi, are you thinking what I'm thinking?" Le Fanu asked.

"If you're thinking planter then, yes."

"It's too neat, too easy," Caldicott commented, half perched on the edge of a desk. "We couldn't be that lucky, or any villain that stupid, surely?"

Le Fanu agreed. "We started with assumptions that served us poorly and we've had to start again, so let's not assume anything here, either. What more do you know, Habi?"

"Not a lot, sir, minor details. I've asked the police station nearest to the seller to gather more information. I haven't explained why I'm asking, either. The story might come out innocently, then we'd end up with a planter running off to the Chief Secretary or, worse, the Madras Mail."

Le Fanu wondered how Chester Barnes would approach

that, given his attempts to give the Mail more balance. But he said nothing. Judgment was still pending. The Mail had a long history to overcome.

"Good," he said, "bring us up to date when you hear more. What about you, Jackson?"

"I have a telegram from another London contact. Taylor was in the intelligence services at the start of the war, then was suddenly shipped out here. There was a scandal but no-one's saying too much. He remained active through the war, though, he ran a research service for London using the local Changarore telegraph office."

"That doesn't seem likely, does it?" Le Fanu was sceptical.

"It might be possible. Other people did similar things from Europe. But that's very different from Changarore. Not exactly a centre of activity, was it? And unless he has very special skills, the agencies would usually hire someone closer to home."

"Habi," Le Fanu asked, "were there any special military units up there through the war?" Habi came from Nellore. That was not so far north as Changarore, but Habi retained a vast network of local informants.

"Artillery units were there for most of the war, with little to do. For some reason, after the Emden shelled Madras in 1914 the military bigwigs decided the coast there was a likely attack point. Nothing happened, but the gunners stayed."

"Hardly reason to have an intelligence operation there," Caldicott chipped in. "Seems like London needed a bolthole for Taylor, and decided on Changarore for some reason. Whatever he did after he arrived was probably to justify the decision rather than do anything useful. By the way, I've more information on his trading business."

He had tracked the company registration papers to a safe at the registry office. According to Caldicott, that was unusual security for an ordinary transaction. Taylor's company was supposedly just another of the minor trading outlets set up in small towns and ports along the coast.

There was more, however. "From those papers, I tracked the financial links back to London. Taylor's funding was paid out of a civil service source, but channelled through a third party provider."

"Is that usual?" Le Fanu asked.

"Not at all. That's why it's important, particularly when I tell you the name of the third party."

"Pallampur," Habi pronounced.

Caldicott was stunned. "How did you know?"

"I didn't," the sergeant said, "but after the mysterious planter and the revolver story, the Rajah seemed the obvious answer in yet another coincidence."

"Don't worry, Jackson," Le Fanu said, "Habi does this all the time, he has a knack for intuitive thinking."

"Well, it's a great gift because he's right. My contact says the money came from a military propaganda wing and was channelled through the Rajah's Coutts account, obviously then at the Strand but now shifted to Park Lane."

"And the Rajah then funded Taylor when he arrived in Changarore?"

"Yes, and the company registration papers don't mention that." Caldicott looked pensive. "Not that they necessarily would, but those finance arrangements are odd."

"There's one obvious question," Habi said. "Who authorised the payment to Taylor via the Rajah of Pallampur, and why? And one more: who here in Madras knew, if anyone? With such a thing going on, you'd think someone would be advised."

"Quite right, Habi," Le Fanu said, "we've more work to do. Where do we start, you two?"

Caldicott would probe further into the business registration to determine the exact nature of Taylor's trading. He would also contact additional London financial sources to learn more about the money trail, but was pessimistic given

Coutts' reputation for confidentiality.

"I'll give it a try, LF, but I doubt it'll work. Might have to try something unconventional." He grinned.

"Well, don't tell me until later, if at all, I'll leave that to you. Habi, what's your next move?"

"I'll contact some Changarore people for more information on Taylor, and chase up anything else on that possible revolver source. I'm worried about the picture we're getting. As we agree, it seems too easy."

"Alright," Le Fanu said, "both do what you can through the rest of the day, then we'll meet back here seven thirty in the morning. Have a good evening when you do both get home."

He knew Habi would be fine. Caldicott still lived in a chummery, though, sharing a rambling place near Adyar with other unattached men drawn from commerce, the civil service and the law, including a Presbyterian minister. Le Fanu was not sure how good an evening that could be, even after drinks and dinner at the Club. Which reminded him, he had to fill in until eight when he met the Chief Secretary.

He needed a couple of hours at home, to think. The bike was in the stables so he gathered some things, shut the door and walked down the stairs. A servant wheeled out the Powerplus. Le Fanu put on his recently bought leather helmet and goggles. He doubted they would help if he did come off but put them on anyway, and started up. As usual, it brought out a few servants, and some European colleagues scowled out their windows. Most of them feared the unconventional, along with strong decision-making and logical thought he reflected.

Needing sea air, he took a long way home. He rode south along the beach line to the Adyar River with its eponymous club. Europeans took their families there, not allowable at the Madras Club. Off in the distance he saw the headquarters of the Theosophy movement, which drew followers from around the world. He was not sure why but its leader, Annie Besant, was still influential in Madras even though most Europeans despised her eclectic mix of Western rationality, Eastern mysticism and pro-Indian politics. Rather than return down the outer reaches of Mount Road, he rode through smaller back streets towards Mylapore and home.

The ride reminded him of the India he and the ICS did not see regularly enough. He dealt mainly with people outside the law. The ICS, in the city at least, met the movers and shakers. Out here, many Indian families lived on the street with few possessions and a smaller future even if independence did arrive. Some kids went to school, if they lived long enough. On the outer city limits, shantytowns mushroomed as people flocked in beguiled by the prospect of jobs, money and opportunity which, for most of them, was an illusion.

He passed some of those shantytowns. A friend in the Corporation of Madras told him there were over a hundred officially identified slums. There was no telling how many there really were. Those slums and shanties created more work for missionaries like the one who shared Caldicott's chummery. There were far more of them now than just five years ago. He admired their tenacity if not their purpose. Converting people from Hinduism was a major challenge.

Along the streets, Corporation employees were laying drains and installing other services, but shantytown growth outstripped the government's financial and human capacity as the missionaries, Theosophists and others kept pointing out. Those alternative voices got short shrift in official circles, yet another social division in this small but convoluted European social order. Le Fanu reflected on the cocooned nature of these European sections, and on his own inability to connect with most of them.

By the time he turned in the gate, he felt worse than when he left the office despite the exhilaration of the ride. The mail brought nothing new. And he still had to read Ro's latest. Later. He took a club and a putter out to the lawn and spent an hour practising his short game. There was a competition at the Gymkhana this weekend. He would play, anything to get out of the house.

He was ready by seven thirty, and sniffing a Glenmorangie when the telephone rang. It was Caldicott. James Westshire was summoned to the Chepauk Palace by the First Member of the Board of Revenue, Arthur Jamieson, first thing in the morning. So was Le Fanu. He groaned. Two years earlier, the now-First Member was a pretentious and arrogant Third Member involved in the Jane Carstairs case. He and Le Fanu clashed strongly. This would be a tense reunion. He hesitated, drained the whisky, called the driver, and set out for Mount Road.

Fourteen

Dinner turned out well, despite his fears. The Chief Secretary arranged a table in a secluded part of the garden, away from the pack. Whitney ordered a Bordeaux to settle the food and the preceding whiskeys.

As anticipated, Lord Willingdon knew nothing about the clandestine London emissary, and was furious. New Delhi was being bombarded with "please explains" and, in turn, handing them to London for advice on how to placate an enraged Governor. According to Whitney, Willingdon displayed a magisterial command of all military curses.

They agreed there was little to do immediately other than keep each other informed. Relaxed, they agreed also that the English fare was poor doings given local alternatives. The wine sparked a taste for more alcohol, and more whiskeys allowed Whitney time to expend another two cigars. It was one in the morning before Le Fanu arrived home courtesy of his driver. He recognised the paradox: he was all for increased Indian responsibility, but relied on his servants. He slept well, woke early, had a good breakfast and was in the office when the other two arrived.

They planned the day and agreed to meet in the late afternoon. Now it was time to meet James Westshire.

It was another short trip along the Esplanade to the Chepauk Palace whose British inhabitants, Le Fanu thought, were long on attitude and short on insight. Millions of Indians were affected by their decisions on land, water and tax, yet those Indian concerns were disregarded. As the Indo-Saracenic domes of the University and the Palace loomed, Le Fanu wondered what the current Prince of Arcot was doing over at his family's new home in the Amir Mahal, a couple of miles away. A predecessor lost the Palace to the British in the mid-nineteenth century. Perhaps the present British lot in the south would have been better had the Board and Secretariat bosses back then dealt more creatively with the Prince. Probably not, but it was tempting to think things might have been easier.

They turned in through the gates and he climbed the front steps, looking briefly to the front tower's distinctive architecture. The grandeur paled inside. The place was choked by a legion of clerks who tracked the titles and tax obligations of everyone claiming land ownership in the Presidency. Millions of records were maintained about monies due and accounted payable.

That work was sharper-edged now. During Non-Co-Operation, the Board won the right to seize personal and household goods in lieu of unpaid taxes. It was clever, at one level. In some districts the movement mutated into a non-payment of taxes campaign, so the Government's response was both political and financial. The disadvantage was that the strategy produced even more enemies among an already alienated populace. District superintendents told Le Fanu they encountered fierce resistance to the collection of goods and chattels.

He reached the second floor via a set of stairs thronged by people carrying files. This was the archetypal Raj, people carrying paper from one room to another with no obvious purpose. Reaching the First Member's offices, he was shown into the main meeting room.

Long bay windows showed out to the ocean, but little natural light penetrated back from there so the lamps were already on. They brightened things in mid-room, but shadows stalked the walls lined with photographs and paintings from which stared serious-faced earlier Board officials. Bookcases held the official Board Proceedings, which each District Collector must know inside out. But those rules changed daily, so implementing officials were forever scrambling to keep up. No wonder Board members were held in low esteem by their country subordinates, Le Fanu thought.

He was surprised to see all four Members present, seated along the table with their backs to the windows, which meant their faces were shadowed. Each was supported by an ICS Under-Secretary and several clerks seated along the walls to the side.

Arthur Jamieson sat in the middle, more pompous than ever. He was gaunt, hollow-cheeked and tight-lipped with sunken eyes. The prominent nose accentuated the mottled moustache and thin, pursed lips. Grey, wispy hair stranded across his scalp, well back from the temples. His elevated status had inspired Jamieson to wear a monocle now fixed in his left eye, but not well. It kept falling out.

"Ah Le Fanu, thank you for coming. A pleasure for all of us, I'm sure. We at the Board always appreciate advice from the IPS."

The good river sarcasm was in full flood.

Le Fanu was relegated to a side of the table well away from the Members. He sat opposite another lone figure. That had to be James Westshire. They were not introduced.

The man looked tall, over six feet, wiry thin with narrow shoulders that seemed tinier in the ill-fitting grey suit jacket. A green tie jarred with the suit. It was knotted untidily against a white shirt whose collar was now three sizes too big for the neck. The head was small, nose well shaped. Tension etched the blue eyes staring out from under bushy, fair eyebrows crowned ultimately by a cropped head of greying hair. The hands resting on the table were worn. This man spent more time in the field than in rooms dealing with people like Jamieson.

"As you know, Le Fanu," Jamieson droned, "we have before us an especially troubling matter. That is why we are all here today, and we thank Mr. Westshire for having come down from Ramsheed."

As if he had any choice. Westshire looked across the table at Le Fanu, eyebrows raised.

"Yes, First Member" replied Le Fanu, "but I'm unclear as to why I'm here."

"So are we, Le Fanu," came the immediate response. He had played into Jamieson's campaign. "We see no useful purpose in your being here, but the Chief Secretary thought there was so we hoped you might share that with us." Jamieson looked to his colleagues. They all studiously read their papers, embarrassed by the exchange.

"I, for one, am glad Superintendent Le Fanu is here."

Westshire's voice was deep and resonant. The man was not over-awed being here or by those sitting in judgement. Others in his predicament would have been silent to the point of catatonic. The deep voice continued.

"This is a total fabrication, and needs a police mind to sort it out. Neither the Board nor the Secretariat can sift fact from fiction. Superintendent Le Fanu is better able to do that."

Jamieson paled, the lip line tightening further. "You will speak only when addressed and when asked to do so, Westshire. You're a disgrace to the service and have no rights whatsoever, so kindly keep your views to yourself."

The result of this inquiry was preordained, thought Le Fanu. "Excuse me, First Member," he intervened, "Perhaps the Chief Secretary's idea was that my unit could examine the circumstances, then inform the Board as to the accuracy or otherwise of the matters as reported."

He hated the bureaucratic language, but it was what Jamieson understood. Le Fanu noticed Westshire glance at him, and detected a wry smile.

"We know the situation only too well, Le Fanu." Jamieson's voice lifted, cracked. "This poor excuse for an ICS officer has let down the service by engaging in corrupt activity with the Rajah of Pallampur who sided with the rabble against us."

That was the quintessential conservative European view, and Le Fanu was interested to notice a couple of Members looked uncomfortable.

"You'll know, of course, First Member, that my unit is also inquiring into the Rajah's murder. Sir Charles Whitney has determined it wise to consider that murder and the charges against Mr. Westshire conjointly, for obvious reasons. We must be sure of our facts in all respects, and check any possible overlapping matters."

"Absolute nonsense, Le Fanu." Jamieson was visibly angry. "We will deal with this miscreant and get him out of the service. We must show the Indians we do not tolerate corruption anywhere."

The idea that a senior officer with so much power could, after all these years, consign all "Indians" into one compartment saddened and angered Le Fanu. If this was the level of understanding and knowledge, the British were politically moribund.

"I understand that, First Member, but the Chief Secretary has given me instructions at the behest of the Governor which I'm bound to carry out."

Jamieson winced, knowing he had no choice, but he was unwilling to let go. "This is just caving in. We must act resolutely, and now," he whined.

"And I'm sure you will, First Member. Our inquiries shouldn't take too long. If I may suggest, perhaps Mr. Westshire and I might retire to another room, if you can find us one. We can have a discussion there while you continue here so long as you need. I'll report back to you and the Chief Secretary, and we can then decide a course of action."

The First Member agreed, with little grace. He barked orders to a clerk who asked Le Fanu and Westshire to follow him. They walked to the back of the building, entered a small room with a dusty table, a couple of chairs, and a mountain of files. Le Fanu ordered tea, Westshire asked for coffee. Both arrived minutes later, and they were left to themselves.

Fifteen

"Le Fanu." He reached across the table to Westshire whose return grip was firm, the hand calloused.

"James Westshire. Sorry you've been dragged into this."

"Might be a good thing for you I'm here. You've not a lot of support out there judging by that performance."

Westshire looked at him, perhaps wondering how open he might be with the policeman. "I've heard a lot about you, "he said, "even up in the wilds of Ramsheed. It's a small Presidency. You've a reputation for being straight, and no respecter of rank."

"Not sure I'd put it that way," Le Fanu replied. He found these discussions awkward. "I do my work based on the facts."

"Fair enough. I hope you can in my case, because no-one else does."

Le Fanu thought back to the PCR and decided on a direct approach. "You've a reputation yourself, for being an irritant to all and sundry ever since you arrived."

Westshire laughed. "You've seen the PCR, then?"

"Interesting reading. How'd you manage to make so many enemies?"

"Rumour has it you're not too different," shot back Westshire, "Jamieson likes you as much as he does me."

"The First Member and I had different views on a case a couple of years ago."

"Was he as rational then as he is now?"

"I can't answer that question, but he couldn't see the full range of the options."

"There's a surprise." Sardonic until now, Westshire was suddenly bitter. "The man's a fool, and narrow minded."

"Perhaps so, but he's the one sitting in judgement. What material do you have to rebut the charges?"

"How much time do you have?"

"More than enough. As I said in there, the Rajah's death changed things. I'm instructed to find out as much as I can. That's why I'm here. Use the opportunity to help me see things differently."

Westshire took time to reach full stride, but over the next hour gave Le Fanu a significantly alternative version of events.

He covered all the episodes mentioned in the PCR: disciplinary hearings, admonitions, reprimands, charges and vengeful campaigns. Like Le Fanu, he disliked the Government's increased repression and wanted more support for ordinary people. He rebuked several officials, including Members of the Board.

Westshire supported delaying the water tax increases. The Board conducted the usual survey in his district, fixed an increase, and prepared for collection. Westshire claimed the survey evidence was flawed because alternative information gathered by Congress was ignored. The Board, led by Jamieson, branded him a Congress supporter. The local Congress publicised him as a Chepauk Palace victim, further damaging his standing with the Board. Westshire had a University of Madras economist verify the Congress figures. The Board charged him with insubordination. As Le Fanu knew, the Board and the Secretariat had a gift for ignoring facts when convenient.

"What about the Boer War episode?" Le Fanu asked.

"I was young and brash, and stupid. Honesty looked like the best approach but I should've kept quiet."

Le Fanu recalled his own learning experiences. He and Westshire had much in common. "And the wartime statements?"

Westshire was wary. "Look. Le Fanu, you had a tough war and I respect what you did, but there were aspects of it that had to be debated."

"Wouldn't argue with that." But Le Fanu still harboured a doubt. "What about the Gandhi episode?"

Westshire shook his head. "If it wasn't treated so seriously it would be wonderful Gilbert and Sullivan material."

"What happened?"

"An American journalist wrote an article criticising the treatment of cattle in India. It focused on Hinduism's veneration of the cow. The American, like most Westerners, considered the cows to be neglected, diseased and under-nourished. Gandhi picked up on the article in an essay, arguing that Indians should improve cattle conditions as part of self-improvement."

Westshire thought Gandhi's piece ill-informed. He wrote to the Mahatma, conveying Ramsheed research findings that countered the American's view. Gandhi acknowledged receipt but wrote nothing else. Someone at the Board discovered the exchange. Westshire was sure one of his conservative juniors passed information to the Chepauk Palace. The Board charged Westshire with disobeying instructions and discussing Government policy with an unauthorised person.

Le Fanu saw Jamieson's hand in that sophistry. The Board was notorious for becoming bogged in the letter of the law rather than the evidence. Westshire wrote to Gandhi, yes, but to point out positives in the British case. The Board disregarded that.

"I'll look into that," Le Fanu said. "But you'd better give me your version of this minerals company matter."

For the first time, Westshire's self-assurance slipped. It crumpled.

"I've been a bloody fool," he said. He propped his elbows on the table, bony wrists protruding even further from the flapping shirtsleeves pulled out from the jacket. The small head lowered into the cupped hands. He looked under pressure.

"So?"

"Among other things I'm an amateur geologist. It gives me a break from the work, and from the Board. A couple of years ago I found iron ore deposits in one of the Ramsheed taluks. The deposits were average quality but good enough, and there were a lot of them. As you know, my district's poor, so I saw a chance for a new industry and more jobs. God knows we need them there."

Le Fanu saw a good district man. The best ICS officers went out to these places to make a difference. Creating opportunities and jobs was the best antidote to rising political spirit, not police and military repression. "What happened?"

Westshire shrugged. "I filed a report with the appropriate department, informed the Board, and nothing happened. Usual rigmarole: budget cuts, low on the priorities, blah blah blah. Then I met a local landholder who wanted to take it up. He was close to the Rajah of Pallampur so I saw opportunities, especially with all these rising political troubles."

"What did you do?"

"Made a huge mistake. The landholder claimed he couldn't register a company because of problems he had with the Government. He suggested we file a company in my name to secure the deposits. We would still have to negotiate with the people whose land held the deposits, but this would be a start. Meanwhile, he'd talk to the Rajah who'd take over the company and I'd stand back."

"Interesting idea but not a smart one."

"No, and it got worse. The Rajah was reluctant and no one else would step in. Then Non-Co-Operation arrived, I got caught up in dealing with that and, believe it or not, forgot the company papers were still in my name. That was about a year ago. Then, lo and behold, as all these other charges appeared, those mineral papers became general knowledge. I think the same officer leaked them as payback for something he thought I'd done to him."

"So you didn't make any money out of this?"

"Money? I paid all the fees, so it's cost me money."

"Didn't the Board consider all that?"

"I made several submissions to the Board but it still maintains I broke the rules. Technically, I did, but all I'm guilty of is trying to improve my district."

"You're vulnerable."

"Yes, and even more on this court case issue."

"How so?"

"The Rajah felt guilty over not helping me with the minerals development, so suggested we support other worthy causes. But he needed help, first."

"His retainers?"

"Yes, they'd allegedly roughed up a couple of thugs who took them to court. That was unusual, the thugs usually sort it out among themselves. So these clowns appear before me and it wasn't worth the court's time."

"Bad call, given your reputation."

"Yes. I dismissed it, just the thing my critics were waiting for. It was the right call, according to law, but I should have dealt with it in a smarter way. Put it down to tiredness, carelessness, recklessness, whatever. "

"Were they guilty?"

"Of course not. If they were I'd have convicted them, the Rajah's men or not. The so-called evidence was pure fabrication."

"Did Pallampur give you any sense of why those charges arose?"

"No, but I knew he was worried. The thugs had something on him, I'm sure."

"What did you get in return? That's the key."

Westshire leaned back in his chair, arms raised. "Ha. There's the irony. The Rajah promised nothing, just that he'd help with something when the moment arose."

"You slipped up, didn't you? It's bad enough because the company registration was against the rules, but add that to your history…."

"Don't rub it in, Le Fanu. You think facing the vultures in there is hard?" He waved towards the meeting room. "You should see my wife, she's as angry as hell. I'm not proud of myself."

"What happens next here?"

"They'll decide whether or not to sack me."

"Your wife's connection any help?"

"I thought you'd know about that. No, Marjorie's father is profoundly deaf on this matter. Not one of my strong supporters. He's probably even less sympathetic than Jamieson."

"There's little I can do now," Le Fanu said, "but I'll keep this in mind as I deal with the Pallampur case. If you think of anything else or have any documents that might help, let me know. Meanwhile, don't let them provoke you."

They stood, shook hands. Le Fanu left. Westshire shuffled back towards the meeting room.

Sixteen

Ramachandran's autopsy report was on Le Fanu's desk. Cause of death was extensive bleeding from multiple wounds. No surprise there. The Rajah took several minutes to die, it would have been painful. There was a lot of alcohol in his system. They had to determine the Rajah's state of mind at the Governor's reception, how much drink he consumed there, then determine where he went later. What happened during those few hours was crucial.

Le Fanu called the Chief Secretary on a direct office telephone number. "Good morning, Sir Charles, sorry to bother you. We have the autopsy report. It's as we expected. The Rajah had a lot of alcohol aboard when he died. You mentioned last night you were at the Governor's reception. How did he seem to you?"

"Certainly not drunk, LF. I didn't watch him specifically but it was a small enough affair so I was aware of him. He took a couple of drinks but wasn't washing it back."

"How long was he there, do you think?"

"The show started between seven thirty and eight. I probably spotted him last about nine thirty, perhaps a few minutes later. He'd gone by the time I left just after ten."

"And he was sober, so far as you could tell?"

"As I say, he'd had a couple, but looked fine to me. You should talk to His Excellency as well, he might have a better idea. I'll get you an appointment."

"Thank you, sir, that's helpful. We have a three-hour gap or so between his leaving Government House and reaching his own place. By then he'd drunk a lot more. We're wondering where he, was."

"And what was he up to?" the Chief Secretary said. "We're still getting reports about the gun running but they sound unlikely. It's like a campaign is being waged to convince us about the Rajah. That's the trouble. He was a nice man personally, which makes me wonder about this background picture we're getting."

"There are weaknesses, I agree. Now we have the facts about his death, we'll do more investigation here and I'll let you know when anything new arises."

Habi and Caldicott arrived. Determining the Rajah's movements after the Governor's party was now a priority. Habi would question servants at Pallampur House, Caldicott would check the other guests present at Government House and set timelines there. Le Fanu would revisit the Rani.

***

He hated that he was so nervous. She kept him waiting, deliberately.

Charlotte Lacey swept in majestically. Her long black cotton dress was moulded to her body. A strategically placed gold elephant brooch emphasised her impressive chest. High-heeled black shoes gave her extra height, and that unsettled him. Scarlet lipstick and bright makeup were not standard mourning material. Nor was the patterned silk scarf around the throat.

"Good morning, Superintendent, how lovely to see you."

He was here about her husband's murder, in this house. What was lovely about that? Slithering into a chair opposite, stretching and smoothing the dress to accentuate her legs, she directed him to sit. He wasn't transfixed, yet.

"I'm sorry to follow up so soon, Rani, but there are questions we need answered about the Rajah's last movements."

"Of course, Superintendent, but you know now I didn't see him after late afternoon because I was otherwise engaged." She looked at him, smiling.

"Yes." The thought of what she was doing that evening stuck in his head. "But you may have heard him say something. It might have seemed insignificant then. Do you know where he went after the Governor's reception?"

It struck him immediately: why was she not there herself? It was given by the Governor, after all.

She anticipated that. "Superintendent. I'm sure it's hard for you to understand, but I had no interest in Pally's activities, and that included going to boring receptions. He went all the time, and after the first few I told him I wouldn't go. Even to the Governor's. Waste of my time. Willingdon's nice enough but his wife's a bloody shocker. Sorry to be blunt but you know it's true."

Lady Willingdon loved being at the centre of Madras social life, doing "good works", and being passionate about the colour mauve. Le Fanu understood the message but was startled by its Australian bluntness.

"Forgive me for asking, Rani, but was everything alright between you and the Rajah?"

"Oh, we had sex from time to time, if that's what you're asking. But he was also getting it elsewhere, and as for me, well, you know…"

Le Fanu wriggled.

"I'm sorry I'm so direct, Superintendent, but you need to know, don't you? Pally and I knew exactly what we each needed, and led mostly separate lives but that didn't make us unhappy. It was a perfectly good arrangement. I was something different for him to parade around, and he gave me a lovely lifestyle."

Le Fanu saw an opportunity. "What did you know about his financial arrangements?"

"How do you mean?" She looked puzzled.

"Was he in any difficulty?"

Now she looked worried. "Not that I know of, but perhaps you know differently?"

"What we know, Rani, is that his account with Coutts was shifted from the Strand to their new branch in Park Lane last year. Substantial funds were moved in and out of that account. But we don't know why. Do you?"

The control faltered. Her hands flexed and inflexed. She reached for a cigarette, lit it. "Not really," she replied, staring out a window, "but he muttered a couple of things about big expenses. I asked if that meant my bloody allowance was being cut. He said no, but kept talking about costs."

"Did he say what those expenses were?"

"No, just that they were in the UK and not here, apart from the funds he was frittering away on Congress. But he was worried there could be an impact on estate affairs here."

"And you've no idea about why he was worried?

"Not for certain," she replied, "but he was making payments reluctantly and didn't consider them an investment."

"Why did you think that?"

She consulted the distance beyond the window. "Pally was an enthusiast but he was also shrewd. It was only in the past few months that I saw him differently. Nothing specific, but he wasn't convinced that what he was doing was a good thing."

They needed information from Coutts, a huge challenge.

"And you've no idea where he went after the Governor's?"

"None at all."

"Was the Rajah drinking more than usual lately?"

"Quite the reverse. The money matters bothered him and he wanted to be sober so he could think about them clearly."

"The autopsy report will surprise you. It says he was full of alcohol."

For the first time since learning of her husband's death,

Charlotte Tracey looked distressed. She stood, turned away, dabbed the scarf to her eyes. Walking to the window, she replied without looking at Le Fanu.

"That, that must be a mistake."

"We know he had only a little alcohol at the Governor's. Wherever he went later, it appears he consumed a lot more in a short time."

"No, that was out of character normally, let alone the past few months. There's something bloody wrong there, Superintendent."

He left soon after, a servant showing him out because the Rani went straight up to her rooms. That news had shaken her, he thought, and wondered why. She handled her husband's death straightforwardly from the start. Shock might be setting in, but the alcohol issue triggered something. She might know more about his health than she was admitting, or possibly the alcohol consumption was associated with a particular person.

On the journey back he watched bullock carts hauling goods to the trading houses, and handcarts pushed or pulled by frail men wearing little more than loincloths, turbans and sandals. He was used to these sights, but occasionally despaired of the tough lives led by Indians struggling to make a living and maintain a family. These handcart men lived in the slums. Conditions were appalling. Yet out of those kerosene can, cardboard and mud shelters, neatly dressed and presented kids went off to school every day.

Along the Esplanade, the sea breeze rushed through the windows, lifting his spirits. By late afternoon the beach would be crowded between the Cooum and Adyar rivers. Those slum residents and the thousands of homeless would mingle on the sands with the better off. Food stalls and entertainment venues would spring up. Kids would take pony rides and ice creams, their parents escaping houses or huts for a while. The politicians would be there, drumming up support. Petty criminals would be out, pickpockets and fraud merchants. And along the walkways, further back, a few Europeans would parade, mostly from the commercial sector because few Government personnel would stoop to show themselves. They would be in the solitude of their expansive houses, or being entertained in the home of like-minded thinkers as relief from the pressing political cries down on the sands.

This was an important time, Le Fanu realised. Gandhi's non-violent mass movement had success, but tougher elements were taking over. If the Mahatma could not win back support, a more violent future was possible. This gun running development demonstrated that. Meanwhile the Government vowed to suppress dissent, confusing concession and compromise with weakness. That sentiment was stronger in Madras than anywhere else in India. Even Willingdon ordered up more troops ahead of initiating more discussion. An opportunity was being lost. The Governor could not communicate with moderate local Congress leaders who were keen on a peaceful and gradual transition. Willingdon had few, possibly no advisers capable of helping him do that. Whitney was there, but even he was a traditionalist. It was a serious government weakness.

By the time he reached the office it was early afternoon. The mercury was over eighty Fahrenheit. Most people were at lunch or post-lunch napping to see off the heat. Le Fanu felt flat. Neither Habi nor Caldicott were back, so he entered his latest information and questions, sat back, contemplated the boards, and his options on what to do next.

Seventeen

The ringing telephone jolted those thoughts.

"Le Fanu here." Jepson had issued pages of directions about how to answer the things but Le Fanu had not bothered reading them.

"Good afternoon, Superintendent, Barnes speaking. Will we ever get used to this telephone thing?"

"Doubt it."

"You may be right. Look, I can't talk here as I'm not sure who might be listening. Could we meet later? Perhaps the bar at D'Angelis'?"

D'Angelis was owned and run by one of the small Italian community that had found its way to Madras. It was the hotel of choice for younger European civilians, perhaps because it had a good wine cellar to go with the French and Italian cuisine.

"What time suits you?" Le Fanu asked. He was already considering the wine selection.

"How about six? Have an hour or so before we go our ways for dinner." Barnes rang off.

Le Fanu was glad to avoid a dinner engagement, even though the prospect of another solitary evening at home was unappealing. Barnes was still a largely unknown quantity. Le Fanu knew he developed friendships slowly, but used the excuse of his profession to justify that. Besides, he could always go to the Club from D'Angelis.

Caldicott's arrival ended the contemplation. "Sir, I've finally rounded up all those court files concerning Westshire."

Le Fanu had forgotten them, so worried he might have forgotten other important developments. "Good man. Had a look at them yet?"

"Just quickly, but I'll go through them in full later. First glance suggests Westshire was right to dismiss the charges. There was little solid evidence to suggest the Rajah's people did anything serious or out of the ordinary."

That was no surprise after Westshire's own explanation. "Any idea how it escalated to this full Board Star Chamber?"

"Not yet," Caldicott replied, "and the real answer to that might not be in the files. I'll ask around and see if I can get any Secretariat gossip."

"That'd be good. I'm getting twitchy, because it looks like Westshire's being set up and I'd like to know why. Which reminds me, anything more about the Rajah from your London contacts?"

"No, but I'm trying to find a way into Coutts. Not much more on Taylor yet, either, though I'm promised additional information tomorrow."

"Good. No point us meeting later as I'm meeting Barnes who has something to tell me. Let's gather here in the morning, eight o'clock."

"Certainly, sir. I'll browse these files, then I'll be at cricket practice if you need to contact me."

Caldicott left, as Le Fanu remembered the days when he set off for the golf course at every possible moment. That was before wife, war and lover leaving. A lot of life changes had happened in a short time.

Habi was still elsewhere so Le Fanu refreshed the boards, organised his files, then set off for D'Angelis. The hotel's imposing façade looked on to Mount Road. Giacomo D'Angelis started as a confectioner and ice cream maker but expanded into the hotel business. These days that included Sylk's in Ootacamund, managed by his daughter, and where Le Fanu had encountered the Delhi widow. D'Angelis was the first Madras hotel to have en suite facilities and electric fans in every room, so it gave the Connemara competition.

Barnes was waiting at a table in the corner of the main reception area, one of the places to be seen in the city. He looked right at home.

"Hello, Le Fanu, thanks for coming. I've got us a table out in the gardens."

So he had influence here, too. The French Gardens were coveted by people desperate to be noticed. Le Fanu and Barnes walked through the reception area, turned left into a short corridor lined with old Madras prints and emerged onto a broad verandah. Steps led down into gardens that were so European as to defy the logic of their location. In the middle stood a rotunda where a string quartet was playing.

Barnes grinned. "They're good players but I've got us a table in the corner so we can talk." He walked behind tall shrubs and under a pergola to where a solitary table was set. White cloths and sparkling cutlery competed for space with glasses and jugs of iced water and fresh lime soda. A uniformed servant stood ready to serve. Barnes waved him away, and started pouring.

They sat across from each other, Le Fanu facing the main entrance to the gardens. Force of habit, he thought, keep an eye on comings and goings.

"So, Barnes, what's this about? But first, thanks for doing a good job on the Pallampur case report. I appreciate that. And second, you're right. You are making changes in the paper from what I've seen, though you've still a couple of dinosaurs to tame."

"Thank you, I appreciate the comments. I do still have oddities to clean out, but I've a lot of time to make up for so don't expect it all at once."

"Fair enough."

"Glass of wine?"

"Sounds like a good idea."

A bottle of Chablis soon sat up to its neck in ice, and he poured the first glasses.

"You'll remember, Le Fanu, I said I might be able to help in London?"

"Yes."

"I've had a couple of friends make discreet inquiries. The Rajah had money worries."

"I'm assuming all this will still be between us until I clear anything you might write." Le Fanu commented. "You'll publish only after you've discussed it with me?"

"Yes."

"Right, then. Yes, there is a financial aspect, a big one, coming into the investigation. There were large and regular deposits and withdrawals going on, and the Rajah himself was worried about things. Do you know anything more?" He surprised himself by being so expansive.

Barnes looked at him, evenly. "I know it will take you a while to trust me, but I can tell you the Rajah was being watched by some very interesting people, and has been since the end of the war."

Le Fanu tried to look unconcerned. "Interesting. How'd you get to know that?"

"Le Fanu, I have to trust you, too, so I'll keep quiet on that front for a while, but I suspect you know the information is right."

"Yes, I do, so we understand each other. Are you writing a story on this?"

"My London friends have asked me not to and I'm respecting that until they clear me to publish."

"Good, so I can tell you we know about the watch on the Rajah. His affairs are also being investigated in Delhi by London agents. There has even been an agent sent here. And all this is happening without Madras being told. You can imagine how well that's been received. But that's between you and me."

Barnes poured them each another glass. "I didn't know that last bit. An agent here?"

"So we understand."

"Interesting. Whoever it is would scarcely be sent from London. More likely comes from somewhere closer. Probably Singapore. There are some officers there, I know. I'll see what I can discover."

"That would be helpful."

"This suggests the Rajah was under the spotlight for something seriously big. I might be able to help there, too. Another source tells me Pallampur met some dubious characters at a Soho nightclub just before he returned here."

"Wouldn't be people connected to gun running, would it?"

Now Barnes looked surprised. "Yes, well known people from Belfast connected to the IRA. But why would they be involved here in India, and with the Rajah of Pallampur?"

"Purely business, I think, the chance to make money to fund their campaign against the Irish Free State proposals. As you know, it looks like Northern Ireland will opt out, and the IRA opposes that. Out here, I doubt that even the Bengali radicals have thought to team up with the IRA, but anything's possible. The Madras government thinks that any guns that do arrive might turn Rampa into an armed extension of the Indian cause."

"That seems a bit far-fetched."

"I agree, though I've yet to see all the evidence."

This was as open as he'd been with anyone in a long time, Le Fanu thought, and wondered if he was premature. Barnes was still unproven. Even so, Le Fanu was happy to talk with someone outside police ranks. It helped him think.

Barnes paused, finishing another glass. "My contacts say the Rajah looked unhappy and uncomfortable with his new companions, and might have been there unwillingly. Do you think there's a connection between that London activity and his death?"

"Logic says yes but my instincts are not so sure. There might be a connection, though, in what looks like an attempt to have the Rajah implicated in gun running. We're re-examining some cases where odd things happened. Let's say the evidence did not justify the charges, on what we've seen so far."

"Well, with your permission I'll have my London people keep looking."

"By all means. I would really appreciate it if you can find me a way into Coutts. The Rajah's accounts were there."

"Of course they were, like all the other princes. No promises, but I've an old school contact who works there."

The bottle was finished.

"Shall we get another one?" Barnes said. "I thought I might have dinner here anyway, so if you joined me that would justify another couple of drinks."

So much for going to the Club.

Half an hour later the food arrived, and an hour after that they were at the bar for whiskeys and background. Barnes attended Winchester and was set for Oxford, but rebelled against his family and went to journalism school in New York before returning to Fleet Street. Later in the war he worked in Whitehall as an information officer, then became deputy editor of a small English provincial paper. By that stage he was tired of British politics, saw the opportunity in Madras and accepted the offer.

Le Fanu found a taxi to take him home through the quiet, still streets. The mail awaited, as did Ro's letter of a couple of days ago. He opened it, finally, feeling mellow.

She was to visit Madras for a week, beginning just two days from now.

Eighteen

Her military employer had business in Madras, but was bringing his family and would lodge Ro at D'Angelis so she might meet her friends. Le Fanu was the only person she had told.

Now he was anxious. Her letters arrived regularly, and as regularly he mostly ignored them. He replied occasionally, but in perfunctory and non-committal fashion. He convinced himself it was because he was too busy, but it was really because he had no idea what to say or how to express his feelings. And that was another problem. He was not sure how he felt. No, that was wrong, too. He knew what and how he felt, but without admitting it to himself let alone Ro.

Now she would be here in two days and he had to deal with that as well as the Pallampur cases. He preferred being pitched into work than confronting personal challenges. His ex-wife always said he never knew what she was thinking, and that was true. It was a worrying thought with Ro just two days away.

He went to bed with no hope of sleeping, so at one in the morning he was downstairs in his study, reading all Ro's letters. He might not have replied, but he kept them. She sent one a week for the two years, sometimes missing when travelling with the Hyderabad family or being overwhelmed by work. They were short, recounting her activities. None raised their relationship, but she kept the connection alive and was probably not surprised by his spasmodic responses. She was smarter than him two years ago and would have guessed his inability to confront his feelings.

Time meandered towards dawn. He drank tea dredged up from the kitchen, leafed through the letters again, thinking of earlier times and why he found it difficult to deal with this. His thoughts drifted back to his family in England.

His brother was five years older and, in Le Fanu's mind, always favoured by his father though his mother was more generous. Once his brother had left for boarding school, his father had ignored Le Fanu completely. The house library had become his focus, as well as the disused golf clubs in the storeroom. Whenever he had been left alone, he had either immersed himself in the library or disappeared down the backfield to hack golf balls about and learn the game's basics. Later, he had cycled to the local course where the resident professional had given him free lessons, and his game had developed quickly.

Those two odd strands had saved him. The home library had been excellent. His father had gone to Oxford then become a teacher, but had been a frustrated and unfulfilled don. The shelves had been full of history and what was to become anthropology. So Le Fanu had read Andrew Lang's collections of folklore and fairy stories, and books like J.G. Frazer's The Golden Bough on the rise of culture and religion. There had been many works on India including travel accounts written by people like Bishop Heber, and Francis Buchanan who had been in Pallampur's library. Buchanan had initiated Le Fanu's interest in south India. And Rudyard Kipling had turned him towards the police. Kipling captured ordinary India and Indians like no other writer. He relayed the sounds and smells and mystery and dirt and pulse. Le Fanu had convinced himself that if the civil service or the army would not provide access to that life, it must be the police.

He had also been dispatched to boarding school, which he had hated. His father had decided that if India was a fait a compli, then at least it should be the elite service. The school had been a cramming college for ICS entry, its library the information equivalent of the Golconda diamond mines up near Hyderabad. It had held all the official publications: district gazetteers detailing each small area of India; reports from every conceivable government department; memoirs of retired civil servants; maps, statistics, photographs and more. There had been all the annual reports on provincial police administration, including the Madras Presidency. Le Fanu had read the lot, wondering after Kipling how this fascinating enterprise could be reduced to such dry tones but knowing he had to go there.

That dryness had been leavened by newspapers from all over India: the Times of India, the Civil and Military Gazette, the Pioneer and those from the south like the Madras Mail and The Hindu. The school had expected students to concentrate on politics and national development, but Le Fanu had read all the court cases in search of his India. Despite his father, it was always going to be the police, not the ICS.

He checked the clock. It was still just four in the morning. A long day stretched ahead. He made more tea and returned to the desk, shuffling the letters again.

On the rare occasions he had gone home his mother had been glad to see him, but his father had become colder still, probably because the headmaster's reports revealed a boy becoming a non-conformist young man. As a headmaster himself his father had been embarrassed, and angry as a father. They had disagreed on everything, especially Le Fanu's determination to join the Indian Police Service.

His father had wanted Le Fanu to go to Oxford. He had gone to Edinburgh, for two reasons apart from annoying his father. It was Andrew Lang's city, full of intellectual excitement about new ways of seeing foreign places as the Scots had gone everywhere, including India. Then there had been Edinburgh's golf courses. A university friend had proposed him as a member of the Royal and Ancient Golf Club of St. Andrews up in Fife. Most weekends he had taken the train from Waverley to the golf town and stayed at a guesthouse overlooking the course. He had played twice a day on Saturday and Sunday then returned to Edinburgh.

That had been his pattern for four years. He had gone to the library, and played golf. There had been some friends, none women. There had been few women at the university, and he had spent so little time outside the university there was precious chance of meeting one.

He had refused to sit the ICS examination so his father had cut communication completely. His mother had kept in touch whenever possible. Le Fanu had applied to the IPS, and had left for Madras in 1905. He had always liked and was good at the district work. Promotion had come faster than normal, annoying several colleagues. Early in 1913 his mother had fallen ill and he took leave in England. She had recovered, but while there Le Fanu had met a woman and proposed to her immediately. Within a year the war had begun and he had joined the army. The marriage had struggled from the beginning, not helped by his solitary nature. The war had finished it off.

One of the servants took his breakfast order. It was six thirty. Half an hour later he had coffee, idlis and sambar. He was exhausted, and still undecided on what to do about Ro's visit. Even the bike ride along the marina did not inspire him, so by the time he climbed the stairs to his office he was ready for nothing.

Habi came along from his room. "Good morning, sir. Have you had any sleep at all?"

"You should be a detective, Habi."

"Oh no, sir, I leave that to you smart Europeans."

Tired though he was, Le Fanu smiled. "Hindus might

claim to have invented detection, Habi, but you Muslims were not far behind. We should be learning from you."

"We could have a long discussion about who invented what in India, sir, but I don't think you're ready for that this morning. I'll get some coffee." Habi disappeared out the door.

Le Fanu surveyed his desk, not knowing where to start. He was irresolute, more so because of Ro than the cases.

Habi arrived back with a tray, two steaming mugs of south Indian coffee, and a plate of coconut biscuits.

"Those look good, Habi, where'd they come from?"

"There's a street seller near my house who's been making these for years. I bought them on the way in this morning."

They dunked the biscuits in their coffees, silent for a while.

"You alright, sir?" Habi asked, looking quizzical.

"Yes, thanks Habi. I've a few things to deal with but I'll manage. I'd be happier if we could make progress here."

Habi looked at him. "I don't really think it's these cases worrying you, sir, but we can concentrate on them if you like."

Le Fanu turned his hands palms up. "You read me too well, Habi, I might have to get you transferred."

"Where would I go, and how would you solve cases without me? Now, I've some news. The owner of the revolver for sale is definitely the Rani's friend. We had someone talk to the servant and, yes, his employer is Jason Palmer."

"Well done, Habi, even though that makes things difficult for the Rani." And more difficult for me, thought Le Fanu. If this goes further then Palmer's name won't be kept quiet and the Rani will be unhappy. "What do we know about Mr. Palmer?"

"He's a planter, of course, late thirties, out here about fifteen years. Began as a manager on one of the Nilgiris estates. You know the type - went to Oxford so naturally knows how to run an Indian tea plantation."

Le Fanu could not help but laugh. Habi's sardonic humour was so English. He rarely said much about the British in India, but when he did it was memorable.

"Steady, Habi, innocent people might think you were being critical."

"Not me, sir. I'm sure Mr Palmer makes an excellent cup of tea."

More laughter.

"What else do we know, Habi?"

"After about five years he became a partner and has done well. Active in the planters' association and has said a few things about the present political developments. More conservative than normal, perhaps, but mostly like the rest of the planters. Keeps up all the right appearances. Has a big house up on the plantation, and another one out in Saidapet for some reason."

That was where he and Charlotte Lacey met. Le Fanu imagined them together. "Seems an odd choice, those types normally have something right here in town."

"Yes", Habi replied, "I did some more research. He's never married. Often stays at the Club when he's here in Madras."

Impossible to entertain a woman there, thought le Fanu, no wonder he bought a house out of town. "That's great progress, Habi, keep tracking him and keep me advised so I can feed good news to the I-G. We'll need to interview Mr. Palmer. What about the revolver?"

"We have the servant in sight, so we'll pick him up today, he's due to visit the pawnbroker."

"Good work."

Habi was leaving when Caldicott arrived looking far fresher than Le Fanu felt, as well as pleased with himself.

"Good morning, Caldicott. What are you so cheerful about?"

"I have a story for you. Habi, don't go yet."

Nineteen

"What do you know about intelligence organisations here in India and the UK?" Caldicott settled in a chair, leaning back, elbows on the armrests, fingers steepled under his chin. Impeccably dressed and manicured as always, he looked like a civil service boss.

"The basics, I suppose, picked up through the war," replied Le Fanu. "What about you, Habi?"

"Probably the same, but a bit less, sir. I've heard a couple of things from friends in Delhi but that's all."

"Caldicott, run us through it. You look like you're ready to tell a tale."

Caldicott looked pleased. "Right, sir, but I need to give you some background, because it bears on what we're dealing with now." He looked like a teacher now.

"Intelligence gathering is quite new, at the formal level anyway. And its development has been co-ordinated between India and home. In 1909 Whitehall set up the Secret Service Bureau to watch anarchists and the like, because of what was brewing in Europe. At the same time, they established the Indian Political Intelligence Office in Delhi but with operations in London as well."

"In London?" Habi asked. "Why was that?"

"Good question," replied Caldicott. "London was worried about the violent outbreaks in Bengal and elsewhere, bombs and shootings and so on. Some of that was orchestrated from outside India, so the office in London was to watch Indians in the UK and in Europe."

"I never knew that," Le Fanu said, "and I thought I knew what was going on."

"Well, it was supposed to be secret, after all, even from well credentialed policemen in south India." Caldicott smiled, a rare point scored.

"Fair enough. But were the police ever involved?"

"That needs more background, because things changed once the war began. In 1916 the Secret Service Bureau split into two sections known as Military Intelligence 5 and Military Intelligence 6, MI5 and MI6 for short. You've heard of those." Le Fanu and Habi nodded. "The first kept an eye on things at home, the other overseas."

"And where does India fit?" Habi asked.

"Getting to that. Through the war, Delhi was involved with the Indian Political Intelligence Office and had strong links to London. Those links strengthened after 1917."

"The Russian Revolution" Le Fanu interjected.

"Precisely," continued Caldicott. "London and Delhi both worried about the rise of socialism and communism, and about the interest taken in those views by Indians at home and overseas. In 1919 MI6 created these wonderful positions called Passport Control Officers who were sent around the world. They're spies, pure and simple. Then just last year, the Indian Political Intelligence branch was established in Delhi. But it's controlled both by London and Delhi. It liaises directly with MI5 and with Scotland Yard, which is where the police angle comes in."

"So," Habi said, "MI5 and Scotland Yard have a direct line into India because they're worried about political change. Where does the IPS fit in?"

"Another great question," Caldicott acknowledged. "The IPS is rarely consulted or informed about these activities, even when those other agencies are operating in India, like the chap who came to see us. That's all controlled through the Foreign and Political Department in Delhi. The relevant police authorities are advised only when absolutely necessary."

"Which," Le Fanu said, "is hardly ever, I'm guessing."

"Yes," Caldicott continued, "which is why we have our present situation."

"Do you know any more about that?" Le Fanu asked.

"Yes, and that's why the history lesson was necessary. Remember: MI5 and Scotland Yard have an interest in India, and so does MI6. One of my London contacts confirms that the Rajah was being watched by both MI5 and MI6, and that those sections argued constantly about who had priority. For us, though, the real question is why they were interested in Pallampur in the first place."

"Who are these people running around Delhi and here in Madras without anyone knowing?" Le Fanu asked.

"The one in Delhi is MI5 and is known only to a few very select people there, perhaps the Viceroy, the Secretary to the Home Department and the Secretary to Foreign and Political. I'm told nobody in the IPS knows, we're the first."

Habi laughed. "You British are always too clever for your own good. We have a spy running around Delhi and no-one knows?"

"It gets worse, Habi," Caldicott continued. "The one who came to see me is MI6, and absolutely no one knows he's here. No one. Not even the Viceroy, or Willingdon. We're the only ones, and we don't know his name or where he lives. He was posted in Singapore and came over here using a false passport, to watch the Rajah at this end."

They looked at each other. The Rajah's activities were so serious that MI5 and MI6 both had officers on the ground in India. Willingdon would be apoplectic. Le Fanu needed to see the Chief Secretary as soon as possible.

"Caldicott, this is excellent," he said, "but do we know why they were and remain so interested in the Rajah?"

"Not yet, but I've been thinking. The IRA gun running connection is still possible, but none of us are convinced by that. So I wondered what else might cause both 5 and 6 to take an interest. I'm working on that and have a couple of ideas to develop. Maybe you two can do the same. I'll be back in the telegraph room later to ask a few more contacts what they know. But we're definitely sitting on something big."

"You're right," said Le Fanu, "so we need to keep this investigation moving. And somehow I need to keep all this from Jepson. Habi, can you keep following the revolver and the Jason Palmer stories. Caldicott, you keep talking to your murky friends. I'll inform the Chief Secretary, then work out what happens next."

"There's one thing, though, sir," said Habi. "If this is all spies and secret service, it doesn't fit the way the Rajah died. As Dr Ramachandran says and we observed, there was no control or discipline to the killing. The Rajah was killed in a rage. That doesn't fit the patterns these other people would demonstrate."

"Good point, Habi," Le Fanu said. "What do you think, Caldicott?"

"I doubt the secret services killed the Rajah. They were hoping he would lead them to others. It's more likely those others were responsible. But we don't know yet who they are, and they're probably violent. Habi makes a good point. I'm not sure what we do with it yet, but we should keep it in mind."

Le Fanu made the familiar car journey down to the Secretariat. Along the way he wondered more about what to do concerning Ro than about who had killed the Rajah and why. Keeping focus would be difficult over the next week.

Whitney was outraged. "You mean to tell me we have a bloody spy floating about Madras and no one's bothered to tell us? At least your lot's on the ball, LF, otherwise we would still be in the dark. Would you care to come with me to tell Willingdon?"

"Not really, sir, handling an enraged Governor doesn't fall into my assigned tasks. I do need to see him about the reception, but I might leave that for now."

They laughed, knowing Whitney's day was about to get difficult. "Fair enough, LF. We're best off with you keeping up the good work elsewhere. But come back here later, about six. I can update you from my end but now I also need you to keep me briefed."

"On that, sir, what do I tell the I-G?"

"I think you know the answer, LF," Whitney replied, brandishing his usual cigar. "We can't tell him any of this, he'll charge in and create a mess. At the very time we need a safe pair of hands, we have Jepson." It was the most direct criticism Whitney had made of the I-G in Le Fanu's hearing, so Jepson's tenure was tenuous.

"I'll dream up something to tell him, sir, we have more news on the revolver and some possible connections. That should keep him satisfied for another day, perhaps two. We'll find something else, then."

"Good. You know how ugly this might get, LF. If we make progress on the Pallampur killing, that will dull the impact of the secret service nonsense. Not much, but it will help. If that got out we'd take a public caning, so Jepson's the last person we need involved. The Governor will stir Delhi, that I can promise, and that has to be kept quiet, too. What will you tell your new friend at the Mail?"

Le Fanu was speechless.

Whitney was pleased. "Don't worry, LF, I don't know anything, I have no spies. I just put two and two together. His report on the Pallampur murder was so balanced it could only have come from you. Well done. Nice to have that lot on side for once."

"You might get some background done on Barnes, too, Sir

Charles. He's remarkably well informed at the London end, with the same interesting contacts as Caldicott."

"I'll do that, LF, thanks for the tip. Right, I'd better go. I'll see you later today."

They left the office together, and Le Fanu returned to police headquarters. Once in his office, he wrote notes about the morning's revelations and activities, signed and dated them, and locked them in the safe. Some details would not appear on the case boards in case of unexpected or unusual visitors.

He went over it in his mind. The Rajah had been murdered in a vicious frenzy, and they still had to find out where he had been between leaving the Governor's and arriving home. It was very likely there were links between Pallampur, Westshire and Taylor. Those links had a London dimension, and were so important as to warrant MI5 and MI6 agents being placed in Delhi and Madras. The Rani had a secret lover who was now apparently trying to sell a revolver of the type stolen from the Rajah's desk. And they still had to find the murder weapon, almost certainly the Rajah's missing Highland Officer's sword.

The next moves involved interviewing Jason Palmer, probing the Pallampur connections to Westshire and Taylor more deeply, and identifying the fund sources for the movements in the Rajah's accounts. On top of that he had to keep Jepson in the dark, and decide what to do about Ro. He sighed, and wished he could go home to sleep.

Twenty

He needed to see Jepson as soon as possible, so he telephoned ahead. The I-G was again waiting when Le Fanu arrived. This was becoming a habit.

"Thanks for coming over, Le Fanu, I appreciate it. Any updates?"

"Yes, sir." He gave Jepson as anodyne an account as possible, hoping the new conciliatory mood precluded questions. It did.

"That all sounds like good progress, Le Fanu. Finding the murder weapon would help enormously, but I know your people are looking for that."

"Yes, sir, Habi and several constables are looking now. It could be anywhere, of course, given we haven't found it around the house yet, but the search is thorough. I'll keep you informed."

"Thank you. We're getting an easier ride from the Mail, too. You have anything to do with that?"

Le Fanu was cautious. "The new editor asked about the case, and we agreed that if he acted responsibly, I would give him whatever information was possible. It's a trial arrangement but is working so far."

"It is. Very good thing for us, so well done."

Le Fanu found it more difficult to deal with the new Jepson than the old one. At least the old one was consistent, there was no doubt about what was coming. With this one, Le Fanu was braced constantly for the inevitable eruption that had still to arrive. As Le Fanu left the office, Jepson added a further surprise.

"You know, Le Fanu, we've not always agreed on things." There was a candidate for understatement of the year. "But your unit does excellent work. Once this crisis passes, we must talk about expanding your activities."

Now Le Fanu was totally confused. Either Jepson had undergone a complete personality transformation, or was exceptionally worried about his future. The former was unlikely. If the latter, then Jepson could be more dangerous than ever. As he left the building, Le Fanu almost wished he was followed by the usual expletives and buckets of bile. Almost. At least Jepson was at bay for another day.

Habi had an update on Jason Palmer. "A most interesting man, sir. I think we should interview him soon."

"Why's that Habi?" Le Fanu was looking at the boards, thinking about the material consigned to the safe and that Palmer was the least of their concerns.

"Sir, he's upset several European men around Madras. The Rani of Pallampur was not the first woman to have found him charming, or to have visited his house. One of my Saidapet informants tells me there've been several incidents."

"Like what?"

"Palmer has been assaulted at least twice. He made no reports but it was well known out there. One attack was by a gang of goondas hired by an aggrieved husband." Habi smiled, smugly.

"Alright Habi, astonish me."

"Yes, sir. The man who did the hiring is now First Member of the Board of Revenue, Mr. Jamieson."

"You win, Habi, I'm astonished. I'd never have guessed that. Why did I not hear about that?" He had to reconsider his views on Jamieson, his wife, and Palmer for that matter.

"It was when he was Third Member, sir, around the time of the Jane Carstairs murder. The Board was under pressure and did not need further bad publicity. The matter was hushed up and Jamieson got promotion. In fact, he got two promotions in short order."

"Why did Palmer not protest?"

"He was told that if he did, other charges would be laid by leading figures and he'd have to leave India. That would have hurt him financially, a lot."

"The warning didn't curb his enthusiasm for married women, though."

"Quite so, sir. My spies tell me the Rani began visiting his house about a year ago. Palmer even keeps his servants in the house during visits, so there's no doubt about what happens. And other women visit him, too. The Rani isn't the only one. Very sociable these European ladies, it seems." He looked studious.

"I wouldn't know, Habi, no use asking me."

That affair was longer standing than Charlotte Lacey suggested, Le Fanu thought. Perhaps the Rajah had not been as relaxed about the arrangement as she suggested. He might have had money problems and unsavoury friends, but she was still his wife and the most attractive woman in Madras. Her being with Palmer must have upset him. Le Fanu realised he was putting himself in the Rajah's position, but could not imagine any man doing otherwise.

"You're right, as usual Habi. We must have a chat with Mr. Palmer."

"That will take some organising, sir. Mr. Palmer left for the Nilgiris and his plantation last night. His servants say there are no dates set for his return. We might have to go to him if we think it that important."

"Check it, Habi, and we can discuss later."

Le Fanu's main thought was not about Palmer but about timing the interview. Ro was due in Madras for a week. He could not go to the Nilgiris immediately or she'd think he was running away, again. At least, he would have to see her first and not go off immediately. Even then, he would have to plan well. He realised that meant he was anxious the reunion went well, and dared not think what that implied.

The other problem was how he and Ro could meet. From the start the issue was her being Anglo-Indian, the mixed race hated passionately by the mainstream European community. He had caved in to that, and had felt guilty ever since. If she stayed at D'Angelis they would need to be careful about meeting in public. That news would reach every European dining room within half an hour. She could come to his house, but he would have to dispatch the servants. Most were loyal, but would share gossip with fellow servants in other houses. Ro's visit would be too tempting a subject. Somehow he had to find a solution.

He switched his thoughts back to Palmer. The Rani was with him at the time the Rajah was murdered. Well, technically, all they knew currently was that the Rani was allegedly at Palmer's house when her husband died so violently. They had no precise information or guarantee that Palmer was there, or her for that matter. She told Le Fanu she was there, and that was more assertion than proof. They had yet to confirm that Palmer and the Rani were, in fact, at Palmer's house.

Le Fanu thought that would be a formality. Palmer had no reason to kill the Rajah. Tupping the wife was complication enough. Killing the husband would have created far too much difficulty. There was little urgency about interviewing the man, then. The thought passed his mind that he might again be assuming too much, to simplify his personal life. He dismissed the idea.

Habi was assessing the logistics of getting to the Nilgiris. It would be an overnight train trip, at least a day there and another overnight trip back. That was just one day but, importantly for Le Fanu, two nights. He had some expectations of what might happen while Ro was in Madras, then. That made him feel even more guilty about his non-replies to her letters.

He added the Palmer dimension to the case boards, thinking about their slow progress on the cases. Uncovering secret service involvement was good but he couldn't tell anyone. To the outside observer, then, they had no murder weapon, no suspect, no real clues apart from a blood-soaked library, a mutilated body and a fractious Australian Rani.

Caldicott arrived from another telegraph office room session. Le Fanu realised it was mid-afternoon. He'd gone without lunch but he wasn't hungry.

"You alright, sir?" Caldicott asked. "Looked like you were a long way off."

"Yes, I'm fine. Just wishing we had more progress we could report publicly. This secret service material is fine but we can't tell anyone."

"Unfortunately, I can't help. I've some information on Westshire that's not for public consumption, either."

"Wonderful. Perhaps I should just go to lunch." Le Fanu crushed his face in his hands. The lack of sleep was beginning to tell.

"Oh, it's not that bad, sir. I've had people looking over the court files, and more examining material in Ramsheed. There are some interesting developments."

Le Fanu grabbed paper and a pencil. "Go on, just more to add to the puzzle."

"First, there've been strangers lurking around Ramsheed in recent weeks. We're tracking them down, but one of my people reckons they're connected to criminal gangs here in Madras."

"That's odd. Those gangs deal mostly in extortion and protection activities with the odd foray into drugs and low-level prostitution. What on earth would they be doing up there?"

"No idea but we're following up. Not sure there's a connection yet, but it does seem Westshire was set up, as you've suggested. We've also checked the businessman who persuaded Westshire into the minerals company arrangement. The man has a record, including for that sort of action."

"Does Westshire know this?"

"No, I wanted to let you know first. Westshire's returned to Ramsheed, so he may get wind of it."

"We should probably go up there to have a look around, given that news. But I'm not sure when. We might have to go to the Nilgiris and interview Jason Palmer as well."

Le Fanu gave Caldicott a quick version of Habi's discoveries, along with his own speculations.

"I agree with you, sir" Caldicott said, twirling a pencil through his fingers. "Palmer's an unlikely candidate. The Ramsheed developments are more important. We could be up there tomorrow morning."

Le Fanu shifted on his chair. "We'll meet here first thing tomorrow morning to assess where we are. I need to see the Chief Secretary again before we do much more. The political dimension's a worry and we don't need any rockets from our side. I'll try to do that tonight."

Caldicott was puzzled. "You're in charge, sir, so we'll do it that way. I'm worried, though. We might lose time and possibly even the trail up in Ramsheed. I'm curious about those strangers, I must say."

"I agree, Jackson, I agree. But we can't leave Madras if there's any chance of an explosion while we're away. We won't lose too much time." He could not tell Caldicott he was contemplating an even longer delay.

Caldicott left to continue his investigations. Le Fanu reformulated the boards. Whitney agreed to meet him again at the Club, so he filled in time until seven.

Twenty-one

He banked the bike into the club's sweeping driveway off Mount Road along from the banks, shops and institutions that symbolised the Raj in the south. The only local touch came from The Hindu, which was balanced enough but supported political power being given to Indians. Further up the road at the Thousand Lights mosque, many of faithful were deserting the British for the Congress.

The bike drew disapproving looks from the few Europeans near the entrance to the three-level, whitewashed affair with verandahs around the ground floor and rattan blinds on all the balconies. A servant rushed up, anxious to take responsibility for what was here an exotic machine. By the time Le Fanu walked in, his presence was noted. He was accosted in the bar by civil service and commercial people, all demanding justice for the Rajah. Le Fanu thought they were seeking guarantees for their own safety, which, somehow, was imperilled by what had happened to the Rajah. He fobbed them off, bar a couple he trusted. He told them enough to pass to the others. That way he might be left alone.

Chester Barnes was talking with a senior Secretariat officer whose brow furrowed as Le Fanu approached. The man made excuses and left.

"Sorry to break up your chat, Barnes" Le Fanu said.

"You do divide opinion among the worthies," came the

bemused reply.

"Oh, you know, anything different is frowned on here. Must be the bike."

"Your mode of transport was commented upon."

"I'm sure. How are things at the Mail?" They walked towards a corner of the largest bar in Asia, and sat at a small table. A waiter approached.

"A drink, Le Fanu?" Barnes asked.

"A quick one, I'm meeting Whitney."

"I won't ask. But he has another guest with him."

"Who?"

"I can't say."

Le Fanu had ordered a whiskey, Barnes some cocktail concoction. The drinks arrived.

"Are you sure you can't give me warning?"

"Sorry. Now, any update at the London end?" The question seemed simple, and Le Fanu was still wondering about who was with Whitney.

"No, but we do have connections into some new organisations."

"You mean like 5 and 6?" Barnes looked straight at him.

"Yes, but that's definitely not for publication. And how do you know?"

"A couple of my school friends found their ways into those wonderfully secretive halls."

"Can't be too secret if they're telling you!"

Barnes laughed. "True, but you know the power of the old school tie. Unlike me they went to Oxford, attended all the right parties and ended up with opportunities to become unlike everybody else."

"I don't suppose these friends are telling you why they're interested in Pallampur?" The mystery man in Madras might be one of Barnes' friends, he thought. "And I don't suppose one of those friends is based not too far from here? Close enough to come to Madras for a holiday?"

The smile on Barnes' face could not have been broader. "You mean from somewhere like Singapore? That's not far from here, just a few days sailing."

"Exactly what I was thinking. If he did happen to drop in, I'd welcome a chat off the record. "

"I'll keep it in mind and let you know. In London, there's still talk around the guns issue, but rising chatter about some other dimension I'm looking into."

"Well, thanks for the drink, and keep me up to date. Don't forget, if you're talking to your holidaying friend…."

Barnes raised his glass in salute as Le Fanu finished his, stood, and headed through the nearest verandah window in search of Whitney who, no doubt, was adding cigar aroma to the freshening night air.

He was at the same table as before complete with cigar, glasses and whisky bottle. The other person at the table was Lord Willingdon.

"Good evening, LF. Thought you might like the chance to ask HE about that reception."

"Good evening, Your Excellency, Chief Secretary. Thank you."

"LF," the Governor said, "I want you to know there's no blame on you for this spy fiasco. It just underlines how useless Special Branch have been. If it wasn't for your team we'd know nothing."

"Thank you, sir, we may be getting more on that, too."

Whitney broke in. "The waiter tells me you were having a chat with Barnes. How's that going?"

"You've been checking on him, I suspect. He may know our spy here in Madras, possibly an old school chum. I've asked Barnes to see if we can have a chat with mystery man."

"Charles," the Governor said. "I really do have to go so perhaps I can brief LF on the Rajah's appearance at my place?"

"Of course, HE."

"LF, the Rajah was in good form at the reception. He had no more than two drinks. I checked with the waiters. He seemed bright enough but had something on his mind, that was clear. No idea what, because he didn't say. And he may have been buttering me up, but he claimed to be rethinking his support of Congress. He said that was partly because of what some Congress leaders were doing, partly because they were pestering him for money."

"Sir, that's excellent information, especially that last piece. It confirms that he did have serious money issues. Did he say where he was going when he left you?"

"Just that he was going home, and I assumed immediately."

"We haven't heard that before, either," Le Fanu said. "That suggests he went somewhere he'd not expected to go. And met someone at short notice."

"Sorry I can't help more, and I have to go now. Let me know if you need anything else, LF, and thanks again for alerting us to the spies." He walked away and into the building where he would be fawned on by most people present.

Whitney watched him leave. "He has calmed down a lot. Earlier today was a spectacle, I can tell you. Delhi and London, what a combination."

"I hope to have more on the Singapore man as soon as possible, and I'll pass that on."

"You'll know far more than me and the Governor." Whitney was still chafing at the thought of an unidentified spy roaming "his" city.

"Damn spies. Willingdon's been onto Delhi and they're referring to London. Meanwhile, these cowboys are still roaming our prairies."

A large puff of richly scented smoke headed towards the night sky.

"Sir, what do you know about Jason Palmer?"

"Wondered when you'd have a look at him. You know the Jamieson story?"

"I've only just heard. I'm astonished it's been kept so quiet."

"Wasn't easy, and I hated the man being promoted. He's a dolt, but Palmer gave him an importance he didn't deserve. Jamieson persuaded everyone that a convenient veil of discretion would be in everybody's best interests. I'm afraid to say that's an argument I lost."

"Because of the political conditions." Le Fanu doubted the Chief Secretary lost too many battles.

"Yes. Not what I'd have done but there you are. Palmer's brainless, of course. He escaped that Jamieson affair with a few cuts and bruises, then started the same game with other women. There were at least two before he latched onto the Rani and there are a couple of others besides her. The other planters are unhappy and want him kicked out of the country, but he's fireproof for now, thanks to Jamieson." The lips pursed after expelling more smoke, and Whitney poured two whiskeys, Macallans.

"What's he like?"

"Got more oil than a ghee factory, seems to me. The women go for it, though. My wife tells me it's mainly because he talks to them as if they matter, and they like the attention. Don't understand it myself."

"What about his business?"

"Doesn't spend much time at it, mostly down here playing musical chairs, or beds." The disapproval was obvious. "He has bank problems. Had to pay out a couple of partners who no longer wanted to work with him. One of the bank managers comes to the Club. He told me Palmer has large debts."

There were few secrets between senior club members. This was the city's unofficial government. Le Fanu remembered the large sums going into then out of the Rajah's Coutts account. What if Palmer owed Pallampur money? Bedding the wife but being indebted to the husband changed the settings. There was a motive for murder.

"I know what you're thinking, LF and, yes, it should be checked. But I doubt he's your man. He gets at men by taking their wives."

"Did he serve in the war?"

"Of course not. He was deemed to be in an essential industry. The war would have been lost had the tea supply dried up." The sarcasm was close to bitterness. "You don't need my advice, LF, but focus on the central facts. Palmer didn't serve, and should have, but few if any people here put in as much service as you. You're atypical, not them, more's the pity."

None of them learned as much, either, Le Fanu thought.

They talked for a while, then dinner arrived. When the roast beef was served, they looked at each other. Whitney was the bureaucrat and supported the Raj mission but even he wondered how a Madras club, in the Hindu heartland, could eat the meat of that religion's most sacred animal. Le Fanu left most of his on the plate. He was not a vegetarian, but these days he ate little beef.

He was home by ten, to find two telegrams waiting. The first was from Ro. She would arrive from Hyderabad the morning after tomorrow, at nine. Her room was booked at D'Angelis. She gave him the number. He should make contact. Le Fanu tried to decode any signal she might be giving, and speculated again about what arrangements he should make.

The second telegram was from his brother. His father had died earlier that day, suddenly.

He half filled a tumbler with a twenty-year-old Ardberg and went to the garden. As he sat there and sipped the malt, his thoughts became disjointed. He had not seen his father for nine years, because when the war had ended he had declined home leave and returned immediately to Madras. The excuse had been that he needed to buy the house, but the main reason had been to avoid his father. With his brother's Foreign Office career wrecked, his father had sought reflected glory from Le Fanu's MC. Returning to Madras had denied that. Perhaps he should have gone home.

There were no fond memories of his father. Le Fanu could not recall one moment of warmth, affection, encouragement or support. His brother had always come first. Le Fanu had made his own way, at a cost. His narrow life in the library and on the links had stunted him personally. He realised that now. It explained the quick, stilted marriage. It explained his narrowed personality and his difficulties dealing with Ro. It explained his becoming a policeman. He loved the work, but chose the police initially because he was given no serious alternatives as opposed to ultimatums. Any leadership skills he had he had learned in the army, not at home or school.

Yet, indirectly, his father had given him learning. He had also given Le Fanu resolve. That was why he was a good policeman. For all the frustrations Le Fanu still liked being a policeman, and applying Hans Gross' investigative approaches. Being a policeman gave his life meaning. That was why he was so unsettled. He could not think of anything else to do if he had to leave India and stop being a policeman.

The light was gone. So was the whiskey. He went in, refilled, returned to the garden. The sky was clear, the air clean, and it was warm. It was so different from where he grew up, and different again from Edinburgh, which he loved despite the quirky weather. He could live there. Perhaps he could join the Edinburgh City Police. The golf would be alright. Or perhaps he could go elsewhere in the Empire: Singapore, the Straits Settlements, Australia, New Zealand.

Ideally, he would remain happily in India doing what he was doing. In small part he owed that to his father, estranged though they were for so long. He would not be there to farewell the man who had made his life so complicated.

As he swallowed a good measure of the Ardberg, the tears began.

Twenty-two

He was in the office by six thirty the next morning, having scarcely slept again. For the next hour and a half he summarised progress. The results confirmed his thoughts at three in the morning: they knew a lot, but not much. At least, not enough to believe they were close to identifying the Rajah's killer, or why the intersections between the Rajah, Taylor and Westshire warranted the presence of two British secret service officers in India.

Caldicott arrived at eight. "You look as tired as yesterday, sir. Are you not sleeping at all?"

Le Fanu wondered if he should mention his father's death, but kept quiet. He could not deal with sympathy, or suggestions he should be at home rather than work. Home was the last place he wanted to be.

"The case is on my mind. If we get a stronger sense of who killed the Rajah I'll sleep better."

Caldicott was unswayed. "This has been going on for a while. If you get too tired you'll miss whatever clue comes along to give us the break. We need you fit. Play some golf. Get some fresh air."

"I might play at the weekend." He doubted that. Ro would be here. And then they might have to visit either Ramsheed or the Nilgiris or both. He couldn't delay those trips too obviously or Habi and Caldicott would become suspicious.

"Not soon enough in my book, but at least it's something." Caldicott looked to continue the discussion so Le Fanu diverted him. "What more do you have on Taylor?"

"Oh, glad you asked. Early in the war, according London, Taylor was recruited into MI6. In fact, he joined the branch before it officially existed. He had been with the Foreign Office working on the Ottoman Empire. Turns out he speaks fluent Turkish."

"That's useful in Changarore."

"Indeed. But as we know, he didn't last long. The details are vague, but a major intelligence failure led to a battlefield disaster. Part of the Dardanelles fiasco that hit our Indian troops so hard, as well as our Australian and New Zealand friends."

"Taylor was responsible for that?"

"Well, this is where it gets interesting. According to my source, Taylor advised against implementing the campaign, and predicted the results. However, that view was not shared by the military mind behind the plan, so Taylor was overruled. When it all went wrong, the general responsible could not be sacrificed so Taylor became the victim. Ironic, eh? He predicted what would happen, was overruled, then got blamed for the result."

"Why? Even by London standards that was cynical."

"There was no one else available. In return, he received the Changarore option, sweetened by a very large sum of money. Part of that went to him via the Rajah for reasons I don't yet know. Another lump ended up in a UK account."

"Why Changarore? I could understand Madras, but up there?"

"The idea," Caldicott said, "was to raise as few questions and generate as little interest as possible. In addition, having him somewhere like that, they thought he could continue intelligence work without anyone else finding out."

Le Fanu shook his head. "But again, why Changarore? He

could have been sent anywhere."

"It was ideal. Strangely enough, it has excellent telegraphic connection to the international lines because of some quirk of nature. A boffin discovered that about the time they were deciding where to put Taylor."

"Did he work through the war?"

"He was one of the main people involved in intercepting and deciphering code coming out of Constantinople. His work helped turn our fortunes in that region."

Le Fanu wondered if that work involved Shaiba. No, that battle was in April 1915. Taylor was probably still in London. He would check, though. Those days flashed through his mind. The nightmares were receding, gradually, but the battalion losses still haunted him. Too many Indian soldiers were left there. His father had been ridiculously proud of the MC won there, but that counted for little to Le Fanu. The recognition did not outweigh the losses. He walked to the window, emotion welling.

"LF, are you sure you're alright?" Caldicott was concerned.

"Wartime flashbacks. I was at Shaiba and wondered if Taylor worked on that. Doubt it, probably a bit early."

"He arrived in Changarore late in 1915. That battle was earlier, wasn't it? He might have been involved. Were you there? I don't know much about it but heard it was bloodier than most."

"Yes, I was and, yes, it was." He turned away again.

"Sorry, sir." Caldicott looked embarrassed, unsure of what to say next.

"That's alright, Jackson, I'm fine. As you say, I'm probably too tired. I'll try and get more sleep tonight." But that was unlikely, he thought. Ro would arrive tomorrow. And he'd still not decided how to handle that.

Caldicott left, to resume discussions with London. Le Fanu sat for a while, then reached for the telephone and dialled a number.

"Is that D'Angelis? Oh, good. Listen. I'd like to book a room for a week starting from tomorrow. Is that possible?"

He listened for a while. "Very good. But, um, I've an odd request. A friend stayed with you recently, and said the room was the best he'd stayed in anywhere. Sounds silly, I know, but I wonder if that room is available."

He listened again. "Room 305." He looked out the window. "It is? That's excellent. If you'd book me into that room I'd be most grateful. I'll see you tomorrow."

He replaced the telephone in its cradle, his hand shaking. He wondered if the clerk had worked out what he was doing. He'd look silly if Ro ended up in a different room. And he was not sure she wanted him next door anyway. Or even in the same hotel. As always, he had no idea and no way of finding out. At least he had made a decision.

Just before lunch time the telephone rang. It was Barnes. "Le Fanu, can you get away for lunch? I need to talk to you."

"Sounds mysterious, and urgent."

"It is."

"In that case, we'd better be careful. Do you eat local food?"

"Not much but I'm prepared to try because I'm guessing you're an expert."

He directed the editor to Krishna Rao's in Acharappan Street. "It won't be what you're used to," he said, "but the food is good and no European will see us there. I'll be there in half an hour."

A couple of minutes later he slipped down the back stairs, walked out to Edward Elliott's Road, turned left then right a couple of hundred yards later where he knew there was always a pony cart. He was at the restaurant in fifteen minutes, waiting for Barnes just inside the door.

Barnes arrived in a chauffeured car. He looked doubtful until he saw Le Fanu. The elegant suit and shoes were well out of place

"I know you said it was not what I was used to, but even so...."

"Hold judgment until you've eaten. And we won't be seen here by any Europeans."

Krishna Rao sat them at a corner table, away from the other patrons who were curious but trying to look disinterested. This was a rare sight, two Europeans in a Georgetown restaurant.

Le Fanu ordered standard dishes he thought Barnes would like. "Out of curiosity, have you eaten Udipi food before?" he asked.

"Probably not. The truth is I haven't eaten much local food at all. Too much time at the Club and no reliable guide, until now."

"Well, I think you'll like this. But there's no alcohol. Have a fresh lime soda."

Krishna Rao gave them snacks to start.

"So what's the big intrigue," Le Fanu continued, "you sounded nervous."

"Not really, but I have some information. The gun running story might be a front for something else." He looked around the room. "It is safe to talk here?"

"Yes."

"As you guessed, I do have a friend holidaying here from Singapore. I met him last night and he'd like to meet you."

"When?"

"Tonight, eight, at the Connemara, room 263."

"You'll be there?"

"Yes."

"What's he likely to say?"

"I'm not sure, but he hinted the gun running was a false lead in the Pallampur case. The story seems more complicated than that."

The food arrived. Le Fanu instructed Barnes on what it was and how it should be eaten. He also introduced the editor to Krishna Rao.

"You know," he said, as Barnes began enjoying the food, "the Mail should run some articles on the range of local food available in restaurants here."

Barnes almost choked. "I can imagine my readers opening their morning editions to that. I'd have more protests than if Home Rule for India was announced. Pity, though, it's a good idea. This food is excellent."

"Of course it is. We come out here and expect local cooks to do great English food when all the ingredients are wrong and they have no tradition to follow. It doesn't fit the local climate or the palate. It stands to reason they're best cooking their own food in their own style. You can't tell me you enjoy the Club food."

"Well, no, it's dreadful. Don't most people put up with it because it's British and familiar?"

"They think that stodge is superior to local offerings when this food tells you otherwise. It's just another way of imagining English superiority, and resisting change."

"You sound more like an anthropologist than a policeman, Le Fanu."

"Better call me LF."

"Thank you, I will."

"I'm not really anything other than a policeman, but I've read and thought a lot about things. I just wish my countrymen in high places would do the same."

"Perhaps I'd better have the Mail run a special column by the Radical Detective?"

"You've met the Inspector-General, I think? How d'you reckon he'd take to that? About as well as your readers would to Udipi food."

They agreed to meet at the Connemara just before eight. Le Fanu had a taxi drop him near the office, and walked back upstairs. Habi had left sheets of notes on Jason Palmer. Le Fanu started reading, but thought mostly about the meeting later that evening and the one tomorrow. He knew which one interested him the most, and it was not tonight's. This was a first, putting the personal before the professional.

Twenty-three

Le Fanu decided to go home rather than back to the office even though it was mid-afternoon. He would sit in the study and rethink the case, no notes, just thoughts. That would fill in time until he met the spy and help clarify his analysis. The lack of a tipping point bothered him. There was a murder, converging lines of interest that linked people in odd ways, but little more.

By the time he arrived home his resolve had softened. Perhaps he would think better while fiddling about on the lawn with a niblick and a putter. Focus on that and allow his thoughts to wander. The problem was that those thoughts wandered to Ro, and to his father.

He had not expected to be so affected by his father's death. Their relationship was so poor, yet he'd made something of his life despite that emotional poverty. He'd never contemplated his father dying. Being moved by the loss was unexpected, and unsettling. All those missed opportunities to talk, to resolve differences and reach understanding. He should use these reflections to create a better relationship with his brother. As he chipped balls towards the flagstick, Le Fanu wondered how life could combine so many challenges at once. That included Ro.

He did not know what he wanted to come out of this reunion. Over the past two years he had blocked out any honest analysis of their relationship. He wanted to sleep with her again, hopefully tomorrow night. But that was the physical rather than emotional response. The emotional one bothered him. Somehow between now and tomorrow he had to clarify his real feelings. He missed her a lot, but had never told her that in his spasmodic and perfunctory replies. She had said nothing directly to him, either, but the regularity and warmth of the letters suggested she cared. He had to decide if he did.

If he did, there were significant consequences. It would mean a relationship out in the open, running the gamut of European prejudice towards Anglo-Indians. When he first arrived in Madras he had stayed in a hotel for a week. The guests had included an Irish railway manager and his Anglo-Indian wife. They had existed in a bubble. No other guest had spoken to or even looked at them. The European disdain was obvious. When Le Fanu had talked to them, he had received the same treatment from guests and even staff. Things had changed little since.

If he and Ro were to be together that's what it would be like, and provide his detractors with even more ammunition. That would not alter his approach to work, but it would complicate his life. Ro had left in the first place because she did not want him under that pressure. On top of these complex and intertwined cases, he had to unscramble his thoughts during the next twenty-four hours to deal with her presence for a week.

And it might not be a week if he had to go to the Nilgiris or Changarore or both. He still did not see Palmer as the Rajah's killer. But that left no other obvious candidate. Pallampur had been mixed up in something serious in England but it was hard to see how that led to his murder in Madras. The Taylor connection to the Rajah remained a puzzle, as did the attempt to compromise Westshire in the mineral sands company matter. If those two strands tied to the Rajah, then the picture was even more complicated, and Palmer an even less likely suspect.

Le Fanu checked the time. Somehow it was six o'clock. He collected his golf gear, put it away, then walked around the garden for a few minutes. After a shower, he put on his Prince of Wales checked suit, matched a dark blue tie with a white shirt and the anonymous black shoes. In the mirror he saw a banker rather than a policeman. He should dress more smartly more often. But that was impractical at murder sites like the one in the Rajah's library. Those scenes returned. He drank some water.

Back downstairs he removed the suit jacket, sat near a reading light and skimmed the latest Mail edition. A brief reference to Pallampur suggested simply that inquiries were continuing. The main stories concerned local politics, the threats to business by Congress demands for devolution, and reports from garden parties hosted in Madras by Willingdon and in Delhi by the Viceroy. Such was British Raj life. He read until a quarter to eight when his car arrived, and set out for the Connemara.

The hotel was busy. A trade conference brought industrialists from across India and they all seemed to be staying at the Connemara. He saw several local civil service figures connected to labour and industry and avoided them. Assuming Barnes would go straight to his friend's room Le Fanu started up the stairs, hoping no one saw him. It occurred to him it would be like this tomorrow night, too.

Room 263 was towards the end of a wide corridor with windows to the outside and a wall lined with old Indian scenes inside. They were mostly by Thomas and William Daniell, and looked like eighteenth century originals.

The door was the same neutral cream colour as the walls. He knocked.

Barnes opened the door immediately, as if he'd been waiting. "Good evening, LF. Admirably prompt." He showed Le Fanu into the room, which was a suite. They stood in a reception area with a bedroom off to the right, and what looked like a writing room to the left.

"Drink?" Barnes was holding a tumbler of whisky.

"A smaller one of those, thanks."

Barnes ushered him towards the sideboard and poured a large whisky.

"Come through and meet my holidaying friend." He went into the writing room.

Whatever Le Fanu had expected, he was disappointed. The man was four or five inches shorter than him and leaner, whippet-like in the face. His mouth was small and thin-lipped, the nose prominently long and accentuated by the steeply receding chin. Brownish hair clung to the skull in clumps, accompanied by unfashionably long and greying sideburns. The man wore grey flannel trousers, a cream linen shirt topped with a Harris tweed hunting jacket set off by brown brogues. This did not look like a spy.

He extended his hand, looking up at Le Fanu. "Miles Watson."

"That your real name?"

The man smiled, without humour. "Yes. I use it because I forget all the aliases. Chester told me about you, says you're trustworthy."

Le Fanu nodded. "Thank you, I do my best."

Watson directed them to three club chairs placed around a low table bearing two thick files and place mats for the glasses. Le Fanu was glad to see no ashtray.

"Superintendent," Watson began, "First, I apologise for being in your city unannounced."

"I'm not the one who's bothered. You might make peace with the Chief Secretary and the Governor before you leave."

"Perhaps, but you're most directly involved in the Pallampur case."

Le Fanu hesitated. "Why have you come all the way from Singapore to investigate him? You're MI6, I understand. You must have more important things to do." He looked at the files.

"The files concern Pallampur. I'll go for a walk to the bar shortly and you can have a look."

Chester Barnes was uneasy. "I'm not sure I should be hearing this," he said. "I might be tempted to publish."

"I don't think so," Le Fanu shot back. "We've started a better relationship between the Mail and the police. You don't want to damage that long term. Stay and listen and we can fashion something for you later."

Now Watson looked bothered. "We'll need to ensure I don't appear in dispatches. This is only happening because Chester and I are friends." He pulled the files towards him.

"Before you take that walk," Le Fanu said, "give me a general idea why you're so interested in Pallampur. Was it because of the guns and the IRA?"

Watson calmed, a little. "No, not the guns. They initially attracted Indian Political Intelligence attention and that drew in 5 and 6. But then we discovered some of Pallampur's other friends and became much more interested."

"Why did he make those friends anyway?" Le Fanu was still searching for a link between the London activities and the Rajah's murder.

"Usual story, really. Money troubles. When the war broke out he made a big play investing in New Zealand scheelite ore that contained the tungsten used in making armaments. He thought he'd make a fortune. Unfortunately, he didn't realise that the vital part of the processing could only be done in Germany. When the war started, Germany was off limits, of course, so the scheelite couldn't be shipped there. All shipments ceased and he was left with a lot of iron and much less money."

"He was very well off. That doesn't sound like something that would cripple him."

"He bought £3 million's worth."

"Oh."

"Oh, indeed," Watson continued. "He made arrangements with Coutts to keep himself afloat. They reconstructed his account and shifted it to the new Park Lane branch when that opened."

"Why was that?" Le Fanu asked.

"Simple enough. Coutts didn't want him seen at the Strand, but saved his face by promoting him as one of their eager new branch clients."

Barnes listened intently. "Where did these new friends come in? If Coutts were protecting his interests he would have been alright. He'd have to spend more carefully, but he'd have been fine."

Watson tapped the files. "It's all in here, but this is the short version. He had to be a very careful spender because Coutts set demanding pay-back schedules. But the Rajah couldn't bring himself to tell his wife who was used to spending large sums unhindered. He had to support her, so needed other forms of income."

"He did raise the spending issue with her," Le Fanu interrupted. "She told me that and, yes, she wasn't pleased. It put distance between them, so the Rajah dealt with it alone." He did not mention Jason Palmer.

Watson resumed. "Now for the next bit. What do you both know about the Green Gang?"

Barnes looked puzzled, Le Fanu surprised. "Well, the only Green Gang I know is in China, based in Shanghai, I think. A friend of mine in the British Quarter police there told me about it."

"That's the one," Watson replied.

"But how does that have anything to do with Pallampur?" Barnes asked.

"Bear with me. Big Eared Du Yushang is the mover and shaker in the gang whose activities, believe it or not, are facilitated by the head Chinese detective in the French Quarter. It makes its money in the usual gang ways: drugs, gambling and women. The gang also helps suppress communist and trades union groups as directed by the Kuomintang political movement. That's why MI6 got interested, because London now has a big interest in communists after the Russian Revolution."

"That's fascinating," Le Fanu said, "but I still can't see the Pallampur connection, or how this links to his murder."

"Getting to that," Watson said, "it's intricate. The Green Gang runs mainly in Shanghai, but is building a big branch in Hong Kong which is another reason 5 and 6 got interested. Given that Hong Kong is a key part of the Empire in Asia, any change in gangs or addition to the triads there automatically comes to attention. Especially a gang with mainland political connections. But because it is Hong Kong, the Green Gang is emphasising one particular business activity."

"Prostitution," Barnes immediately said. "I saw a wire report the other day."

"Full marks," Watson replied, "and that's where the Rajah came in."

"He was involved in prostitution?" Le Fanu was astonished. "I don't believe that. He was misguided, but he was also decent and not stupid. How could he get involved in Hong Kong prostitution, anyway?"

"Quite easily, it turns out. Some important Green Gang clients in Hong Kong wanted a change from Chinese girls. They still wanted Asian ones, but not Chinese. Among other places, they looked to India."

"And that's how the Rajah got involved?" Barnes asked.

"Yes," the spy replied, "but not directly. Because of the Kuomintang connection, the Green Gang also deals in guns, and to do that they linked with the IRA. All the deals were done in London. Pallampur met some of the more refined IRA negotiators in a nightclub. Coutts had just put pressure on him, money was tight, the Rani was whining about her allowance, and the nightclub talk turned towards opportunities."

"That's still a long way from being involved in prostitution," Le Fanu said.

"There's more," Watson replied. "The IRA boys suggested it would be easy for the Rajah to ship girls from his area to Hong Kong. For a fee, the IRA would arrange transport. the Rajah would get the girls. It was the IRA's idea to divert attention by putting up the arms smuggling cover story. We're not sure why they did that. The Rampa uprising being next door helped – it kept the Government's focus there and away from whatever else was happening. That's how the arms story emerged."

"That trade in girls actually happened?" Le Fanu had neither seen nor heard any reports of such activity.

"Yes. It began about a year before the end of the war, but the Hong Kong authorities were slow to pick up on the development. By the time they did the war had just ended, 5 and 6 were looking into some related political things, the Rajah was spotted with the IRA in London and immediately put under watch."

"But why not tell Delhi or Madras," Barnes asked. "Surely action here would have helped? And this is where the girls were being procured."

Watson looked thoughtful. "You know, I'm not sure. I'd have felt more comfortable being here with someone's knowledge."

"How long have you been here, anyway?" Le Fanu asked.

"About eight months."

Le Fanu thought immediately of Special Branch, and the Willingdon /Whitney concerns about its ineffectiveness. "Eight months," he repeated, "and we knew nothing about you."

"And he only told me he was here yesterday," Barnes chipped in.

"Sorry about that but I was under tight rein. I got permission to make an approach only after the Rajah was murdered, because we hadn't anticipated that."

"What else do you know?" Le Fanu was more annoyed with Special Branch than Watson. The man did his job brilliantly and the Branch did not.

"It's all in the file, but we've a good idea where the girls are recruited, kidnapped really, and where they're shipped from. It's up north. A district called Ramsheed is a main source, and a town called Changarore a major dispatch centre."

Le Fanu looked up. "I think I'd better read those files now."

"Then it's time for my walk," the spy replied. "Chester, I think Le Fanu has just learned something important. Come and have a drink downstairs, and he can concentrate. Not often he gets to see an MI6 file, I bet. Le Fanu, we'll be back in an hour."

They left. He drew the files towards him, turned them around, opened the first and began reading.

Twenty-four

Half an hour later he picked up the telephone sitting in a corner, called the receptionist and was connected to the Chief Secretary's private number.

"Sir Charles, Le Fanu here. Sorry to bother you." He looked at his watch. It was now ten. "If you're available, I'd like to come and see you. There are things you need to know immediately."

"LF, if you're ringing me at this hour I know it's important. Come over when you're ready."

"Thank you, sir, I'll finish here in fifteen minutes to half an hour. I'll come somewhere between ten thirty and eleven. See you then."

He returned to the files and finished reading. Then he went through them again, adding here and there to notes he'd written on the Connemara's complimentary stationery. There were several small pages. They would go in the safe in the morning.

The door opened. Watson and Barnes came in, each carrying a whiskey.

"Too crowded down there," Barnes said, "all those industrialists. It was too dangerous to talk after a while." He flopped in a chair.

"Interesting reading?" Watson stared at Le Fanu.

"You chaps are efficient. Is all this information accurate?"

"As correct as possible," the spy replied. "Sometimes it's difficult to be one hundred percent sure. But it's as close a record of what's happened as you'll find." He finished his whiskey and visited the sideboard for another.

"Refill, Le Fanu?"

"No thanks, I have to leave, but thanks for the discussion and the information. It's even more useful to us than you think. Are you staying in Madras?"

"No point now the Rajah's dead, so I'm returning to Singapore the day after tomorrow."

"In that case, come with me now. I'm going to the Chief Secretary's, and it will help any future ventures if you settle him. He might be rough at first, but he knows you and 5 have been helpful. Better to have him onside."

"Good idea." Watson put down the glass. "Chester, you and I should have lunch here tomorrow."

Le Fanu and Watson went to the car, Barnes started walking along to the Mail offices. Le Fanu wondered if he had a home somewhere, and how he managed to look so neat. Questions for another time.

It took fifteen minutes to reach Whitney's home.

"Le Fanu, I hear you had a good war."

"I'm not sure there is such a thing, Watson, but I survived. I've that to be thankful for." He tried to remember the most recent nightmare. A few nights ago now. Perhaps he had too many other things to worry about. "What about you?"

"Stuck in London for most of it, following aliens around. They were mostly harmless so the work was boring. Frustrating, too. Didn't think I was doing enough."

"Why'd you stay on when the war finished?"

"Got promised a good posting and that turned out to be Singapore. I like it there and there is important work to do. Have you been over?"

"No, I haven't left India since I came back from the war, and no prospect of doing so."

"This Pallampur thing might change that." Watson picked at his cufflinks.

Le Fanu wondered at the comment. "Is there something you haven't told me?"

"It's all in the files, for the most part. However, girls are still being shipped and we're not sure who's directly involved. The IRA is organising it but we don't know who they're using to actually get the girls. The Rajah was the front. The Hong Kong gang are involved but they'll have recruited locals up in the districts. There could be some overseas complications."

The driver turned in the gate.

"Can we finish that later?" Le Fanu asked. "It might be important for our investigation."

They got out at the foot of the steps. Whitney was at the door, still in three piece dark suit, blue shirt, red tie, carnation in the lapel, spruced shoes. The cigar was lit.

"You've brought me a visitor, LF. That's a bonus."

"Sir Charles, this is Miles Watson. Watson, this is Sir Charles Whitney, the Chief Secretary." The two shook hands.

"Sir Charles, "Le Fanu continued, "Watson is our friend from Singapore."

"Is he, indeed?" Puffs of cigar smoke headed skywards. "Well, LF, as usual you're way ahead of us. Mr. Watson, we've been looking for you for the past two days, once we learned you were here." The last words carried an edge. "We're anxious to entertain you. But do come in, we can't talk out here all night."

He took them into the same small room Le Fanu had been earlier. A servant hurried to bring in an extra glass and additional sweets for the plate that graced the low table. Le Fanu saw Watson surveying the photographs and ornaments as he had previously. Whitney saw them into chairs, poured whiskeys, then turned to Watson.

"Tell me, my mysterious friend, how long have you been in Madras."

Watson told him.

Whitney turned to Le Fanu. "It seems Special Branch has been as efficient as ever, LF."

"Yes, Sir Charles. Watson and his colleagues are very good at this, of course, but we do need to improve our intelligence wings."

"Wouldn't really call them intelligent," came the growled reply amidst a cloud of smoke that he waved to disperse. "More like the Unintelligence Wing." He puffed furiously.

"Chief Secretary," Watson said, "don't be too hard on them, though I'll admit that going undetected for so long surprised me. The war experiences gave us a big start and your men are just beginning. And please do accept my apologies for being here unannounced. That was not by choice."

"Thank you. Apology accepted, I'll pass that to HE. Kind of you to defend our chaps, too, but there'll be words exchanged over this. Now, what do I need to know?"

Between them, Le Fanu and Watson briefed him on the Pallampur story. That took about fifteen minutes. At the end of it, Whitney went to a box and retrieved another cigar, clipped the end of it and lit it from his extant one. He poured three more whiskeys and returned to his chair.

"The Governor's going to love this. A major landholder and political troublemaker married to a spendthrift foreign wife gets murdered because of connections to the IRA and Chinese gangs involved in prostitution. What a wonderful story." It was a story he evidently did not relish passing on to Willingdon.

"Sir," Le Fanu said, "we don't know for sure he was murdered because of those connections, or that he was directly involved in the prostitution, even though it looks a possibility."

"Not a good time for any of this to become public," Whitney commented.

"Sir," Watson said, "you can rely on Barnes not to publish

anything. Le Fanu has him squared away. You can control the others, probably."

"I hope so." The reply came from behind another cloud of smoke.

"Sir Charles," Le Fanu said, "the immediate issue is solving the Rajah's murder. The most likely trail is up in Changarore and Ramsheed, so I'll take my people up there and investigate. We're still looking at Jason Palmer because he's been with the Rani, but he's an unlikely suspect. Perhaps some local police down there might pay him a preliminary visit?"

"I'll fix that. We don't need Jepson getting involved." Whitney ignored the questioning look on Watson's face.

"Now, LF, when do you think you can visit the north?" The face was neutral but Le Fanu sensed an awareness.

"Perhaps the day after tomorrow, sir. That'll give us a chance to prepare."

"Quite so," came the reply. "No sense rushing off and upsetting other arrangements."

Did he know about Ro? Probably. His sources were excellent. Le Fanu mumbled a reply, trying not to blush.

"And what about you, Spy Watson?" Whitney turned to the other man.

"Sir, I sail for Singapore day after tomorrow, too. Sorry to have caused you all this bother."

"Bother? You've been no bother, and that's what upsets me. One thing, though. If you do come back, feel free to come and see me. Pass that on to your superiors as well."

"Thank you, sir." Message received.

They finished the drinks and Whitney escorted them back to the front door. "Good night to you both," he said. "Pleasant voyage, Mr Watson. And LF, I hope you have a pleasant evening tomorrow before setting off north." He smiled, waved, and went back inside.

"What was that all about?" Watson asked when they were back in the car.

"Let's just say that the Chief Secretary would make an excellent MI6. His intelligence sources are excellent, which is why he was upset you slipped in undetected."

"Yes, but what was it about?"

"I believe he knows about a meeting I have tomorrow night."

"Business or pleasure?"

"Classified information, Mr. Watson. Sorry. Now, tell me what you know about the north, even if it's not much."

Watson provided a few more details, but there was no solid evidence beyond what Le Fanu had already. The Rajah's name was invoked by the gangs but they were in control, and MI6 had little hard intelligence concerning the ground conditions.

They arrived at the Connemara. Le Fanu stayed in the car where they shook hands. "Watson, you've been a mine of information so thank you."

"Sorry it took a while before I could help."

"Not at all. Have a pleasant trip back."

Watson disappeared inside the hotel, and the driver made for the house. There were a couple of lights burning when they turned in the drive, and he welcomed the peace and calm. Le Fanu went inside, made tea, found some snacks and retreated to the verandah where he sat for half an hour, pondering the next day.

Twenty-five

He was ready for breakfast by six thirty, anxious to get on with the day. The food seemed bland. It was his mood, he knew. Two cups of south Indian coffee improved the taste buds, but he left half the idlis and sambar. Back upstairs he packed a small bag with clothes and shaving kit. He could always come back to the house for anything else, and he might not be long at D'Angelis anyway.

A telegram arrived by special delivery, from his brother. The funeral would be three days from now, usual service and arrangements. Taking another coffee, he walked outside and sat overlooking the lawn. Last night's emotions returned and he still did not know why. He regretted his father's passing, but the childhood memories were so unhappy that being this sad was inexplicable.

He had a servant cycle to the nearest telegraphic office to send off a scribbled and barely adequate response. The issue was as much about his brother as his father. All he had heard from his brother was the need for money to maintain both parents. Now it would be about supporting their mother. As he remembered her unsent present, he realised he should send her a message, too. He wrote another telegram, promised to write as soon as possible, and sent another servant after the first. It might take a few days to write that letter, given everything about to happen. He needed tranquil time to write what he wanted to say, but that seemed a long way off.

By seven thirty he could not sit still so left for the office. Ro would arrive by train from Hyderabad at ten and go straight to the hotel. He did not know what time he should arrive there, but thought later. She might have family tasks even though she was supposedly on holiday. He was more comfortable with office tasks than making a decision about meeting Ro.

Habi arrived soon after.

"Sir, that Webley-Wilkinson turned up at the pawnbroker's. The servant arrived late yesterday afternoon and the dealer let me know last evening, but I knew you were busy. The fellow is definitely a servant for Mr. Palmer. As we know, Mr. Palmer is in the hills, but the servant is still in Saidapet. Shall we go to see him?"

"That's good news, Habi. Yes, take Caldicott and see this fellow. We need to know whether or not he's acting on Palmer's instructions and if so, why? Once we know that, we'll decide if we have to go to the Nilgiris."

He hoped not. One less complication would be welcome right now.

"Sir, do we leave the revolver with the pawnbroker, or collect it?

"It's not the murder weapon, but we should have it in safe keeping. Get it off the pawnbroker, bring it here but tell him he'll get it back if everything's in order. We'll put it in the safe. That's a dangerous weapon."

"You speak from experience, sir?"

"I had one through the war. I didn't bring it back because by then I'd seen more than enough of revolvers and rifles and weapons in general."

Caldicott arrived. "Good morning sir, Habi. I've come from my telegraph room, been there half the night."

He looked as well dressed and groomed as ever. How did he do that?

"What was that all about, Caldicott?" Le Fanu asked.

"Another of my friends, of course. I'll know later today, but I think I've found a way into Coutts so we can access the Rajah's account."

"Should I ask how?"

"Probably not. Let's just say MI5 have powers unavailable to us or even to Scotland Yard. I've found someone who can authorise bank access and he'll get to work when business hours open in London."

"What are we likely to find?" Habi asked. "Will there be names and contacts listing where all the transfers?"

"That's what I'm hoping, Habi" Caldicott replied. "If so, we'll have a money trail that leads us to all the business connections. Could be interesting reading: Madras, London, and who knows where else? Perhaps even Changarore and Ramsheed."

Le Fanu was drifting until those two names were mentioned ."I need to tell you," he said, "my meeting last night tied Pallampur to Ramsheed and Changarore. And you can add Hong Kong, Shanghai and maybe even Belfast or Dublin to your possible list of money destinations."

He recounted the story. By the time he finished, the other two were mesmerised.

"Sir," Habi said, "we know Special Branch is incompetent, but we've had a spy wandering about Madras all that time."

"The Chief Secretary makes the same point. Sometime about now the I-G will be at a meeting in the Secretariat, perhaps even Government House, and that won't be pleasant. When he gets back he'll be unhappy, so we need something new to tell him. Habi, that revolver story's a good one, and so is the Coutts angle, Caldicott. Do we have anything else? I can't tell Jepson about my meetings."

They assembled a story. Jepson would learn about the Palmer involvement, but that they did not think him the murderer. He would hear about the Coutts angle, but not the groups and destinations involved. They might tell him about the prostitution later. Le Fanu would ask Whitney just how much Jepson knew before briefing the I-G.

It was nine thirty. The train arrived at ten. Filling in the next few hours would be difficult.

"Sir," Habi said, "are you ready to travel to Changarore already?"

Le Fanu was puzzled. Habi pointed to the bag sitting behind the desk. Le Fanu cursed himself for being careless.

"Ah, yes, well, no. Just a precaution in case we have to move quickly."

"Looks like a holiday bag," Caldicott said. "I've one like that I take away at weekends. Mind you, haven't done that in a while."

Le Fanu hoped the discussion would change. It didn't.

"It's good to be prepared for a change of scenery." Habi seemed serious but Le Fanu knew he suspected something. Habi's intelligence network was even better than Whitney's, so was his instinct.

"I agree, Habi," Caldicott said. "What's that saying: a change is as good as a holiday?"

"It is, Mr. Caldicott, and I'm told Europeans particularly like having a change at a hotel."

He knew. Knowing him, he probably knew why as well.

"Are you two going to gabble on about holidays or do some work?" They grinned, especially Habi.

"Oh work, of course, sir, but good to see you're prepared," the sergeant commented. "Too often people don't think far enough ahead."

Caldicott recognised a nuance, even if he did not know its source. "I'll get back to my desk now, sir."

"It's alright, Caldicott," Le Fanu replied, "Habi's stirring me. I'll tell you about it sometime. Before you go, let's sort out what we might need to do over the next forty eight hours."

The main task was to visit Ramsheed and Changarore. Le Fanu had delayed that trip until the day after next. That left him two nights in the D'Angelis at least. Tomorrow, he would question Charlotte Lacey to see if she knew anything about Pallampur's newly discovered activities, and how much she knew about Palmer's background. Le Fanu expected she knew more about the latter than the former, but would deny knowing anything. He had two challenging women to deal with inside a day.

The train had arrived. A porter would be carrying her luggage to a taxi for the ride to the hotel. He tried to imagine how she was dressed, how she looked.

Habi and Caldicott went off to their tasks. He shifted the bag out of sight. Stable doors and bolting, he thought, but did it anyway.

For the next four hours he tidied his office, walked the corridors and talked to other officers and constables, went to the headquarters library, which he had not done in years. Jepson's secretary said the I-G was "off at a meeting" which Le Fanu assumed was a rocketing about Special Branch inefficiency. He went to the stables to check on the bike. The attendant treated it like his own and polished it every day, sometimes twice. Le Fanu thought about beginning the letter to his mother, but that would be futile, he could not concentrate for long enough.

By early afternoon he had exhausted his list of fill-in activities. He looked at the bag, then his watch. He walked around to Jepson's office. The I-G was still at the meeting. He would be in a foul mood when he returned. Le Fanu returned to his office, picked up the bag. Put it back down again. A few minutes later he picked it up again, looked out his office door. No one in sight, especially not Habi. Le Fanu went downstairs and out the back door towards Edward Elliott's Road. He wondered what anyone watching from the windows would make of this.

His usual pony cart driver was up the road. Le Fanu threw the bag into the cab, climbed up and asked the driver to go towards Mount Road. It was quiet as they wended through the tree-lined back streets. Restaurants were seeing off the last lunch customers. Some locals slept on rattan racks in front of their tiny dwellings. A few kids played in the streets. Shops were shut. It was not the hottest time of the year but it was the warmest part of the day. Even the kites hovering on air currents above seemed more languid than ever. The pony clip clopped on, watched by lazy dogs and resting cows. A few rubbish fires burned here and there, adding to the smoke and haze.

When they emerged onto Mount Road, Le Fanu specified the D'Angelis. He pulled at his tie. It seemed tighter than usual. His jacket was on the seat beside him but he was still sweating more than normal. The driver pulled up outside and a footman arrived to take the bag. Le Fanu paid the driver and followed his bag into the reception desk, trying to look inconspicuous. He checked in, collected his key, and imagined the desk clerk was scrutinising him extra carefully. The footman led the way up the stairs. They reached the room, the footman unlocked it, stood back and allowed Le Fanu to enter. Le Fanu tipped the man before he could spend too much time fussing about, then shut the door on him.

It was large and comfortable, the bed standing against the left hand wall. The bathroom was off through a door. A desk stood under the window, flooded with natural light. There was a wardrobe in one corner, small tables either side of the bed. He stored his few clothes and put his toilet things in the bathroom that had only a bath, not his favoured shower. Le Fanu sat on the bed, wondering what was happening on the other side of the wall.

Twenty-six

After shuffling around the room for half an hour he got up, put on his jacket, straightened his tie, smoothed his hair, put the key in his pocket, shut the door behind him and inched towards the adjoining one.

He knocked quietly.

After what seemed an age, the door opened.

She had changed, but only for the better.

He was speechless.

"I see you are as articulate as ever, Chris. You speak as frequently as you write. Come in." She was smiling.

Ro short for Roisin McPhedren still kept her dark hair short to frame the fine boned, deep olive complexioned face. Those spectacular green eyes were more striking than ever. A dark green cotton reached the floor where green flat shoes peeped from underneath. The body was still strong and trim. A high collared plain white blouse showed her form perfectly. She was more beautiful than Charlotte Lacey.

"I, well, you know, its…"

"Oh Chris, it's wonderful to see you."

She walked over, opened her arms, and hugged him. He hugged her back, clinging for time to get rid of the tears.

"Come and sit down," she said. Her room was a suite like the spy's at the Connemara. They went through to the sitting area. She telephoned for tea, then sat in a chair across from him. A low table separated them.

"Chris Le Fanu. I keep hearing about you and occasionally read about you, usually involving blood and gore. You haven't changed much there. Still handle the blood as well as ever?" Her laugh was rich, warm and inviting.

"Unfortunately, yes. Ramachandran still treats me with kid gloves and Habi still teases me. You look wonderfully well."

"I am, thank you. Hyderabad is lovely, and so is the family I work for. They have put me up well here. As it stands, I have a free week. How is your house?"

He was becoming more confident. "Honestly, Ro, it's not been the same since you left. Bigger and emptier."

"Less food available, too, by the look of you. You're almost gaunt."

He hadn't thought it that bad.

"You should come and see the house if you've time," he replied. "Though it has not changed at all. I've done nothing new."

She smiled again. "Knowing you, you haven't been there often enough to make any changes. Has your golf handicap improved?"

"It did for a while but has slipped again recently."

There was a knock at the door, a servant arrived with the tea things, set them on the low table and left. Ro poured, handed him a cup and touched him on the arm.

"I'm surprised you're here in the afternoon," she said. "I wasn't sure when I might see you. You're usually at the office until late."

"Well, I wanted to see you so came in earlier." He hesitated. "In fact, I've checked into the hotel, though I'm not sure I'll be here the whole week. I've got a murder case on and have to go north, probably day after tomorrow and be away two days."

She looked at him. "You're in the hotel? That's enterprising of you, Chris. Which room do you have?"

He reddened. "Well, um, right next door actually."

She began to laugh again, got up, came around the table, leaned over and hugged him again. "Le Fanu, you are quite something. You let me go off to Hyderabad, answer very few of my letters, then take the room right next to mine." But she looked pleased.

He wasn't sure how to take that. "Ro, I have to apologise for the letters. I wanted to reply, but somehow I couldn't find the right thing to say or to explain how I felt."

"So you thought the best approach was to say nothing at all. Even by normal male standards, that's a dumb strategy."

He nodded, couldn't think of anything to say.

"You know," she continued, "your upbringing really handicapped your personal life, didn't it?" She sensed something in his face. "Chris? Is there anything wrong?"

"Sorry, I heard the night before last that my father had died. The funeral is in a couple of days."

She hugged him again, for longer. "Is there anything I can do? I know you weren't close to your father, but the death of a parent is a life moment."

He began talking about his father, and his own surprise reactions to the death. That led to his childhood, and upbringing, the rivalry with his brother, his defiance in joining the police and his lack of friends in Madras. He told her of his fears about what might be coming and where he might go next.

Le Fanu was surprised by his openness. Ro had heard some of this before, but he'd never put it altogether for her. He'd never put it together that way for himself. It was long overdue.

"Realising all that might make things easier for you," she said.

"How do you mean?"

"You've always been an excellent policeman and a struggling man. You could never tell me what you were really thinking. You might now understand a few things about yourself. I might even forgive you your abysmal letter writing skills." She laughed again, and he felt better.

"I wanted to write," he repeated, "but couldn't do it." He thought about how he was delaying writing to his mother. Perhaps he could do that more easily now.

"What did you want to say?" The question came softly.

"Ro, the moment you left I felt a guilt that never went away. You made the decision for me, and I weakly let that happen."

"Do you still feel that way?"

"Strongly. We discussed it all, yes, but I let you walk away."

"Why is that so important?"

This was the moment, he thought, when he was honest with Ro but more with himself.

"Because I let you leave even though I cared for you very deeply. I still do."

She leaned over, kissed him lightly on the cheek.

"Thank you. But tell me about your having to go away for a couple of days."

He told her about Changarore and the case that began with the Rajah's murder. He told her everything, including the spies and the overseas connections.

"Tell me about this Australian Rani. Is she attractive?"

"Yes, but not nearly as much as you."

"Chris, I'm impressed. You're learning. Thank you again." He hoped she would not ask about any other women.

"Well, er, you are a beautiful woman, even I can see that." She brushed his arm again. "Perhaps," he continued, "we might have dinner this evening, if you have no other plans."

"That's a lovely idea, but where would we go? You've improved over a couple of years but I doubt Madras society has changed its opinion of Anglo-Indians. Can you be seen with me?"

This was a test, he realised. "You know, I think I can, or should. You prefer Indian food, I think? "

"Of course."

"In that case we won't eat in the hotel. I'll introduce you to a new friend of mine. Runs an Udipi restaurant over in Acharappan Street. You'll like it."

"Will they let me in there?"

"He lets me in, and you'll be with me."

"Well, alright, if you think so. I like this new Le Fanu."

He knew it was as much a commentary on his past as compliment to his present outlook. That was fair, he thought. This would not be easy, though. There would be no Europeans at Krishna Rao's, but gossip would circulate fast about a senior policeman eating there with an Anglo-Indian woman once his housekeeper.

He was ready for that. In a way, it was time. He criticised his European colleagues for not accepting change. Yet he did nothing to challenge attitudes in an area that meant so much to him and affected his life. It was time for him to stare down prejudice and stand up for people like Ro. Without the Anglo-Indians there would be no railway services in India, yet the Europeans declared them inferior. There was no justice in that. Krishna Rao's might be an odd place to start a rebellion, but as good as any.

"We'll go at seven thirty," he said. "Wear a shawl over what you have now and you'll be perfect." He hesitated. "You look beautiful."

"Thank you Chris, that's lovely of you to say so. Now tell me about what you'll be doing in Changarore."

For the next hour the discussion went from his work to what she had been doing and how she enjoyed Hyderabad. They explored family histories and shared city gossip.

At six he left to allow Ro time to prepare, and himself to think about the afternoon. It had gone unexpectedly well, but the coming days could be difficult.

Twenty-seven

He telephoned headquarters and was put through to Habi.

"Where are you, sir?"

"Ah, I'm looking into a few details, I'll be in tomorrow morning."

"Oh, I hope those details are interesting, sir. Any clue as to what they might be?" The hint was in the voice.

"Um, no, not yet Habi, I'll advise you tomorrow."

"Very good, sir. Now, on other matters."

Habi had checked on the servant selling the revolver. He was in Saidapet but Palmer was still in the Nilgiris. The servant had previous convictions. Nothing serious, mainly petty theft from earlier employers, and served a short sentence for taking part in a 1921 Chingleput Non Co-Operation demonstration. He was a formal member of the District Congress Party.

They agreed there was something odd here. Given that record, most European employers would have dismissed him. Yet Palmer employed him directly after he left prison. That was worth investigating. Either Palmer was more liberal than most planters, or the servant had other qualities that made him valuable. If those qualities included the ability to pass on firearms then there might be more to this.

Habi would interview the man in Saidapet, but they might

also have to go to the Nilgiris to interview Palmer, after Changarore.

"Habi, is Assistant Super Caldicott in the office?"

Habi went off to find Caldicott, and brought him back to the telephone. "Good evening, sir, Habi tells me you're off checking details?"

Soon Caldicott would know as much as Habi, thought Le Fanu. He might as well take out an advertisement in the Mail. Barnes would probably give him a discount.

"Yes, thank Habi for me, will you? Anything further from London?"

"Potentially good news. One of my MI5 contacts talked to a friend at Coutts and explained the Pallampur account transactions have potential criminal links. That's stretching it, at present, but it helped. The Coutts woman is taking advice from a director but is confident we'll get access. The report should arrive in a few hours, so I'll stay at the telegraph room. First thing in the morning I'll update you. Where should I telephone?"

Le Fanu was not sure what to say.

"Ah, don't worry. I'll be in the office in the morning so we can catch up then."

Caldicott would be curious because Le Fanu normally wanted results immediately. Habi would become even more intrigued, and informed. He should just have announced he was at the D'Angelis and let them speculate.

It was time to collect Ro. He had told her to dress simply, so he chose a pair of dark linen trousers, a plain linen shirt and light jacket, and light canvas shoes. He had been in India a long time, he reflected. The jacket was to ward off the chill of an evening that would not drop below seventy Fahrenheit. He looked in the mirror. The hair looked alright but he was tired, drawn, and nervous.

He knocked on her door. She was dressed simply but she looked wonderful. The dark green pants matched the long top that was fully sleeved with a high neckline. The green flat sandals matched that. The outfit was flowing but not enough to disguise the figure. Small gold earrings were the only jewellery.

"Ro, you look…gorgeous," he managed to get out.

She smiled. "How do we get out of here?" she asked.

"Down the stairs," he said.

"Are you sure? There could be talk."

He had thought about this. "Perhaps there will. I'll deal with that if you can. But if you want to take another approach we can."

She paused. "Let's take it slowly. You go down, organise a car, and I'll meet you at the front."

"Are you sure? I have my car down there. The driver left it for me."

"Good. You get the car and I'll be there."

"You really do look wonderful."

"Thank you."

Le Fanu walked down the stairs and through the reception area, feeling thousands of eyes on him. They weren't, of course, but they would be on Ro when she came down. Those visiting industrialists would notice a beautiful woman.

He had the car at the entrance steps when she emerged through the doors with a couple of men, inevitably, who just happened to leave the building at the same time. The doorman ushered her into the front seat, and they were ready to go.

"You had some attention, I see," he said as he pulled out of the hotel grounds and turned left into Mount Road heading towards Georgetown.

She laughed. "You men all share two characteristics: great interest in us women, and an inability to deal with us."

"You should be a philosopher."

Mount Road was quiet. A few trucks and bullock carts were completing the last of the day's deliveries to commercial houses. Street dwellers were selecting their doorways for the night, shawled up against the cool. Lights blazed at the Madras Club, welcoming the privileged and repelling the unqualified. Cows wandered the streets unhindered.

As they neared Broadway the streetscape changed, the High Court buildings further along marking the end of British Madras. The great trading houses were here, but Georgetown was Indian Madras. When he had arrived in 1905 it was still Blacktown, the name given three hundred years earlier to identify the Indian quarter. It had become Georgetown in 1911, not through embarrassment at the racist implication but to mark King George V's elevation to the throne. The area had duality, an Indian substance and a British veneer. It seemed incongruous to do an English thing like "go out to dinner" there.

He negotiated carts and cyclists, pedestrians and stray dogs, piles of rubbish, and smouldering dung fires that street families used to cook by and keep warm. Some days he worried that he was inured to the enduring inequality. It was impossible to alleviate poverty entirely but the British could and should do more, as he should.

Ro was quiet, looking out to a city she had not seen for two years. "Georgetown looks worse than before," she said, "although perhaps I'm spoiled by Hyderabad."

"In what way?" he asked.

"The Nizams made Hyderabad a great city, and the British settlements in Secunderabad complemented that. My military family live in Secunderabad, and days go by when I never see anything like this. The poverty's there, yes, but less obvious than here."

"I need you to remind me of that," Le Fanu commented, recalling his earlier thought. "I see this every day and sometimes assume its normal. It's not, of course. The slums have become worse. There's not enough money to provide adequate facilities. There are more people living on the streets than ever."

They turned into Acharappan Street, and he parked outside Krishna Rao's. There were still few cars in Georgetown, especially at night. Europeans owned most vehicles, but they were seen rarely in Georgetown outside business hours.

Krishna Rao was waiting for them. "Superintendent, thank you for coming this evening."

"Good evening Krishna Rao. Allow me to introduce a very good friend of mine, Mrs McPhedren." He felt strange introducing her by her married name, and jealous.

"Mrs McPhedren, I'm honoured to have you here and I hope you'll enjoy my food." He began showing them inside.

"Oh, I'm sure I will," she replied," Chris, Superintendent Le Fanu has told me a lot about it and he's a very good judge." They spoke in Tamil, and Le Fanu had forgotten how well she spoke the language.

They sat at a corner table, and Krishna Rao arrived with the first dishes. Le Fanu thought his chef friend had ensured the food was even better than ever.

As they ate, picking food from the banana leaves with their fingers, the conversation moved easily to Ro's life in Hyderabad, which she enjoyed, and occasionally back to his in Madras, which was mostly about work. His world was too narrow. Ro explored Hyderabad extensively because her family allowed her lots of leisure time. She knew the city's history, rulers and contemporary politics. Princes like the Nizam supported a permanent British presence that gave them certainty and continued wealth. If self-rule came, many Congress members would want to abolish princely rights. That was discussed widely in Hyderabad, according to Ro, who thought a balance must be struck or India would see conflict.

She talked about the city and its treasures, the Charminar pearl shops and the jewellers who made the city famous. Her earrings were made by a man who came to her family's house. He arrived on a bicycle carrying a small charcoal burner on the back. That was lit and once hot, he turned the gold above it, fashioning exquisite pieces with a couple of basic tools. She loved Hyderabad.

"Do you think you'll stay there?" he asked.

She hesitated. "I'd like to, but we all know things change. I'm happy there, mostly, now. I wasn't at first."

He wondered if he should ask. "Why?"

"Chris, you know why. It was my decision to leave, but I wasn't happy. I loved being in your house, you must know that."

He nodded. "So did I while you were there, but not since. It's my house and I'm still glad I bought it, but it's not been the same since you left."

Le Fanu could not have imagined saying that back then, when he was mute. They had only just met up again yet already he was more open with her. She picked up his thoughts.

"Chris, you are becoming positively articulate. How wonderful." She reached over and touched his hand.

"Well, the past couple of years have not been much fun," he replied, placing his other hand over hers. "Work kept me going but the other hours were a trial. I played a lot of golf, that's about all."

"At least you could play," she said, "you'd have been a mess without that."

This was the most relaxed he had been in years, and it was because of her. "I really am sorry I was such a poor correspondent. I didn't know how to deal with it."

She reached out and squeezed his hands. "I know, you always were hopeless but somehow you've improved. That almost makes two years away worthwhile, almost." The wisp of a smile revealed the humour.

They finished the food, washed their hands in the communal basin, thanked Krishna Rao who beamed at the praise and showed them out to the car.

As they drove back, little was said. Peace was made.

"Drop me at the front door," she said.

He watched her ascend the steps into reception, and imagined her crossing the room, watched again. She made it easy for him, he realised, and he was grateful. He parked the car, entered the hotel and went to his room. There was no sign of her. Should he knock on her door?

There was a slip of paper just behind the bottom of the door.

Thank you for a wonderful evening. It was lovely. I'll see you in the morning. Ro.

He looked at his watch, surprised to see it was midnight. A couple of minutes later he was in bed, light out, thinking about tomorrow.

At ten past twelve his door opened quietly. A second later the covers on the other side of his bed were drawn back, and she slid in beside him.

"Chris, I said I'd see you in the morning. I just didn't say how early."

Twenty-eight

He awoke alone, as he did when she lived in the house. After bathing and dressing, he went down for breakfast. Back up stairs he prepared for the office. Outside his room he hesitated, then knocked on her door softly. It opened and he went in quickly. They hugged.

"Are you alright? he asked.

"Oh, excellent, thank you, Chris. And you?"

"Better than in a long time, two years in fact. But I have to go to the office. What will you do today?"

"I'm meeting the general and his family later this morning but I'll be back here later this afternoon. We can catch up then. Don't hurry, I'm not going anywhere."

By the time he reached the office Habi and Caldicott were already updating the case boards.

"Good morning, sir," Habi said, "I do hope all those details were sorted out satisfactorily last evening." He looked innocent, which meant he was not. "Tricky things, details."

"Yes, Habi, they are, but only if not handled the right way. Caldicott, how are you this morning."

"Well, sir, thank you. And I've news. We have access to the Rajah's Coutts account. The officer there is being very helpful. The first copies of the transactions have arrived and I've started going through them."

"There are a lot of details in them, sir" Habi added.

"Very well, Habi. If you must know, I'm staying a few nights at the D'Angelis, and I'm working from there so your instincts are right, I'm not at home."

"The D'Angelis is a very nice office, sir" Habi replied. "Assistant Super Caldicott has to make do with the telegraph room."

"And I'm sure he doesn't mind so long as he's chasing criminals, Habi, as I know you like to do. Caldicott, anything new in those documents yet?"

"I need more time, but my London connections suggest the IRA control some of the accounts from which the Rajah received funds. That supports the gunrunning story, at least superficially. But there are oddities we're chasing up. According to the Coutts officer, they were concerned about and investigated some transactions. In several cases, the IRA accounts were merely transition channels. The money came from elsewhere, the IRA were used as a channel. That's what we're looking into."

"What about the payments out?" Habi asked. "Have we any information on those yet?"

"Yes. Some went to Taylor in Changarore, until quite recently. That's something we hadn't thought about. We know the Rajah funded Taylor earlier, but we didn't know some of the payments continued. And the Rajah made payments to other parties up there and in Ramsheed. None to Westshire I've seen yet, but certainly to other people."

"That's good progress," Le Fanu observed, "we might be closer to understanding this puzzle." He paused. "But it doesn't get us any closer to who killed the Rajah. What news do you have, Habi, or are you too focused on details to see the bigger picture?"

Habi roared. "Very good, sir, very good. I do have some information. When that revolver arrived at the pawnbroker's yesterday, we had a plain-clothes constable there. It was Mr. Palmer's servant who sold the weapon. We have the man here now. He sold the revolver on behalf of Mr. Palmer who paid him a commission."

"Good. It just means he sold the revolver, though. It's not the murder weapon. Palmer might have needed cash. Did he get a good price?" Le Fanu thought about how much his own revolver might have been worth had he kept it.

"A very good price. The pawnbroker paid him £400, because he can sell it in England for £700. Everyone is happy, except Mr. Palmer if he found out the UK price."

Caldicott chimed in. "It would be good to know why he needed the money. He probably knew the real worth but sold anyway. There must be a reason for that."

"I think you're right," Le Fanu said. "But his problems are probably not connected to our present ones. We need to get up to Changarore for a look. We'll focus there rather than Ramsheed, and talk to Westshire later. We'll leave first thing in the morning as planned. Habi, are the arrangements made?"

"Yes, sir, the train is booked, and a hotel for tomorrow night. It's not the D'Angelis, though. And our Changarore colleagues have given me the names of people usually mixed up in things like this. We can start with them."

"Good. Caldicott, you keep up with the London end today and unearth some more on those accounts. They're turning up some excellent links. Habi, you come with me because we need to ask the Rani more questions about Jason Palmer."

It was ten when they reached Pallampur House. The temperature was creeping up. They were shown into a room on the first floor, along from the library. Le Fanu still found it strange that she stayed in the house, and would conduct this meeting so close to the library.

Charlotte Lacey came in soon after they arrived. Le Fanu and Habi rose but she motioned them back into their chairs. "Gentlemen, so nice to see you."

She wore a brocade jacket over a floral blouse, the jacket matched by a long straight skirt accentuated by the black, high heeled shoes that made her look even taller and more statuesque. "What would you like to know now?"

"We need to ask more questions about Mr. Palmer, I'm afraid," Le Fanu replied.

"Jason? Why?" She looked worried, probably the fear of publicity.

"Sergeant Habibullah will start."

"Your Highness, Mr Palmer has just sold a revolver. One of his servants sold it to a pawnbroker who will sell it in England, at a big profit. Have you ever seen Mr. Palmer with a revolver?"

"I still don't understand why this is important but, no, I don't think so. He has a shotgun and a rifle in his Saidapet house, but I've no idea what he has up in the hills. Why are you asking?"

Le Fanu developed the point. "Rani, a revolver went missing from here the night your husband was killed. It wasn't the murder weapon but we need to know where it went. It's probably a coincidence, but the weapon sold by Mr. Palmer was the same model that went missing. We've no idea if it's the same one, but you'll understand our interest."

Now she was bothered. "But that's absurd. Jason wasn't even here so how could he steal the gun? That suggests you consider him a suspect and that's even more absurd. Pally knew Jason was shagging me. As I told you, Pally and I had an arrangement about these things. Why would Jason come here and upset him?"

"Did Mr. Palmer have money worries?" Habi asked.

"Not that I know of, but that doesn't mean much. I spent my time with Jason in bed, not talking about life and money or discussing the latest novel."

If she hoped to embarrass them, she failed. Habi was learning how to deal with these modern European women. Le Fanu thought she was overly defensive.

"He didn't talk about having to sell things or about having

a cash flow problem?" Habi continued.

"Not to me, so I think that line of questioning is exhausted."

"Perhaps we can change direction, then, Rani, "Le Fanu said. "How much did you know about Mr. Palmer as a person. Did you know he's not very popular here?"

"I do now, but not when we first met."

"So you know his reputation for entertaining married women?"

"You put it so quaintly, Superintendent." She turned in profile, trying to distract him. He ignored her, but thought about Ro back at the D'Angelis. "Yes, he has a gift for giving women what their husbands couldn't, or wouldn't. And those sad husbands resented him. I doubt the women did, he's very good at what he does."

"Do you know he upset some senior members of the civil service, and that one of them set a gang of thugs on him?"

"So he provokes men by servicing their wives satisfactorily? Thanks to Marie Stopes, women now know they should be satisfied. Jason does that very well."

Le Fanu doubted Married Love was standard reading in Madras' European households let alone in those of senior ICS officers like the First Member of the Board of Revenue. If it was, Jason Palmer might not be in such demand.

She continued. "And satisfying a few women scarcely makes him a murder suspect. Pally was actually grateful that Jason took me off his hands, as it were, now and then. Pally was the one with the worries, and that didn't help my life. And when he and I did get together, I was pretty keen having learned a few new tricks with Jason. So again, why would Jason kill Pally?"

The Rani of Pallampur had certainly read Marie Stopes. He should ask Ro if she had.

"Rani," he said, "you've been very honest, so I'll be honest, too. Mr. Palmer's not at the centre of our investigation, but we need to cover all possible connections to your husband's murder. We'll talk to Mr. Palmer to confirm his movements. You told us he was with you, I know. But we'll ask him, just for the record."

"Thank you, Superintendent, I'll help all I can, obviously. Jason's not the man, I'm sure of that. He just has a gift for providing certain services not provided by neglectful husbands. By the look of you, I doubt you're one of them." Her eyes travelled top to toe, slowly. He did not blush, a triumph.

"Thanks for the compliment, Rani, but you'll know I'm divorced."

"I doubt that stops you performing well."

He thought of last night, or early this morning. "I think we'd best be on our way, Rani."

Habi watched this exchange bemused, but missed nothing.

They left Pallampur House, Le Fanu doubting much would come of this line of inquiry, and thinking more towards Changarore.

Twenty-nine

The driver dropped him at Fort St George, would take Habi to headquarters then return in an hour. Luckily, the Chief Secretary could see him.

"Thanks for coming, LF, the Governor's taking keen interest in this as you'd imagine. So I appreciate you keeping me up to date."

"How does he feel about having a spy here and not knowing?"

"Ha, I think you know the answer to that. He has bombarded Delhi daily with 'please explains' but little has come back. They're embarrassed at being found out, I think. But then, only one or two people up there knew about it. Some other lordly figures are unimpressed, I gather."

"Sir Charles, we now know more about the accounts." He passed on Caldicott's information, then the gist of the interview with the Rani.

"She sounds very modern, LF." His eyes sparkled. "Would shock a few of the local matrons, no doubt."

"Oh yes, she would."

"I agree with you. I doubt Palmer's the man we're after, even if a few chaps in this town would like to settle scores with him. The Pallampur money trail looks far more promising. What are you planning?"

"Habi, Caldicott and I will go to Changarore in the morning and come back the following day. The local police have given us some names, so we'll follow those. And we'll interview Taylor. Hopefully, that will get us further ahead."

"Might interrupt your social life, though?" Sir Charles was smiling.

"Sorry, sir?"

"You know my networks are good, Chris, even if they missed that damned spy. I know there's a guest at the D'Angelis known to you, and I know you're booked in there. I hope it all works but, as ever, mind how you go. Attitudes have changed a little, but most people still hold the old prejudices."

"I'll bear that in mind, sir, thank you." It was fair advice, the same he'd acted on two years earlier. He was different now, but still had to prove that.

"Keep me informed on Changarore," the Chief Secretary continued. "That would be good. The telephone's not be the most secure way, mind. All these spies running around have changed my ideas. If there's anything urgent, call me on the private line and I'll find a way to contact you."

"Thank you, sir, I will, and I'll update the I-G as soon as I get back to headquarters."

"Very good idea. And, Chris, do pass on my best wishes to Mrs McPhedren."

Le Fanu was surprised. That was a covert declaration of support, defying local antipathy. It also did not fit Whitney's public image as a throwback to the nineteenth century.

"Thank you very much, Sir Charles, I will."

Le Fanu sat in the back of the car as they exited through the narrow fortress gate onto the Marina road. Checkpoint staff were more relaxed than a few days earlier, especially with traffic leaving. He needed time to think. Le Fanu directed the driver past the University of Madras and around to the cricket ground, then into a myriad of back streets. Along the way they stopped at a roadside food stall to buy vadas for lunch. He finished them as they reached the Elliott's Road entrance to headquarters.

Le Fanu went upstairs, washed the food off his hands and mouth, then went to Jepson's office. Once more, he was shown straight in.

"Good afternoon, Le Fanu." Cordiality again. "Are we making progress?"

"Yes, sir, we are."

He updated Jepson and emphasised the Palmer story, knowing from past experience that was the one the I-G would latch onto. The presence of spies and some of the Pallampur developments he skirted around carefully.

"However, sir, we're going to Changarore tomorrow. There are some Taylor details we need to confirm. There were possibly odd links between Pallampur and Taylor and some people up there might be able to enlighten us."

"Very good, Le Fanu, I'll see you when you return. I have an interview with the Governor the day after you get back, so I'll need to be on top of things."

Normally, Jepson would have boasted about seeing Willingdon, but now he was rueful. Remembering Whitney's earlier remarks, Le Fanu imagined this would be a progress review of Jepson's performance. The man must be struggling to remain calm.

"I'll let you know as soon as I get back, sir, day after tomorrow."

As he left, Le Fanu considered himself lucky Jepson was not at his roaring, bullyboy best because that would have made matters even more difficult.

Caldicott was waiting. "Sir, more information from London. MI5 have been working with the Coutts officer. Most of the IRA funds that went to the Rajah came originally from Hong Kong accounts. Authorities there confirm that those accounts belong to the Green Gang. So it appears the Rajah was paid to facilitate young women from Ramsheed and Changarore being taken for prostitution."

"How long have those transfers been going on?"

"Since early 1919, it seems, and there are large sums involved, about £400,000 traced so far."

"That's not a patch on his losses, but it does suggest there's a large trade going on. Which again raises the question about why none of this was noticed locally."

"I've checked. In all that time, there were no more than normal missing persons reports registered. There's nothing in Special Branch files. And there's nothing in any of the District Super reports. It seems unimaginable that large numbers of missing women were neither noticed nor reported."

"The most likely reason is that corrupt local officials are involved. If so, that's another development the Government will have to keep quiet, and that won't be easy."

Le Fanu thought for a time.

"Can you imagine what's happened to those poor women? How they've been treated? They've been taken away from homes and families, held below decks on small boats, shipped to Hong Kong via God knows where. The boat crews will have had a go at them while they were captive. Then they end up being abused in Hong Kong. How the hell did the Rajah get involved in that? All reports have him being a decent man."

He wondered how the Rani would react when she found out. The Rajah's money troubles must have been extreme.

"One aspect puzzles me, sir, and I'm sure you've had the same thought." Caldicott was being diplomatic. "Why was the Rajah paying Westshire and Taylor? It seems inconceivable they would be part of anything like that."

"Very good point, Jackson. We've yet to meet Taylor, but I can guarantee Westshire wouldn't condone the trade. Yet it was going on in his district and he seems to have known nothing. We know those district offices are riddled with informers, but they make money by giving advice on how to avoid paying tax, not by hiding serious criminal activity like this. There'll need to be major inquiries into all office activities up there. And soon."

"It looks like the Rajah was paying compensation. But if he was, why and for what purpose? Then there's the issue of who was orchestrating the activity in those districts."

"Yes," Le Fanu said, "and that makes our work over the next thirty six hours even more important. We have the names of likely suspects so we'll round them up for questioning. This is so big, though, the real leaders are probably well out of view."

They discussed the possibilities for a few minutes.

"Well, Jackson, why don't you head off and get ready for tomorrow? There's little else we can do today."

"Thanks, sir, I will. What about you?"

"Back to the D'Angelis. I'll meet you at the station in the morning."

Caldicott looked ready to ask another question but stopped, said goodbye and left. He could be trusted, le Fanu thought, so he might confide in him as a friend, soon.

Habi arrived, they finalised the travelling arrangements then he, too, left for home.

It was five, so Le Fanu had the driver take him home and wait while he collected clothes and equipment for the journey. Then they went to the D'Angelis. The driver would return at eight the next morning.

Le Fanu went to his room, threw his belongings on the bed, then went and knocked on her door.

She hugged him, hard. There was an uncertain moment before he kissed her. They relaxed, and sat at the small table.

"Shall we eat together this evening?" he asked.

"Of course, the only question is where."

"We could go out again," he said, "but I also wondered if we might eat here."

She looked surprised. "Are you sure? That news will cross the city in minutes."

"Would you mind?"

"I think the problem is yours. I'll just be branded. You'll make enemies who might damage your work. Are you sure you want to do this?"

"Would you like a drink? I'm having a whisky off your sideboard."

"I'll join you, neat please."

He handed her the drink, and placed an arm around her shoulders before she sat down.

"Ro, it's never just been about the sex with you." She looked startled.

He recounted the interview with the Rani and her references to Marie Stopes and Palmer's attributes.

Ro was helpless with laughter. "How on earth did you handle that, Chris, you're hopeless with those things. Talking about it, I mean. I'm sure you're Palmer's superior on the actual doing front."

Now he blushed. "Well, thank you. But I handled it better than I would have before, and that has to do with you. As I said, it's not just about sex with you, it never was. I care for you, and know I made a mess of it last time. I've been miserable ever since."

"This is a very new Chris Le Fanu," she said.

"Seeing you again confirms what I knew when you were in the house, and how I felt when you left. I don't want to go through that again. You're very important to me." He leaned over and kissed her.

"Chris, I'm so glad because I've missed you. But that doesn't change things. For many people I'm beyond the pale, literally, and if you're seen with me you're vulnerable."

"At some point I have to face that. If we're to avoid a repeat of the last couple of years, we should face it sooner rather than later. That's why I think we could eat downstairs."

"Not only am I Anglo-Indian, we're not married. Being seen in public will scandalise people. This is Madras, Chris, the bigot's bastion. We could get food delivered to our rooms then eat together."

"Ro, you left two years ago because I wouldn't make a decision. You made the decision for me by leaving. I've thought about that every day since. I don't want this week to be something we have for a few days because you're in Madras briefly. You mean more to me than that. Maybe it's time for me to demonstrate how I feel."

"Are you sure?"

"Yes – but dress in your finest."

"Yes, sir."

He arranged a table for two in the dining room. An hour later they entered, arm in arm. He wore his dinner suit and looked like every other man in the room, but Ro stopped the conversation. She wore a royal blue silk evening dress, matching gloves, shoes, bag and shawl. The short hair was tousled, highlighting her face. A string of Hyderabad pearls sat at her throat, matched by huge single pearl earrings. She looked stunning.

They ordered a bottle of champagne, enjoyed the food, talked incessantly, noticed themselves being noticed. When they left, they were watched all the way out the door.

Le Fanu walked her arm in arm up the stairs, along the corridor, and into her room.

Thirty

It was an important moment waking next to her. That would not have happened before, and changed the relationship. They had been brave enough the previous evening, but Madras would now know they were together at the D'Angelis. Le Fanu was divorced and Ro a widow. Even so, proper European society in Madras would be displeased, to say the least. But now, he did not care. His life might become more difficult but the relationship was important.

She was still sleeping. He got out of bed and prepared for the train trip north. In an hour he had washed, dressed and packed. She stirred as he came back into the bedroom.

"Chris, good morning. How nice to see you." She sat up, pillows behind her. "Are you abandoning me again already?" She smiled.

He sat down next to her. "I'll be back tomorrow evening so don't go too far. I could get used to this."

"Good." She reached up, hugged him. "See you tomorrow."

Walking downstairs with his bag, he felt conspicuous again even though few people were about. The driver was waiting and soon had Le Fanu at Madras Central. The station was crowded, as always. Half the Presidency's population seemed to be travelling. Most would cram into third class carriages, carrying the food and bedding needed for long journeys.

Some would be going in search of work, others for family reasons. Many were on pilgrimage, going to centres like Tirupati, not far north of Madras and the wealthiest temple in India. Every day thousands of Hindus went there, many leaving behind gold, gems and money to serve Vishnu in his Lord Venkateswara form. At a more worldly level, Le Fanu saw several Congress members travelling in a group. They stood out in their off-white, homespun cotton garments topped with the distinctive Gandhi cap. The women also wore the rough, off-white clothing. Le Fanu admired their determination to win power for Indians despite everything that had been done to them over the past two years.

A police porter took his bag, guiding him through the early morning throng to his carriage. It was a several hour trip and he knew they should have taken the night train last evening, but that would have meant leaving Ro. Le Fanu couldn't remember when he'd last put his personal life ahead of his professional one. That was another important step.

Habi and Caldicott were already in the first class carriage. From the start, Le Fanu insisted that Habi travel first class, to the annoyance of other European officers. Le Fanu thought any person good enough to be on the team should be treated equally, irrespective of colour or religion. That came from his war experiences, sharing tough conditions and battles with his Indian soldiers during the Mesopotamian campaign. Le Fanu changed a lot in those years. He thought it a pity more of his European colleagues had not done the same. They would be more progressive now.

Le Fanu was surprised to see someone else there, the Chief Secretary. This had to be important.

"Good morning, LF. Sorry to show up like this, but could I chat with you in private?"

They went into the reserved compartment.

"LF, there are a couple of developments you need to know about. I've had an intelligence report in overnight. There are some very serious criminals involved up in Changarore, some real gangsters who've come in from Bihar. They're the people you're looking for."

"That's ominous," Le Fanu replied. "How do we know this? And why only now?"

"Bloody Special Branch, of course, failed us again. The intelligence boys in Delhi picked it up, but only in the past couple of days and by accident. They were tracking some socialists and stumbled on these characters, found mention of Pallampur and informed us late last night. Real thugs, bad records, and suspected of killing several opponents who got in the way. The trail led to Changarore and they're still there, so I thought I'd let you know."

"Thank you, sir, that changes things. Could you send a telegram and ask that revolvers and rifles be available for us at the police station in Changarore. We'd also better have a unit of armed police available to assist us."

"I'll do that as soon as I reach the office. You'll also get precise instructions on where to find these people, they're a bit out of town."

"Right. There's something else, Chief Secretary?"

"Yes." Whitney had a large smile." A message from the Governor. You know he has a less than favourable view of the local civil service and most of the Europeans. Me excepted, of course. He asks that I pass on to you his best wishes for your future." The smile widened.

"Not sure I understand, sir."

"Come on LF, it's early in the morning but don't play the ingénue. Like most of the senior echelon he knows you're at the D'Angelis, and he's heard reports from last evening. He mightn't like it but he admires your stand. So do I. You'll get criticism, so he wants you to know you have support as well. I join him in that."

"Thank you, Sir Charles. I'm embarrassed but appreciate the thoughts, and I'd be grateful if you could pass that on to

His Excellency."

"I will. Now head off but watch your back. This sounds like dangerous territory."

Whitney left, and the other two came in, intrigued.

"What was that all about, sir?" Habi asked.

Le Fanu told them about the gangsters.

"That fits the other reports from London," Caldicott said. "The IRA lot connected to a Bihari gang active throughout northeast India. It sounds like they've drifted towards our patch. They must be the Green Gang's local agents with the IRA funnelling the money."

"If that's so," Habi said, "then this is a big and organised operation."

"They'll also be desperate," Le Fanu said, "so all the more reason to be armed and have that support unit. Habi, I know you've refreshed your firearms training lately, but what about you, Caldicott?"

"Not since I came out here, really, and I didn't have much chance to use them in the other work, either."

"Hopefully we won't have to use them."

"What else did the Chief Secretary have to say, sir?" Habi looked nonchalant.

"Um, a personal matter, really."

"Not those details you've been dealing with, sir?"

"Yes, Habi, details. Right you two, you should know because the whole of Madras will by the time we return, if it doesn't already. I'm staying at the D'Angelis with a good friend, Mrs. McPhedren. Habi knows her but, Caldicott, she was my housekeeper until a couple of years ago. More importantly, she's a very close personal friend. She's also Anglo-Indian."

"You'll get some attention for that," Caldicott said. "But I do hope it works out for you."

"Thank you, I know it will be difficult, but it's important."

"Sir," Habi said, "you're very good with details and Mrs

McPhedren is a nice person. She has a reputation for being very kind to servants. It will work for you, I'm sure. But please let me be in the room when you tell the I-G."

"I'll keep that in mind, Habi. And thank you both, it means a lot."

They settled in for the trip. Habi went to sleep immediately. Caldicott rummaged in a carry bag and pulled out a book.

"What are you reading, Jackson?"

"A tragedy"

"Shakespeare."

"No. Percy Fender, Defending the Ashes. Misleading title, really, should be Not Defending the Ashes. England did lose 5-0 away in Australia, after all."

"Why read it, then? It's obviously painful."

"Partly to see what went wrong, partly because I know some of the players. I went to school with Johnny Douglas. You know what his initials J.W.H.T. really mean, of course?"

"No."

"Johnny Won't Hit Today. That was certainly true in Australia. How will you fill in the time?"

Le Fanu held up his book.

"Somerset Maugham, Rain and Other South Seas Stories, came out last year."

"That's a bit radical, isn't it? I haven't read the stories but hear he puts the boot into colonial types."

"Like you, it's nice to learn where it went wrong. Should be some lessons for us in there somewhere. Have you run across Hilton Brown yet?"

"No. Who's he?"

"An ICS man. He's a Scot with a literary bent, and not much loved by the Board. He writes for Punch, which is bad enough. But the Board members discovered he is about to publish two novels critical of what's going on in India. They're giving him a hard time. Probably safer to read Maugham than Brown in these parts."

"I saw one of Maugham's plays in London. He has a good instinct for people, though a bit too sardonic for me."

"Better stick to Percy Spender."

As he read, Le Fanu occasionally looked up to watch the scenery as they passed from the Tamil-speaking into the Telugu-speaking area. They rolled through Nellore, Habi's home district. Habi remained asleep. They were soon in Guntur, a Congress heartland during Non-Co-Operation. The landscape changed from dry and dusty to irrigated and lush. By the time they reached Vijayawada on the Kistna river, rich green grain fields spread on both sides of the railway line. That landscape continued as they crossed the Godavari river and travelled further north.

The paradox, thought Le Fanu, was that these wealthy lands and peoples owed it all to an irrigation system built in the mid-nineteenth century by Sir Arthur Cotton. Most towns here still had statues for him. Yet somehow the British lost their support. That takes real skill, he thought. Congress had thousands of supporters here. Troops and armoured cars were sent into some places, and several lives were lost to police and military shootings. Somewhere in the top layers of government someone had to produce more creative policies. Right now, there was no indication about who that might be. The British had lost this region.

Habi awoke as they neared Vizagapatam, rested. Le Fanu had read little Somerset Maugham.

"Nearly there now, sir. I like train travel. I sleep really well."

They looked at Caldicott. His book was unread, too, because he was sound asleep. Perhaps it was a tragedy, although Le Fanu wondered about the importance placed on cricket by the English. He'd been hopeless at school, so was probably the wrong person to ask.

He shook Caldicott as they pulled into the Changarore station. They retrieved their bags, and were met by the District Superintendent of Police who took them to a waiting car.

After checking into the hotel they went to the police station to be briefed, pick up their weapons, and link with the armed squad made up of local constables.

The briefing confirmed the names, profiles and location of the people apparently involved with the prostitution ring. They were a mix of known local criminals and the Bihari hard men. As Whitney suggested, they were last sighted in a village out of town that was more in the direction of Pallampur's estates. The District Super was adamant that local police had no information about large numbers of missing girls. Le Fanu could see at least one senior career hitting a reef.

It was late in the afternoon. The armed squad leader specified the locations and issued travelling instructions. They mounted three trucks and set off northwest, with twenty miles to travel.

Thirty-one

Those minimal Delhi intelligence reports placed their quarry in a small forestlands village where Rampa rebels were active. That was a possible link to the gunrunning, but Le Fanu still doubted the connection was solid. But he did know that several anti-government groups were active in the area, well armed and used to navigating the forest. If the criminals they were chasing had joined those groups, then apprehending them would be dangerous. Their opponents had the advantage here, and Le Fanu's team was inexperienced.

As they neared the target area he had the vehicles halted in a clearing and unloaded. They formed a half circle around him.

"Listen up. This is not a routine exercise. It's dangerous. We're hunting professional criminals from Bihar who have joined up with local thugs. They're all involved in a profitable illegal trade, and won't want to let it go. That trade takes girls from here and puts them into prostitution in Hong Kong. These people are ruthless, they've shot their way out of situations like this before. We must be careful. Everyone got that?"

There were murmurs, some younger policemen looked apprehensive. Le Fanu detailed each group's assignment once they reached the village now about a mile away. He spoke to everyone in the groups, making sure they knew what to do, checked their weapons, and ensured group leaders understood instructions.

They would travel a further half a mile by truck, dismount, then approach the village on foot from different directions. They had to know the different lines of approach in case shooting broke out. The light was fading. That would cut visibility in the village, because the forest filtered out low light quickly. They were as ready as they could be. Once back on board the trucks they maintained silence. The vehicles inched forward. Le Fanu would have preferred to walk the full mile. That would have been less noisy, but they would have lost time.

Half a mile on they dismounted. He formed them into separate columns, checked their weapons again. Rifles and revolvers were loaded, and ready. Tension grew. They filed out. Each group walked on an alternate side of the road. One man looked left, the next looked right. Column leaders scanned ahead, those at the rear walked backwards to provide cover. Little light now pierced the thickly wooded forest, so they cast no shadows. Le Fanu sensed some men getting anxious so moved quietly up and down each column, looking each man in the face and touching an arm in reassurance. It was hard to believe he left Madras and Ro just a few hours ago.

Habi and Caldicott each commanded a column, one each side of the road. Habi's was first on the left, Caldicott's first on the right. Le Fanu was in the middle, moving between them all in overall command. He had a Webley-Wilkinson revolver issued in Changarore, and was accompanied by a constable with a Lee Enfield .303, the war stalwart.

The silence worried him. There were no animal or bird sounds, no human noise. In these areas the last was not unusual, but the other two were. They approached the village outskirts. The columns moved off the road into the forestlands, the front two peeling off left and right to encircle the buildings barely visible through the forest. He saw apprehension in several faces. The first two columns would cover the rear of the village, the middle two the sides, and the last pair the front. Habi would remain with his column and control the rear sector. Caldicott would move back one and control that side and towards the front. Le Fanu would control the left quadrant. The policemen were ten yards apart, each man looking alternately in towards the village or into the forest to create a complete defence. Still no sign of the people they were stalking.

Le Fanu slowed progress to a crawl. They had to be in the right place, with every possible exit from the village covered. Looking through the trees he could just see the first buildings, low-roofed and thatched huts. Some had smoke curling out from cooking fires. It was close to mealtime. He fancied he could smell food, but it was probably his imagination. His men were well spaced, some he could not see at all and the rest were shadows. They inched closer, weapons at the ready. Still no sound from the buildings. They should have seen or heard someone by now.

His men were just back from the first row of trees. Their next steps would be into the open ground between the tree line and the first buildings. He signalled those nearest him to stop and they passed on the signal. He had to decide. They might have to search building to building, not knowing what was inside. He had anticipated encountering villagers and asking them about strangers in the area. That was always an imperfect plan. Some villagers could be Rampa movement supporters or even participants, others might be part of the gang. But it was a better option than going into unknown buildings. The absence of credible intelligence made this much more dangerous.

He had them wait, silent. Ten minutes passed. Still no sound, still no sign. The village could be deserted, but he doubted that. Cooking fire smoke suggested otherwise. The alternative possibility was worrying: that the gang was present, in hiding, and waiting. The responsibility of command flooded back, along with memories of Shaiba and its terrors. He remembered the bodies of dead soldiers, his dead soldiers, his dead Indian soldiers.

They had to go in, he knew that. The longer they waited, the darker it would get. If they withdrew, there was no guarantee of safety. If there was a reception committee, better to deal with it front on rather than fight it off while retreating. He signalled for half of each side column, every alternate man, to advance on the buildings, slowly. Clad in their dark green uniforms the men rose silently, barely visible when viewed from inside the tree line. It would be different from the buildings. The troopers would not stand out clearly, but they would be visible. He watched Caldicott lead the advance guard. This was different for the ex-spy, the lone actor now become leader. It was a difficult switch. The advancing men were half way between the trees and the first buildings.

Heavy gunfire shattered the silence.

"Fuck it, fuck it," he screamed, watching the first of his men fall.

Bullets streamed out from three separate buildings. There were many weapons involved. He heard familiar Lee Enfield sounds coming from the buildings. Their opponents had equal firepower, and probably greater numbers.

"Fall back," he yelled, but moved forward with his rifleman who was emptying his magazine towards the nearest building. Le Fanu fired a couple of rounds but knew there was little chance of hitting anything with the revolver at that range. His rifleman reloaded as they crouched behind a tree from where he surveyed the scene. Most of the advance guard had got back to the trees but four men lay in open ground. Only two were moving. He must get them out of there. Firing from the buildings stopped. He guessed the gunmen were the only people left in the village.

With his rifleman, Le Fanu raced along inside the tree line, anticipating a bullet at any moment. None came. He found

Habi.

"Habi, we must get those men back. I need you to create a diversion. In five minutes, you and five men get to the other side so you can fire back into those buildings. That will distract the gunmen. Start firing in precisely five minutes, rapid fire. I want a wall of bullets. But I want them going into the upper walls. If you fire straight in there's a danger our men will get hit. You're just diverting attention."

Habi nodded, crept away, gathered his men and moved them towards the rear of the buildings. Silence remained. The two men were still moving out in the open, but Le Fanu feared the other two were dead. He moved further around, found Caldicott.

"Jackson," he whispered, "Habi will provide distracting fire. When that starts I'll take three men and retrieve those four out there. I need you and your men to hold fire, because we don't want Habi's lot hit by us. Hopefully the gunmen will be distracted enough to allow us time to do the evacuation."

He returned to his original position. The wait for the diversion was interminable, as it had always been at Shaiba. Memories of the past disrupted his present observations and analysis.

Habi's men began firing right on time. A few seconds later the gunmen responded. Hopefully, they were now fixed on Habi's force. He led his three men into the clearing, each racing towards a fallen constable. Le Fanu ran towards his target, a prone figure closest to the buildings. He sensed rather than saw his men doing the same in the gloom. There were no shots but they had little time. At every moment he expected to hear, feel a bullet. He grabbed his man, sat him upright, hoisted him onto a shoulder and began running back. Luckily the man was light. With his back to the building, Le Fanu felt even more vulnerable. The tree line approached. He saw his other men reach the trees. He had a couple of yards to go. Bullets thumped past him, chips flew out of trees. The gunmen had turned. His own team set up covering fire. Habi would know now to fire directly into the buildings. Le Fanu's ears were ringing, gunfire echoing through the forest, the smell of battle all-pervasive.

He put his man down behind a tree, turned him over. A bullet through the left eye had killed him immediately. The other reports came in. Another dead, two wounded but not critical. Medical assistants were tending the wounded but that removed two further men from the attack force.

Le Fanu found Caldicott. They arranged for Habi's group to move back so they could then establish two vectors of fire into the buildings, from northwest and northeast. That way they could maximise fire without endangering their own personnel.

Once Habi was in position, they opened fire. He wished they had grenades. That would have cleared out the buildings. But they had not anticipated this battle. Whitney's warning before the train left was helpful, but too late and sketchy. With more time and information they could have produced better options, and come better equipped. As it was, he had only rifle and revolver power.

After ten minutes he ceased fire. He was not sure, but there might be less intensive resistance from the buildings now. Their own positions were littered with cartridges, the smell of gunfire mixing with the natural forest smells. Smoke haze turned the late dusk blue. Drained faces stared out at him from behind trees.

He had Habi and Caldicott come to him.

"We're running out of light, and probably ammunition," he said. "We must finish this. I need another ten minute burst of fire into those buildings. Immediately that stops, I want ten men charging in there, one commander and three per building. We should be able to take them by shock, I think they've lost a few already. That clear?"

The other two looked at each other. Nodded.

"Right," he continued, "get three men each from your teams and send them over to that point there." He pointed to a spot beyond the buildings, diagonally across from where they were crouching. "I'll lead them in."

"Sir," replied Caldicott, "You're the senior and most experienced man, but that's why we need you here. You have to keep overall command. I'll take them in."

Le Fanu hesitated. "You haven't done this before, have you?"

"No, sir, but neither had you at one point, I'm guessing?"

Le Fanu didn't like it, but knew Caldicott was right. Even if they cleared the building and captured some gunmen, they still had to reach the trucks with prisoners and wounded, then return to Changarore. That seemed a way off yet.

"Right," he said, "thanks, but be careful."

Caldicott took a rifle from one of the wounded men to augment his revolver, then moved towards the rendezvous point with the other men nominated into his team. Within a minute he signalled Le Fanu they were ready.

Le Fanu started the firing again. A further ten minutes of noise, smoke, flying cartridges and whistling debris followed. He signalled to stop.

He watched Caldicott lead his men out of hiding. They raced across the open ground, split up, then took on the buildings, opening fire as they entered. Return fire was immediate. For ten minutes all Le Fanu and his remaining men could hear was continuous gunfire. Slowly, it subsided. He hated this waiting.

Then it stopped. A constable emerged from each building to indicate they had control. Then another man emerged from the furthest way building, waving furiously and shouting. "Medic! Medic!" Le Fanu ordered a man there and sprinted for the building.

He saw bodies, other gunmen under guard, and Caldicott lying on the straw. Le Fanu squatted down. Caldicott's right arm was askew, blood pouring from its mid-section. A bullet had shattered his elbow. He was shaking. The medic bandaged him, gave him painkillers. They helped him to his feet, Le Fanu supporting him under the other arm.

"Get the trucks in here, now" he shouted to a constable. Habi went to organise that.

"Jackson, are you alright apart from that arm? Not hit anywhere else?"

"No sir, this is bad enough." He was pale, in shock as well as pain.

"The trucks are coming, I'll have you and the other wounded sent straight back to Changarore and the hospital. We'll follow. You did a brilliant job."

"We got some prisoners for you, sir, so this won't be a complete waste. But how many have we lost?"

"Four, I'm afraid. But you only lost two, and that's a great result given what you had to do. Losing two is bad, yes, but it could have been a lot more."

Habi had the trucks back. He set out with Caldicott, the wounded and the dead. Le Fanu rounded up the rest of the men, divided them between the other two trucks. There were six prisoners, also divided between trucks. The twelve dead gunmen would have to be collected later, so Le Fanu left two men to guard the bodies.

During the trip back, the aftermath of battle set in. It began about half way to the city. The blood rushed to his temples, pain flashed behind his eyes, his hands trembled, and his body quivered. He closed his eyes, exhausted, and hoped these long forgotten symptoms would pass soon.

Thirty-two

By the time Le Fanu and Habi saw the prisoners into jail, sent the wounded to hospital, the dead to the morgue and the surviving policemen off duty it was nine at night. It seemed an age since they had left Madras that morning. Leaving the police station, they went to the hospital.

Caldicott was in a room by himself, lying back, looking pale, his arm in plaster.

"Jackson, how is it?" Le Fanu asked.

"The doctor's not sure yet, but it's painful. He's plastered it up, a temporary stabilising measure, I think."

"What happened?" Habi asked.

"At first all was fine. We got into the building and my men cleared out most of the gunmen. But a couple up in a loft were harder to dislodge. We got one of them but the other one was firing rapidly. He hit me while I was changing position. I'm probably lucky not to have been injured more seriously."

"What's the doctor saying about the injury?"

"Not much, he's the only one here and is a bit pushed, with minimal equipment."

"Are you in much pain?"

"I'm not sure. He gave me painkillers so I'm not feeling anything much."

"Right. If you're up to it, we'll get you back to Madras

tonight. There's a train at three in the morning, we'll get on that. Habi, can you arrange for the three of us, the prisoners and an escort party to be on that train? Do that, then meet me back at the police station."

Habi went off to make arrangements.

"What are you going to do now, LF?" Caldicott attempted to sit up.

"You sit back," Le Fanu said, "rest up before we take the train. I'm getting Taylor in for a chat to see if I can discover any more about the happenings here. That was an ambush. And that tells me we're on to something, probably the prostitution. But it doesn't explain the Taylor issue."

"I'd help if I could but I doubt I'm up to it."

"You stay here, you've done enough for the day. We'll be back for you about two or so. Get some sleep. Then we'll get you to hospital in Madras in the morning."

Le Fanu went out into the night air and dusty streets of a deserted Changarore. He sent a waiting constable off to rouse Gerald Taylor and bring him to the station. Needing solitude, he took directions from the constable then began walking to the police station, two miles away. He was calmer now. Supervising the cleanup of the battle helped, but he still had the shakes. The walk should have settled him, but all the way he tried to think how they might have done something different and avoided the loss of life.

In the morning, or tomorrow evening four men under his command would be washed, placed in shrouds and taken to the cremation grounds to be farewelled by grieving families. He was responsible for that. They knew police work was dangerous, but he led them into that trap.

By the time he arrived at the station he had, almost, convinced himself the losses were inevitable. They had known too little about the opposition, had had too small a force, not enough information, and once on site had had to push on rather than fall back. They had had neither time nor force strength to sit it out. That had made an assault inescapable. They had won, but at a cost. It was that cost he resented. Losing those constables would stay with him, as did the loss of his soldiers.

He was at a table in the District Super's room. The Super was downstairs questioning the gunmen prisoners. Tea and biscuits helped settle Le Fanu's nerves. A bottle of whiskey appeared but he declined. There was still work to do. A knock at the door was followed by a constable leading in Gerald Taylor.

Taylor was nondescript, another unnoticeable spy. Shorter than Le Fanu, he stooped at the shoulders and was lightly framed. Close cut brownish short hair covered the scalp, just. The bland featured face was clean-shaven. A crumpled grey suit with a blue shirt, askew maroon tie and scuffed brown shoes completed an unmemorable picture.

"Mr. Taylor, thanks for coming in. We're leaving earlier than planned because there are wounded policemen we need to get back to Madras, but I did want to talk to you. Would you like some tea?"

"No, thanks." The voice was reedy, querulous. "I'm not sure I can help you."

Le Fanu was tired, taut. "Mr. Taylor. We know the Rajah was funnelling money to you. He was also involved in prostitution somehow, with a lot of the girls coming from here. The Rajah was murdered. Criminal gangs are involved. A gun battle with some of those criminals has cost several lives today. So don't tell me you can't help. You're at the centre of this and I need to know why and how, now."

The pale face was now bright red. "I'm sorry. If you have some specific questions….?"

"First, why did you receive money from the Rajah? And I know you were, perhaps still are a spy, so don't be shy."

"Oh. Well, it began with the Dardanelles campaign planning. I knew a lot about the Turkish side and thought it a difficult campaign to win, or at least to win quickly, which was the serious point. I kept objecting, senior people became upset and wanted me out." He clutched the chair as if it were a life raft.

"Go on," Le Fanu said, "I don't have much time."

"I agreed to leave but some mid-ranking officers asked me to keep working on the Turkish ciphers, so I had to be somewhere I could do that. Strangely, Changarore came up."

"Because of the peculiar issues to do with the telegraph."

"Yes." Taylor looked surprised. "How did you know that? It's top secret"

"Never mind, "Le Fanu replied, convinced now that nothing ever remained secret, especially with the secret services. "Go on."

"An MI5 officer who wanted my services knew the Rajah. They were together at Sandhurst. So it was arranged that 5 would fund my work in Changarore but channel the funds through Pallampur so that if anyone came looking, it would look just like any other commercial arrangement. That's how I came to bring my family here. The trading company was a front, but had to look successful. That was easy until the crop failures came along."

"Why was that such an issue? I'd have thought you had money enough."

"Simple. What no one knew was that the Rajah already had major money problems. Because of that, he skimmed a lot of the 5 money meant for me. My account came up short at the very time the failures occurred, so the bank people here and in Madras got edgy."

Le Fanu nodded. "I can see that," he said, "but I still don't get how the charges against you came up."

Taylor grimaced. "There was a lot 5 didn't know, as it turned out, and I ended up in a mess as a result. They didn't know the Rajah was also receiving money from the IRA but which actually came from somewhere in Asia."

"The Green Gang."

"Superintendent, you've learned more than anyone else."

Le Fanu ignored the compliment. "How did it play here in Changarore?"

"The Green Gang and the IRA trail puzzled me. I couldn't connect it all. Then one day, I saw one of my clerks talking to some tough looking strangers. I pressured him, and discovered the girls were being taken from the district. The Green Gang representatives took the girls and the IRA provided the transport. Just as I was about to talk to the District Superintendent, I had a visit from the gang's local representative."

"They threatened you."

"There were direct physical threats to me and my family. And the gang set up the short weight charges against me. They used a corrupt court official, and said that if I cooperated the charges would never be enacted. As we know, that wasn't true. And as further guarantee, they arranged more Pallampur money to be channelled in and out of my other accounts so that I looked corrupt. With all the threats against my family, I had to keep quiet."

"It's a good story," Le Fanu said. It also explained the more recent payments, he thought. "We'll check it further once we're back in Madras. You may need to come down there if we need further information."

"I'll do that. If this can be cleared up quietly I'll be very happy, for all the obvious reasons."

"Which still leaves one very large question," Le Fanu said. "I don't see how this explains the Rajah's murder."

Taylor nodded. "I was shocked when I heard. He was not directly involved in recruiting the girls. I met him once, secretly, and he told me he hated the business. I believed him, he was really remorseful. He only did it because he was desperate financially. There was no reason for him to be murdered. Quite the contrary. The local gang leaders were deeply worried when they heard. The Rajah was the perfect front for them, and they needed him alive. That's why they've been trying to identify his killer, too. They knew your inquiries might reveal the full story."

"That explains their desperate measures this afternoon."

"Oh yes. They had a huge money-generating operation that was about to be disrupted. Even killing policemen seemed worthwhile if it meant the business might continue."

"So they wanted the Rajah alive, not dead."

"Yes."

Le Fanu let Taylor return home. Habi was outside the office, all arrangements made for the train. They'd be back in Madras by midday. They went to the hotel, collected the bags including Caldicott's, then to the hospital. Caldicott was now in a chair but looking groggy. The plastered arm was in a sling, and Habi helped him out into the waiting car.

There was silence on the way to the station. They had now been awake for twenty-four hours, and much had happened. After half an hour in the first class waiting room they went out on the platform. Le Fanu stayed with Caldicott while Habi supervised the loading of the prisoners and their guards into a special prison van.

Five minutes before three, the train slowed into the station with a screech of brakes and clouds of steam. Because the prison van had to be attached to the train, there was plenty of time to board. Le Fanu helped Caldicott into their compartment. Then he went to assist Habi. With the prisoners secure, they returned to find Caldicott asleep already, slumped into a corner. They stretched him out on the seat, found a pillow and blanket and made him comfortable. Habi took one corner on the opposite bench seat, Le Fanu the other.

The train set off and was soon into rhythm. Habi fell asleep.

Le Fanu stared out the window, imagining what was out there but revisiting the day and, again, the losses. He was now even more puzzled by the Rajah's murder. The gang wanted him alive. So who killed him? The Taylor story was explained. That left the Westshire puzzle, but it was hard to see how that linked to the murder. Le Fanu needed to talk to Westshire again. Jason Palmer and the Rani were having an affair but that seemed not to be the cause of the murder, either. That left few if any suspects.

Those questions lingered. The train lumbered on towards Madras and as he drifted into sleep, he remembered: his father would be buried in England later today.

Thirty-three

They slept for most of the journey, waking at different times just outside Madras. As the train travelled through the mean northern suburbs, Le Fanu imagined how newcomers reacted to this first look at their new city. The Perambur railway yards dominated an area home to small manufacturers and industries creating smoke, haze and dirt. Closer in it was more light commercial but even the station was unprepossessing having once been grand. Too much traffic, too many people and too many years ensured that. It was a city struggling to cope with growth, and political change.

They were met by two police porters, one detailed to get Caldicott to Government General Hospital immediately. The other helped Habi and Le Fanu to Fort St. George for a meeting with Whitney and Jepson. Le Fanu realised they were still in yesterday's battle clothes and had not even washed.

"Habi, do you think they'll even let us into the Fort let alone see the Chief Secretary?"

The reply was tired. "They may just see us asleep, sir."

They were ushered into Whitney's office, but drew several stares on the way there. Either news of the battle had spread, or they really were on the nose. Jepson was already there, looking subdued.

"LF, Habi, come in, sit down. You look exhausted. Sorry we've dragged you straight in. I'll get in coffee and breakfast.

The usual idlis and sambar? I'll see what else they can find. You look like you could do with some food." A servant went off for the supplies.

Le Fanu watched surprise cross Jepson's face at the mention of south Indian food. "Sorry we're unpresentable, sir, but we've had no chance to clean up."

"Not at all, LF. Tell me, how's Caldicott?" The District Super and the Collector in Changarore had both telegraphed battle reports.

"He's in no danger, sir, but a lot of pain. And being his elbow, he's worried about permanent damage. Cricket's a big part of his life, as you know." Le Fanu was not sure Whitney did know, and positive Jepson did not. "Our real problem is that we lost four good constables and I really regret that. I know Habi and Caldicott feel exactly the same."

He wondered if the funerals were over already, back in Changarore.

Whitney turned dour. "The I-G and I've been discussing that. The losses are regrettable, and we could have done with fewer dead gunmen. But none of that attaches any blame to you, LF. Far from it. You overcame a dreadful situation and we've now some people we can interrogate. If there's any blame, it lies with Special Branch, again." He looked at Jepson whose customary temper appeared briefly then disappeared.

"Sir," Jepson said, "Special Branch did its best, as I've explained. There was not much...."

"Jepson, so you said before. The fact remains: you gave me all available Special Branch information yesterday morning for me to pass on to LF. That evidence was wholly inadequate. There was nothing remotely helpful in it, let alone anything to give our team an advantage. All the advantage lay with the gunmen. That's not good enough. I suggest you go off and deal with it. I need improvements, rapidly. We've dead men to account for."

Jepson turned various shades of purple but stayed silent.

It must have been a tough conversation earlier, and Whitney had just dressed down the I-G in front of subordinate officers. That was deliberate. No one receiving that speech would ever think it a sign of a strong future career.

The Inspector-General steamed out, a servant closed the door behind him. There was silence.

"Sorry about that, gentlemen, we'd just had a difficult meeting, as you might guess. Special Branch can't be defended on this one, or many others come to think of it. You ended up in a battle on the basis of inadequate information, and for that I can only apologise. And I have the Governor's authority to say so. Now, give me your version of events."

The coffees and food arrived. Habi and Le Fanu seized on it, as Le Fanu realised they hadn't eaten since breakfast yesterday.

Habi and Le Fanu described their impressions of what had happened. This was the first chance they'd had to debrief. There was no time immediately afterwards and they'd slept on the train. He would have to get Caldicott's version.

"So," Whitney said at the end, "do you think you'll get anything out of these prisoners?"

Le Fanu turned to Habi: "Habi, you've seen more of them than me, what do you think?"

"Sir, we don't know whether we have leaders or followers or some of each. There was no time to interview them. But we have them in separate cells so it will be difficult for them to match their stories. Hopefully we'll get some additional information."

Le Fanu remembered what the typical Madras Central Prison cell was like: thick stone and brick, a small high window, heavy metal doors, and spartan design dating back to the 1830s. It was impossible for those prisoners to communicate with each other.

Habi continued. "We'll interview them individually as soon as we finish here, Sir Charles. Hopefully we'll have information for you later this afternoon."

"Excellent, Habi, thank you. I've some information that will be helpful before you go into those interviews. The spy in Delhi has been talking. They were less interested in the Rajah than the people he mixed with. The debts made him desperate, so he took money from people he would not have dealt with normally. The IRA link was a smokescreen, as you suspected, LF, and the real target for 5 and 6 was the Hong Kong lot. However, that gang didn't rely on the Rajah alone. They recruited strong arm men up north directly, and used them to both threaten the women and extort money."

"That fits, sir," Le Fanu commented. "Taylor told me last night he was framed over those short weight charges and that his family was threatened. It's not clear he paid them any additional money, but his Pallampur account was raided. He thought it was the Rajah himself, but it might have been this lot who are mainly from Bihar."

"That's my guess, LF. But it leads us to a problem."

"Yes," Habi said. "It gets us no closer to understanding who killed the Rajah."

Le Fanu admired the insight. They had not discussed the consequences of the fight or its implications, but Habi identified the result immediately.

"Quite so, Habi," the Chief Secretary said. "I now see where your boss gets his ideas."

Habi was delighted. "Thank you, sir"

"As I see it," Whitney continued, "we have no obvious suspect. On the good side we've cleared up the Taylor issue and learned more about spies than is necessary. Neither of you see Palmer as a candidate. Westshire seems connected in some way so I know you'll follow that line, but he doesn't look like a serious suspect. He's not that stupid. I'm not sure who else that leaves, especially as we still don't have the murder weapon, I think?"

"No sir," replied Le Fanu. "We're still looking for that. I'll step things up when I get back to my office."

Habi went home to change. Le Fanu went to the D'Angelis.

He knocked on her door before he went into his own room. She opened it, and looked concerned.

"Chris, are you alright? What happened?" She pulled him into the room, sat him down.

"I was going to change before I told you," he said.

"No," she said. "Give me your key, tell me what clothes you want and I'll get them. I know you prefer a shower. Well, there's one in my bathroom. You get started on that."

As she went off he undressed, got into the shower and let the hot water strip away the events of the past day. After a while he opened his eyes. She was standing at the open shower door.

"You don't look too damaged," she whispered.

He began to react.

"Oh, you're not damaged at all," she laughed, "but you've a story to tell so don't get distracted."

He finished, dressed. She had ordered coffee and a proper lunch, and he was surprised to find he was still hungry. As they ate, he told her the story, thinking how good it was to share it with someone who cared. Ro was a good listener, and asked good questions.

"Tell me," she said, "what do you really know about the Rani? If you have no other suspect, then I assume you'll look hard at her again. I can imagine you looking at her, hard." The smile lingered. He blushed. He hated that.

"It's alright," she continued, "so long as you look at me, harder. You certainly did in the shower, so I'm happy." She stroked his arm.

He might not reach the office today at this rate.

"You think she might be a killer?" he asked. "I can't see that. She's cool, and direct like you. But I can't see her killing her husband. Besides, the timeline doesn't fit."

"Are you sure?"

"She arrived at Pallampur House about an hour after the Rajah's body was found. She'd not been home before, the servants confirmed that. She says she was with Jason Palmer until she left for home. We'll see Palmer and verify that, but I can't see how the sequence allows her time to kill her husband."

Ro was making notes and drawing diagrams. "I see a possible gap or two in those times you have. How long would it take her to reach Pallampur House from, where, Saidapet? What time did she really leave there, and does Palmer confirm that time? Was she there with Palmer the whole time? And you still don't know where the Rajah was after the reception and before he got home. You still have work to do, Superintendent, your hard side will have to wait."

Yes, impatiently, he thought. "You're right, we know that we have assertion rather than evidence from her and Palmer on that. I'll have to go and do that additional work. Shall we have dinner later? Somewhere outside?"

"That would be lovely. Can you take me somewhere where there's good music?"

"I'll make a reservation. Eight suit you? That'll give me time to find answers to your questions and some others, then get back here for another shower."

"I look forward to that."

Thirty-four

He went first to the hospital. Caldicott had been seen by the Chief Medical Officer who was also a bone specialist. By the look on Caldicott's face, the news was bad.

"Jackson, you don't look happy."

"LF, I'm alive and I'm grateful for that, our colleagues were not so lucky. But he's not certain the bones will heal."

"What does that mean?"

"There's a danger the bones will freeze, as he calls it. If that happens, my arm would stay bent at the elbow permanently."

"Your cricket."

"Silly, I know, but it has been my life. I turned down county cricket to come out here and don't regret that, but I'd hoped to play for a bit longer."

"I understand that. It would be like golf becoming impossible for me. I don't play that much anymore, but can if I want to. There's the difference, the possibility versus the impossibility of playing. But you don't know yet, stay optimistic."

"He's not certain yet, that's true, so there's still time for change. I'll be back to the office tomorrow, it doesn't stop me thinking."

"Are you sure? If you can that would be excellent but if you're in too much pain stay home."

"More cheerful at work, I think. The chummery is grim if

you're there on your own."

"See how it goes, then, I'll see you one way or another tomorrow. In the meantime, if you're short of something to do, think back over these cases for me. We're conspicuously short of a suspect for the Rajah's murder. If you can find one I'd be grateful."

Habi was at the office. Le Fanu retrieved his private list of questions from the safe, and updated those with Habi's assistance.

"Sir, we need to interview Mr. Palmer."

"I agree, Habi, if only to eliminate him."

"When shall we go?"

This was difficult. Le Fanu did not want to be away for any of the four nights Ro had left in Madras, including tonight. "Habi, when do you think that should be done?"

"As soon as possible."

He was right. "Could you handle it with a constable from here plus local support in the Nilgiris?"

"Of course, but your expertise really is needed."

"You could do it easily. I can't really get away to the Nilgiris for another four days."

"Those details again, sir?"

"Yes, Habi, those details again."

"I understand, sir, and hope those details don't get too difficult. What about we have the District Super there conduct a preliminary interview and report back? If we think there's anything in it, we can either go up there or get Palmer shipped down here. That way, we save time and the details are left undisturbed."

"Good plan. And, Habi, another thing is that my father is being buried in England tonight our time. He passed away a couple of days ago."

"Sir, I'm very sorry. By being here, you British cut a lot of family ties. I experienced that while I was in England and didn't like it. And I don't like the way British families here send their young children back to boarding school in England. It's barbaric. When was the last time you saw your father, sir?"

"Nine years ago. You're right. We weren't close. That started when I was growing up and got worse once I was out here."

"But he's still your father, sir, and that's a loss, no matter what happened in the past."

Le Fanu was finding it easier to discuss things. That was Ro's influence, but it was also easy to talk with the deep thinking Habi.

"The worst thing, Habi, is thinking back on all the lost opportunities to put things right."

"I'm sure he was proud of you."

"In his own way, probably, and the war helped. But we never really talked, more's the pity."

"I'll think of you this evening, sir."

"Thanks, Habi, now I'll arrange for Mr. Palmer's interview. Once that's done, shall we have a chat to these goondas we brought back with us?"

"Yes, sir. After all they sent our way yesterday, it will be a pleasure to give them something in return."

They had the first three prisoners placed in separate interview rooms, and began working through them. Habi began in Tamil, and when some of them spoke Bihari a native-speaker on the local force was brought in. Then another three were processed, and again until all the captives were accounted for. It was slow and frustrating. By late afternoon, however, two prisoners seemed more important than the others, if only because they were determined not to talk.

Habi and Le Fanu had the first one brought back. He was short, stocky and muscular with a pockmarked face and matching demeanour.

"You're facing several possible charges including murder. You'll hang if convicted so you'd better tell me what you know," Le Fanu began.

The man replied in Tamil. "I know nothing about any murder."

Habi chipped in. "First the Rajah of Pallampur, second a number of our colleagues you shot at yesterday. You know a lot."

"We fired because we were told you were coming to execute us."

"Why would we do that, and who told you?" Le Fanu asked.

"One of our leaders up north sent us a message."

"So you ambushed us," Habi fired in. "You were waiting for us, and set a trap. That's no defence. Why did you not just leave?"

"We were ordered not to, we had to stay and fight."

That was odd.

"What do you know about the Rajah of Pallampur?" Habi asked.

"Nothing," came the grunted reply. "Never heard of him until someone said he'd been murdered."

"What were you doing in Changarore?" It was Le Fanu's turn.

"Rounding up girls. That's what we were paid for. Round them up and get them onto boats. No idea where they went then. Our job was done."

"Who's your boss?" demanded Habi.

The man went silent. Looked at his feet.

"Come on," Le Fanu said, "the hangman's waiting. If you're not convicted for the Rajah's death you will be for one of our dead constables. The judges are hard on police killers."

"There's a man in Changarore who gives us orders. He gets instructions from the north, or perhaps from overseas?"

"Why do you say overseas?" Habi was writing furiously.

"Sometimes he gets telegrams from Hong Kong. He left one lying around one day, and one of our gang reads English. He told me it was from Hong Kong."

So that was the Green Gang's local representative.

"Did he tell you we were coming?" Le Fanu remembered his dead policemen, again.

"Yes."

"How did he know?"

"One of your local policemen is in his pay. A man in the Changarore office."

Half an hour later he gave them the name of the telegram receiver. Le Fanu requested the District Superintendent in Changarore to make an immediate arrest.

"Habi, I think that's enough for the day. Go home to your family."

"Thank you sir, I will. And I hope this evening is not too tough for you."

"Thanks Habi, and thanks for listening to me."

He knew it would be alright, Ro was there.

Back at the hotel, he went to his room. He ran a bath, then looked in the wardrobe to lay out some clothes. The wardrobe was empty. He wondered if he'd lost his mind. He closed off the bath taps, put on a robe, went out and knocked on Ro's door. She beckoned him in.

"I seem to have lost all my clothes. They were in there, I swear. Now I'm not sure what I'll wear to dinner."

She opened the wardrobe door. There were his clothes.

"Since you'll be spending more time in here than in your room, it's more convenient to have your things in here, too. Welcome home. Now, Mr. Hard, I've still to complete my inspection of your physical health."

They were late to dinner. He had booked at a new hotel featuring black American jazz musicians, some of the first to come to India. The place was packed when they arrived, but their side table had a good view of the orchestra. Le Fanu's preordered champagne arrived promptly, and they had just clinked glasses when a shadow loomed at the table.

"Good evening, Superintendent."

It was Chester Barnes, elegant as ever.

"Barnes, nice to see you. Allow me to introduce you to Mrs McPhedren. Ro, this is Chester Barnes, editor of the Madras Mail. Believe it or not, he's dragging it into the twentieth century.

"Mrs McPhedren, I'm delighted to meet you."

"And me, you."

"Barnes, join us for a champagne, unless you're busy?" Here was a chance for them to behave normally in public.

"That would be very pleasant."

Le Fanu called for another glass, poured a drink.

"LF, I hear you were in a skirmish up in Changarore yesterday. Glad you're alright, but very sorry you lost some men. I assume Mrs McPhedren knows about this so we can speak? I won't stay long."

"Yes, thanks. I'll tell you what I can, as always."

"Does it involve the Rajah of Pallampur?

"We think so, but that's not clear yet. Don't print this, we're not certain the battle was connected directly to his death, but it might be indirectly. He was connected to some international criminal gangs, and that business might have been a factor."

"That would be the Green Gang and Hong Kong," Barnes observed.

"Mr. Barnes, you're well informed." Ro's voice was light, warm.

"Ro, Chester has interesting contacts in London as well as here, and has been very helpful."

"And I want to continue that way. LF, Mrs McPhedren, Ro if I may, I'm interrupting your evening, but thank you LF. May I come to see you tomorrow?"

"Yes, come in the morning, about ten. I should still be in the office then."

"Thank you. And LF, my congratulations on your dinner companion. Ro, it is delightful to meet you and I hope to see you again. Hope you enjoy the music, too."

"Thank you Mr Barnes, I'm hoping we'll see you again, too."

Le Fanu watched the editor retreat to another table to join a couple of senior commercial men. "Well, we're in public now," he said, "hope you don't mind."

"Chris, I'm impressed and alarmed that you're doing this. I don't mind at all, you're the one running all the risks. But Mr. Barnes thinks highly of you and approves, so that's a good start."

"It is, and I appreciate that. He's well thought of even in official circles. Oh, and I forgot to tell you. Sir Charles Whitney asked me to extend his very best wishes to you."

She tipped her glass towards him. "You are doing well, Chris, thank you. But I fear tougher challenges ahead among some of your less enlightened colleagues."

"You're right, we should eat so we're strong enough to deal with the challenges."

The food was Italian, and the accompanying Montepulciano D'Abruzzo smooth, as were the musicians. The evening flew by as they talked, ate, reminisced, and wondered what would come next.

As they prepared to leave, she leaned over and touched his arm. "Chris, I know your father is being buried about now. I know, too, that you're wondering what happened to that relationship. He would have been proud of you, so there's nothing to be sorry about. Just remember he was your father."

They left, noticed by a few remaining patrons. Barnes would have identified Le Fanu for those people who did not know him, and there would have been talk about Ro. It had begun, but more would come.

Thirty-five

His first task the next morning was to inform Jepson about the latest developments, such as they were. "Good morning, sir, there isn't a lot that's new to report but I thought I'd report in anyway."

Jepson looked deflated. "Thank you, Le Fanu. How's Caldicott?"

Another twist, Jepson concerned about the welfare of a junior officer.

"Fine in general but worried about his arm. It might have permanent damage but that's not yet clear. He hopes to back in the office quickly to keep up the paperwork. We won't have him chasing around the countryside, though."

"Good, I hope his arm will be fine, he's a good officer, as are you, Le Fanu."

Was there no end to these surprises? "Thank you, sir, I appreciate that."

"What more do we know?" Jepson was asking the right questions but with no obvious interest in the answers.

Le Fanu told him about the immediate plans: check on Palmer, talk to Westshire, follow up with the Rani, but nothing about the deeper background. There would come a time when Jepson would have to know, and Le Fanu doubted the calm would continue then.

"Good, good." Le Fanu wondered if Jepson actually heard

any of the explanations.

"Sir, is there anything else I can help with?"

Jepson looked up from his desk. "Not unless you have a miracle cure for the ills of Special Branch. I'm fielding complaints about them from everyone between here and Delhi. Even London's had a go. The mess you ended up in has frustrated everyone, including me."

This calmer Jepson appeared because his future was threatened. His favourite unit's abysmal performance did not help his cause, especially on top of his well-known loathing of Le Fanu's Crime Unit. Given Le Fanu's success, perhaps the I-G was reluctantly changing his view. That seemed unlikely.

"Sorry, sir, no miracle cures available. I don't even know much about what SB does."

"That's the problem, for some reason it's not doing much, or nearly enough."

"Sorry again, sir, but if you think of a way I might help, let me know."

No harm in trying to get the man onside before he discovered the secret service aspects of the present problems.

"I will, but that might be a way off." Jepson hesitated. "Won't help me much personally, though."

Le Fanu was wary.

"My wife is ill, rather serious. Has to go back to England."

Despite his disdain for Jepson, Le Fanu could understand that pressure, the awful combination of professional and personal problems. He knew all about that.

"I'm sorry to hear that, sir, I hope all goes well."

"Thanks Le Fanu. I hear you've just lost your father so you know what it's like."

"Yes, sir."

"One more thing. I hear you're at the D'Angelis and were seen at that new hotel last night. It's none of my business but I hope you know what you're doing. These things are awkward, and some people take them too seriously. My advice is to be careful, but you're your own person, I know that. Just be careful."

Le Fanu was amazed. Where had this Jepson been hiding all that time?

"Thank you, sir, I'll bear that in mind. And I do hope Mrs Jepson will be alright."

He found it hard to concentrate when he reached his own office, but Habi's arrival brought focus.

"Good morning, sir. Does the D'Angelis continue to be comfortable?"

"It does, Habi, thank you."

The sergeant grinned, white teeth contrasted amidst the forest of the black beard. "I hear the food there is very good, if you like that sort of European thing."

"You should take over Special Branch, Habi, you're better at spying than anyone else I know."

"Thank you, sir. Perhaps you can recommend me?"

Le Fanu did not want to lose Habi, but he would be excellent at the job if the hierarchy ever contemplated appointing a Muslim.

"Not a bad idea, Habi. The I-G was just telling me that Special Branch is his prime problem. You could help him sort it out."

"I thought you were a friend, sir" flashed back the reply.

"Do you have any good news?"

"Some. The District Super in the Nilgiris reported back. He met Mr. Palmer late yesterday afternoon and spent some time with him. From what he said on the telephone a few minutes ago, the Super does not like Mr. Palmer at all."

"Why not?"

"First, Mr. Palmer has been actively applying his special skills down there, too. A neighbouring planter threatened to kill him, and said the neighbour's wife was shipped back to England indefinitely. Mr. Palmer cannot show his face in the club there without someone wanting to injure him."

"He sounds a real charmer."

"You might even call him a snake charmer, sir."

"Very good, Habi. Go on."

"The second thing is that the Super was unsatisfied with some of Mr. Palmer's answers. He thought he was evasive, and especially vague about times."

They had sent the Super a set of questions about timings that might help pinpoint the Rajah's whereabouts, especially in those lost two hours, and his wife's.

"Really? If Palmer had nothing to hide, those questions should have been easy. Unless he's trying to cover for someone else, but I can't think who that might be."

"That was my thought, too, sir. The Super said he asked those questions in several different ways for over an hour, but knew no more at the end than he did at the beginning. He thought Palmer was being deliberately unhelpful."

"Very interesting. What does the Super recommend?"

"That we interview Mr. Palmer ourselves. If you approve, sir, I'll have him brought here by train tonight, as we agreed. That way you can keep attending to those D'Angelis details." He grinned again.

"Thank you, Habi. Mrs. McPhedren will be most grateful."

Not long ago he would never have shared that information with even Habi, the person he trusted most in Madras. Now he'd admitted the situation to Habi. Whitney, Barnes and even Jepson knew about and acknowledged his position. Ro was having an impact, a far better one than he'd created two years earlier.

"Very sensible, sir, you've wasted two years already, you don't want to waste anymore."

"You always were a help, Habi, now go off and get Palmer down here before I recommend to the I-G that you're just the man for Special Branch."

"Immediately, sir, anything but that."

"One other thing, I'm not sure we know anything more about Westshire. Caldicott was handling that. I'll ask when I see him at the hospital, but could you check if any additional information has come in?"

Le Fanu had the driver take a shortcut to the General, but it was too clever a move. They got stuck behind a temple procession. A large wooden temple cart creaked along under the weight of an enormous Lord Siva idol. The cart had white ropes attached to front and back, each attended by a worshipper in simple white loincloth with shaven head, bare chest and legs, bare feet, Saivite markings to the face and ash on the body. They were accompanied by musicians and devotees, crowds along the road showering them with flowers and garlands.

Normally, Le Fanu would have enjoyed the spectacle, but this time he was frustrated at taking an hour and a half to reach the hospital. He used the telephone there to postpone the meeting with Barnes.

"Jackson," he said when he reached the room, "what are they saying now?"

Caldicott looked worried. "The CMO will take the cast off and have a closer look. He says bullet wounds like this sometimes do more hidden damage than expected. He may even operate if he gets worried enough. That will all happen this afternoon."

"I'm sure it will turn out well. I've heard good things about him. You're in the best possible place."

"I know that, LF, but I'd rather be back in the office."

"That will happen, but speaking of the office – was there any more information coming to you on Westshire? We still haven't identified his role, and I'd like to keep moving."

"My London contacts were to provide more, but I thought our best move would be to interview him again, given what we know after Changarore."

"Fair enough. I'll see if the Chief Secretary can get him

back down here on the quiet. We don't want the Board of Revenue involved again. Hopefully, you'll join us at the interview."

"I hope so, I hate lying around waiting for something to happen."

"I'd have thought you'd had enough action for the moment."

"Well, yes."

"Rest up, I'm sure it will be fine."

Caldicott looked unconvinced, and even the new Le Fanu ran out of reassurances.

The driver returned him to the office. It was not Le Fanu's day for travel. They encountered a political demonstration just after they reached the beachfront road. It was small enough, Government policy now prohibiting larger gatherings. But it blocked the road. Most of the participants were university college students. Only a few wore the Gandhi clothes, but they all shouted Congress slogans and carried the standard signs: the British should leave India, the police were brutal, Indians should rule themselves, the lower classes deserved better conditions.

He agreed with the sentiments, apart from the police brutality one which always irritated, even though he knew some colleagues dealt too harshly with demonstrators. These students were peaceful, sitting in the middle of the road to disrupt government-related travel, like his. Board Members would be furious, so Jepson would field more complaints about police inability to control situations like this. It was not his day either.

The crowd would not disperse soon, so Le Fanu had the driver turn around, retrace their earlier route and find another one back. This was becoming a standard problem in Madras these days, Le Fanu thought, another sign the Government was losing authority.

By the time he got back, he was exhausted as the past two

days caught up. He could try and nap here. Or he could get the bike out of the stables, go home for a couple of hours, rest up, and plan the next moves.

The Powerplus roar and the feel of the wind in his face was reinvigorating. It seemed weeks since he'd done that but it was just a few days. By the time he reached the house he felt brighter already, and looked forward to a couple of hours peace, even if Ro was not there.

But there was a car in his driveway, and a visitor waiting on his verandah.

Thirty-six

Charlotte Lacey was lounging in a chair. The flowing white cotton dress extended to her ankles, with high neckline and long sleeves. But it was slit both sides, so fell away sharply from legs crossed at the knees to reveal the attractive thighs. She was leaning forward, smoking. Her face was half covered by the curved brim of the large straw hat from under which puffs of smoke drifted away. Two short gold chains clung to the throat, a matching gold brooch sat high on her left shoulder.

"Took you bloody long enough," she said, "I've been here half an hour." She flicked cigarette ash into the garden to join the remains of three or four predecessors. Her tone was harsh but not the intent.

"You're lucky I'm here at all, Rani, this was a spur of the moment idea to come home. How do you know where I live, anyway?"

"Think you're the only bloody detective in town? Pretty much anyone who's anyone in Madras knows where you live. You're notorious. Even more notorious after last night, from what I hear."

He could never fault the city for knowing everyone else's business, often before they did.

"Oh yes, why's that?" He should know the popular gossip.

"Your flagrant shagging, obviously. If I'd known you were

on the lookout I'd have given you a go myself. All you had to do was ask."

"I had dinner with a friend, that's all."

"Of course you did, with extra dessert later." Her gift for frankness grew by the day.

"I'm not sure what you mean and, besides, you were already busy."

"Good riders keep several horses in the stable, Le Fanu. I certainly do. You could be in that stable anytime." She stubbed out the cigarette, tossed another butt in the garden.

"Now," she continued, "offer me a cold drink then I can get to the point. I didn't come here to discuss your sex life. Well, not exclusively anyway."

A servant brought lemonade for her, lime soda for him. A plate of sweets came with the drinks. He took one, she resisted.

"What's so urgent that you come to my house?" he asked.

"I hear you're still after Jason. The poor man telephoned last night after his police interview. You're chasing the wrong man, Le Fanu, Jason and Pally didn't even know each other. They knew of each other, you know that. But Jason had no reason to kill Pally. His death was connected to his money worries. That's obvious."

He detected a rawness. "You said you knew about those worries, Rani. Did you know what he was doing to alleviate the problems?"

"You mean the guns?"

"We believe the guns were a smokescreen. And you never mentioned the guns before."

"You never asked."

He breathed deeply. That sort of game playing annoyed him. "Rani, I asked if you knew anything at all about his activities. You said no. You lied to me."

"So spank me."

"I'd rather you were honest," Le Fanu said, fighting anger.

"You mean, do I know he was involved with shady characters with Asian connections shipping Indian girls into prostitution."

"It would have helped had you mentioned that, yes. When did you find out?"

She was anxious now. "Just a day before his death, and not from him. A London friend saw Pally in odd company. She asked some police connections about these characters, and they came with the answer. Well, more secret service than police."

Le Fanu counted, slowly, the lives lost because she had not told him this immediately. They might even have caught the killer by now.

"Why the hell didn't you tell me? I've got dead constables on my conscience because I didn't have that information."

"That's why I'm here." Her confidence and brashness disappeared. "I heard what happened. I should have told you sooner. I wanted to say sorry. It's not much but it's all I can offer. I'm sorry you lost your men. I'm sorry I've caused this trouble."

Le Fanu was on the edge of losing control. "Your self indulgence has cost the lives of four policemen, and injured several others. Because of all your fucking game playing, you helped cause that. Do you have any idea how dangerous this gang is, or about what they were doing to those women, and how they threatened your husband? Or are you too worried about your own pathetic existence to give a shit? "

She lit another cigarette, shakily. "I, that is, can…."

"Don't even try to explain, I'm not interested. But I am interested in what else you know. If you don't tell me now, I'll throw you in a cell myself."

She refilled her glass. "I know little more, I'm afraid. But Pally was ashamed. That's the main reason I kept quiet, trying to keep it hidden as he would have wanted. He'd been silly with the investment gamble but he was a decent man, and he hated what he had to do. And I am sorry for the damage my silence has caused."

"You knew about the source of your husband's problem, then?"

"Another friend told me a few days before the murder. Mostly I didn't want to know, but Pally was so precious about my expenses I became worried and started asking around. After that big hit to his finances he became desperate, which was why he ended up with the prostitution ring. He didn't want that. But in return for the gang advancing him money, he had to guarantee the supply of girls."

"How do you feel about that?"

"Terrible. I'm a player myself, but I choose with whom I play. Those poor girls could not. God knows who was doing what to them."

"Yes, indeed. Now, back to your grubby friend, Mr. Palmer. Why wouldn't he tell the District Superintendent about his exact movements? He was extremely vague."

"He was with me, Le Fanu. Men lose track of time when they're with me. You could have discovered that." The brazen one was back.

"Don't bother trying to sidetrack me. You are in serious trouble. Can you account more accurately for your movements and his, and I'm not talking about what you did in bed."

"It was on a sofa outside, actually, but I'm hazy on times myself. I had a few drinks."

Le Fanu was beginning to calm down, so listened. Her story was as before. She had arrived in Saidapet around eight, having left home as the Rajah had set out for the Governor's. Palmer had opened a bottle of wine, they had had drinks then went to the sofa. About nine thirty they went inside for dinner and more drinks. They talked, went back to bed, talked, drowsed, and she arrived back at Pallampur House soon after Le Fanu reached there.

There was a gap in the story he couldn't identify. He would

have to corroborate the sequence with Palmer, so hoped he would see it more clearly after that.

The Rani finished her drink, extinguished yet another cigarette, and made for her car. Le Fanu accompanied her.

"Really, I'm sorry, Le Fanu. I should have told you earlier. But Jason's not the killer, I'm sure of that."

She undulated into the back seat. "Remember," she said, "I'm always on the lookout for another stallion, but I think you're already mating." He slammed the door on her. She still waved as the car moved off.

Le Fanu watched it turn out the gate then went inside, thinking how different the situation might have been had he received that information sooner. For two hours he roamed the garden, events jumbled in his mind. He was making a stand with Ro, but the case had turned nasty. He missed his own father's funeral, and the Hindu services for his fallen constables because he brought the injured back to Madras. That was all made worse now, knowing their deaths could have been avoided. Right now he did not care if the relationship with Ro wrecked his career. But he had no idea what he would do if he lost his job. Australia or New Zealand flashed through his mind again.

He went in, poured a blended whisky and splashed it with soda. Not his favourite drink but it fitted the day. After a while he sat at his desk, then began writing the letter to his mother. It was easier now. An hour later, several pages explained how he'd felt about her, his father, his brother, his job, and why India was important. And he told her about Ro, and the challenges that brought. His mother had been sad when his first marriage broke up though she had never warmed to his wife. She would understand that Ro meant much more to him.

Gathering up the fabric he bought for his mother days ago, he placed it and the letter in a small cardboard box which he wrapped, sealed and addressed, and left for posting.

The "in" tray contained only the day's edition of the Mail.

With a few minutes left before he needed to leave, Le Fanu skimmed the news. Barnes ran a small, bland story on the Changarore skirmish, and a separate update on the Pallampur case progress. Otherwise, the paper was full of letters and comments, mostly derogatory, about the city being disrupted by demonstrations like the one this afternoon. The tide of European sourness was rising.

Towards six, the telephone rang. It was Habi. Palmer would leave the Nilgiris by train that evening, accompanied by a police officer. He would be at headquarters by nine in the morning. Palmer was unhappy about his treatment but, it transpired, several married planters were glad to see the back of him. The police were pleasing at least some people.

The driver returned him to the D'Angelis. This was Ro's second last night before she returned to Hyderabad. He had not thought about that yet. His life would not return easily to the drab existence he had before she arrived.

He walked through the lobby, upstairs, knocked on her door. She opened it immediately, and reached for him.

"I'm so glad you're back, Chris." She was upset.

"What's the matter?"

"Half an hour ago I received a nasty telephone call. It was a European woman, wouldn't give me her name. She advised me to leave the city and take you with me. Her exact words were 'there's no place in Madras for filthy scum like the pair of you, and especially not for a chi-chi slut'."

For all the support from Whitney and the others, general bigotry was still in command. This was the classic elite loathing of Anglo-Indians.

She began to cry. "Chris, why are people like this?"

"If only we knew. You've no idea who it was?"

"None."

"Well, we knew people would be outraged, but this is extreme."

"Chris, I should go back to Hyderabad immediately. This

could ruin you."

"No, you did that last time. We're making a stand here, we must keep doing so. That's what I want to do."

"Are you sure? These people will crucify you."

"Remember, people like Whitney and Barnes and even Jepson are prepared to tolerate us. They like us enough to overlook the stereotype. That's enough for me. This town has to change if Europeans are to have any sort of future, and I want to make that change. You can help."

"I don't know, Chris, this is horrible. I knew it would happen but it's still a shock."

"I know. Look, we could have dinner up here, but I think we should go back to the dining room and show them how determined we are. We'll have a drink at the bar, then make another grand entrance. The bad news is you'll have to dress up again."

An hour later they were in the bar, sipping champagne and fielding the looks, some of which were admiring.

Thirty-seven

The evening went well enough and Ro regained confidence. Some people who knew Le Fanu came to say hello, a positive, and someone who knew Ro's employer did the same. Ro would stay the remaining days.

Le Fanu left early in the morning to prepare for the Palmer interview. Habi arrived so they planned the questions and their approach. Palmer was in the interview room already, but they left him there alone until nine. If he was angry or upset, he might be more open.

They entered the room just after nine. Palmer stood up. Le Fanu had little sense of what attracted women to men, but saw how they might be attracted to this one.

Palmer was trying to be cheerful. The smile was cheeky, engaging. He was over six feet tall, well proportioned, athletic, lively. His fairish hair was longer than fashionable, and had to be flicked back regularly from the eye line. That emphasised the eyes, Le Fanu realised, dark blue and arresting. Palmer was in planter garb: fawn safari jacket over no shirt, similarly coloured trousers and well-worn light boots.

"Mr. Palmer," Habi began. Palmer was surprised, he had looked automatically to Le Fanu for the opening. "Please sit down."

They faced each other across the table. Le Fanu stared at Palmer, already less sure of himself.

Habi was absorbed in his papers. After several seconds he looked up. "Mr. Palmer, I am Sergeant Habibullah and this is Superintendent Le Fanu. We're with the Crime Unit, and we're investigating the murder of the Rajah of Pallampur. Thank you for coming to help us."

Palmer was off balance. It was good opening with Habi. Le Fanu said nothing, but stared at Palmer who was shifting uneasily.

"We believe," Habi continued, "that you've had problems with other men, including senior civil servants, because of the undue attention you pay to their wives."

This was something not discussed with an Indian, judging by the look Habi received. Palmer appealed to Le Fanu. "You shouldn't listen to gossip, there's been a lot of misunderstanding." The voice was attractive, too. Resonant rather than deep, a breathy quality, refined accent. Le Fanu stared at him.

"It's not gossip, Mr. Palmer." Habi forced Palmer's attention back to him. "You're on record as an assault victim because of your activities with one senior lady in this city."

Palmer was becoming irritated, perhaps because of the questions but more likely because of the questioner. "Not really any of your business," he muttered, hands clasped together, white knuckles evident.

"Oh, but it is, sir, if we consider it relevant to our murder inquiry. You also have a relationship with the wife of our murder victim, so that makes you of considerable interest to us as well. Can you tell us about that relationship?"

"It's not a relationship, we're just friends."

Now fixed on Habi, Palmer did not expect to hear Le Fanu who cut in.

"I should tell you, Palmer, we've had a frank explanation from the Rani about your friendship. She was very graphic, as I'm sure you know she can be."

For a reputed Lothario, thought Le Fanu, the man became unusually embarrassed unusually fast.

"Those are, ah, well, private matters," he spluttered. "Nothing to do with you."

"Let me see," continued Le Fanu, "you're shagging the Rani the night her husband's murdered, and you think that's nothing to do with us. Seems to me there's a motive for a fight in there, as a result of which the Rajah ends up dead."

Palmer jumped up. "That's nonsense. I'd nothing to do with him. I'd never met the man, had no interest in doing so."

"You were just fucking his wife as a social service." Le Fanu was being provocative.

"Sit down, sir" Habi said, "we need to know where you were and at what time on the evening and early morning of the Rajah's death."

Palmer treated this as the voice of reason, glaring at Le Fanu who leaned back in his chair.

"The Rani arrived at my house in Saidapet just after eight. We sat around for a while, had a couple of drinks…"

"Lay around, you mean" Le Fanu said, "on top of each other. She told me about the sofa. Do you give your other women the same treatment? We know you have the house out there purely for entertainment purposes."

"None of your bloody business," Palmer screamed, "this is an outrage." He was losing control.

Habi pulled him back in. "Perhaps, sir, if you concentrate on the timeline. What time did you have dinner?"

"About nine thirty, I think."

Palmer and the Rani were consistent, thought Le Fanu, so had probably prepared their stories

"Good," Habi said smoothly, "and after that?"

"We sat around again." He scowled at le Fanu. "That would have been until midnight or so. Then we retired for the night."

"No sleep, though, eh? Bit of a goer that Rani, I think. She told me she's an enthusiastic rider. " Le Fanu watched Palmer closely.

The planter tried to contain himself but failed. "What's wrong with you?" He was in full voice. "Not getting enough yourself? Jealous? Typical bloody copper." The refined accent slipped into one Le Fanu had heard in the British other ranks. They needed deeper background on Mr. Palmer.

Habi resumed. "Times, Mr. Palmer? What time did the Rani leave? Did you leave the house at any time? Anything unusual you can remember?"

Palmer shook his head. "No, nothing at all. I was there all night. So was the Rani. No one else visited. She left, oh, I don't know, sometime after five in the morning."

That fitted the pattern. Time to change direction.

"Tell me, Mr. Palmer, "Le Fanu murmured, "why did you have your servant pawn your Webley-Wilkinson? And where did you get that revolver?"

Palmer looked startled. He was concentrating hard on the timelines and accounting for his movements. He was off guard again. "Oh, I, um, I had no further use for it."

"Really," Le Fanu said, "it's a significant weapon, hard to part with something like that. Yet you have your man sell it just a day or so after the Rajah was killed. Did you steal it from his drawer? He had one just like that."

The man was struggling now. "It was mine, I had it from the war."

"With which units did you serve? I thought you stayed here on the plantations for the duration. People like me went off and survived as best we could." He loaded his voice with as much sarcasm as he could muster.

"We did important work here. I had the revolver in case of emergency."

"Like some enraged husband turning up to beat you? That sort of emergency? Probably just easier if you kept your cock in your pants."

Palmer half rose, thought better of it, thumped back into the chair. He was edgy.

"Did you buy the revolver?" Habi asked, making Palmer change focus again. "Expensive weapon, that."

"I could afford it," Palmer shouted back.

"So you did buy it?"

"No, it was mine from the war. You're confusing me." Palmer was sweating, damp spreading in the armpits of his jacket.

"No," Le Fanu said, "I think you stole it from the Rajah, after you murdered him."

"That's just not true! I didn't kill him. And I didn't steal the revolver."

Le Fanu paused, and Habi came back in.

"Perhaps the Rajah brought it with him when he came to your house after leaving the Governor's reception."

Le Fanu looked at Habi, wondering why he had not thought of that himself.

Palmer was rattled now. "He was never at my place."

"I think he was, Mr. Palmer." Habi was calm, cool. "He came out there, the Rani was upstairs with you, so you went down to confront him. He had the revolver. You plied him with drink to calm him down, and it all got out of control."

"That's not how it was," screamed Palmer. "Yes, he did come out, around midnight, just after the Rani and I went upstairs. He already had a few drinks aboard."

While marvelling at Habi's genius Le Fanu was also calculating where else the Rajah might have been. If he arrived at Palmer's at midnight, there was still a gap after he left the Governor's.

Habi prompted the planter. "Very good, Mr. Palmer, now we're getting somewhere. What happened next?"

"He was very upset, not with me, but with something that had just happened. He wanted to talk to Charlotte."

"What happened to him?" Le Fanu asked.

"From what I could make out, he'd left the Governor's and was somewhere off Mount Road when another car forced his driver off the road. Three men dragged him out and took him away in the other car."

"What did they want?" Habi asked.

"He wouldn't say," Palmer replied, calming now. "I asked him. But they forced him to drink a lot of whisky. A clumsy attempt to make him talk, I suppose. He was very shaken."

"Did he have the revolver?"

"Yes." Palmer was uncomfortable. It must have been in the Rajah's car.

"And he left it when he went away?"

"Yes."

Le Fanu changed direction again. "Why did the Rani not talk to him?"

"She was frightened, and didn't want to hear about what had happened. He'd received threatening letters, was cutting her allowances, and was being difficult. This was too much for her. She was very unhappy. That's why she spent time with me."

"So you let him go off," Habi interjected, "and leave his revolver behind?"

"Yes."

"So tell me, Mr. Palmer, why didn't you give us all this information after his murder?"

"Because of the Rani," came the hesitant reply. "She wanted to keep us away from the investigation."

"That's why you left for the Nilgiris, then?" Le Fanu doubted they were getting the full story.

"Yes. I wanted to get away. She thought she could brazen it out." By being provocative, Le Fanu thought.

"But the real thing is, the Rajah was alive when he left my house, and still had his sword."

Habi looked at le Fanu, then asked "why is that so important, Mr. Palmer?"

"Because that's what killed him, not the revolver."

Le Fanu waited several seconds. "We never made that public, Mr. Palmer, so I'm curious as to how you know."

"It's common knowledge," Palmer screamed. "Everyone in Madras knows that, and Charlotte told me as well."

That last point was plausible, but there was still something odd here.

"Mr. Palmer," Le Fanu began.

"No more," Palmer said, standing abruptly. "No more until I have a lawyer present. This has gone too far."

"Very well," Habi said, "you'll have to stay here while we arrange that. Do you have a lawyer?"

"Yes, I do. Someone will need to contact her." He named the only European woman lawyer in the city. Probably another beneficiary of Palmer's skills, thought Le Fanu, now in uncharitable mood.

They left him there with coffee, and retreated upstairs.

"Habi, perhaps I should nominate you to run Special Branch. You are brilliant. That was a masterstroke to ask him about the revolver. It opened him right up."

"Thank you, sir. But not Special Branch, please, not while it's still controlled by the Jockey. That would be a terrible reward."

"Point made. But do you think Palmer killed the Rajah? I've always dismissed that possibility but now I'm not so sure."

"I've nothing concrete, sir, but he's probably too weak to be a killer. Or at least to kill someone the way the Rajah was butchered. It takes a very tough person to do that to another human being. At best I can see Palmer pulling a trigger in a rage, but I can't see him carving someone up and getting soaked in blood."

"That's a good assessment, Habi, but it puts us back where we were."

"Sorry, sir. I said I didn't think he did it, sir. I didn't say I thought he knew nothing. He's asked for a lawyer. He has more to tell. I'm just not sure what that might be."

Thirty-eight

Palmer's lawyer was unavailable until mid-afternoon, so Le Fanu and Habi went to the hospital to find Caldicott better physically but still subdued.

"Good afternoon, sir, Habi, thanks for coming over."

"The niceties can go, Jackson, the three of us went through the battle together so no rank here," Le Fanu responded. "Habi and I are concerned about you. What's the latest news?"

"The CMO's had another look, and thinks he should operate. There's internal damage he wants to look at before doing anything else."

"He's very good." Habi said. "He operated on one of my friend's employers for a broken leg and it went very well. The man's still out in the field, not stuck behind a desk."

"Good to know, Habi, thanks." Caldicott looked unconvinced. "How are we going on our case?"

Le Fanu and Habi recounted the morning's events and news from the previous evening.

"So," Caldicott said, "are we looking more at Palmer, or are we still none the wiser about who killed the Rajah?"

"We need to do this afternoon's interview before answering that properly," Habi said, "but we're not convinced it's Palmer. But we're not sure who else it might be, either. The Changarore gang didn't want him dead, and neither did Palmer or the Rani."

Le Fanu resumed. "We'll talk more to Westshire this evening, but he's not the killer, either, even if he was caught up in the Rajah's predicament. We've more work to do yet."

"Sorry I'm stuck in here, LF. I'd say I can help but when the painkillers wear off I can't concentrate." He'd not had a good morning. "And going back to the chummery wouldn't be a comfort, either."

"We have to get you better digs," Le Fanu responded. "Habi, get your spies out and see if there's anything around the city that might work for Jackson."

"I'll get right onto that."

Habi and Le Fanu left soon after.

"Sir, he doesn't look too good. I do hope he comes back to us."

"So do I, Habi, but this has shaken him. I'll leave it a day or so. It's more than the elbow. I saw this a lot in the war. He's injured, but knows it could have been much worse. And he's feeling guilty that he's alive while some of our men are not. That's tough to deal with."

He sent Habi home for lunch. They would meet back at headquarters when Palmer's lawyer became available. Le Fanu thought about going to the D'Angelis but he knew he should go back to the office.

Once there, though, he became distracted so went to brief Jepson again to fill in time. The I-G's office door was wide-open, gatekeeper gone. Le Fanu looked in. Jepson was in his chair, staring out the window, half his normal blustering self.

Le Fanu knocked on the open door. "Sir?"

"Le Fanu. Come in, please." Jepson spun his chair, pulled up to the desk, motioned Le Fanu to sit.

"Sir, how is Mrs. Jepson?"

"She sailed this morning, Le Fanu. Down to Colombo to connect for Southampton. Not sure when she'll be back, or even if she'll be back. She's quite ill." If there was a scourge left for the British in India, it was illness in many forms.

"I'm sorry to hear that but I'm sure she'll recover."

"Thank you, Le Fanu, I hope so."

Le Fanu imagined that it was Ro, and found himself sympathising with Jepson. He also thought about the hard and unacknowledged life most Raj women had in India. Mrs. Jepson had good care in Madras, at least. That was not so for wives and daughters living up country. Out there they faced loneliness, sickness, hardship and challenge. They had little support even though they were as much a part of the British enterprise as their men.

"Sir, I have a little more to report."

He told Jepson about the Palmer interview and the Rani's admissions. Jepson seemed not to care. "Good, Le Fanu, good. Keep it up. I'm sure you'll get to the bottom of it soon."

"Sir, should you be here? You've a lot to think about. Would you be better at home?"

"Le Fanu, I suspect you know the answer to that better than me. It's odd, suddenly being alone. Home doesn't feel like home. Being around the job provides familiarity, even though it's hard to focus on the tasks."

And then there are pressures applied by the Governor and the Chief Secretary, Le Fanu remembered. The bullyboy was getting his own back but, somehow, Le Fanu drew no comfort. Perhaps Ro gave him a more balanced outlook. Before she arrived, he could not imagine feeling sorry for Jepson.

There was too much going on in his head. It was another warm but not hot day, for Madras, so he left by the front gate, overlooked by Jepson's office, crossed the road and onto the sand. The beach was wide so it was a fair walk to the surf. Away to his right several small, open fishing boats were drawn up high on the sands. Fishermen and their families were sleeping in the shade of sheets stretched between the vessels. A few kids were playing.

Other families lived on the beach, too. Most stayed up

towards the road, hoarding a few possessions and eking out a living. The police building was to the south of the main beach area, so most beach inhabitants drifted north later in the day to beg money or sell a few items to their slightly better off countrymen. It was so different from what he dealt with in the imposing white building two hundred yards and light years away from this daily struggle.

That separation was confirmed by the stares he got from those already on the beach. They rarely saw someone like him here, this was "their" world. A few would be regulars at the now daily beach demonstrations. For most of these people a European was a concept rather than a reality. Most Indians still did not meet or interact with a European. They just knew the Europeans were there and ran the country. The British bureaucratic presence was strong but its cultural one tenuous.

It was time to return. He crossed the sands to the road edge. The odd thing was that many Europeans in passing vehicles looked at him as strangely as the poor Indians down by the water. An Englishman walking here was not the done thing. These were the people who looked down on Ro, and one of their wives made that dreadful telephone call.

He crossed the road, walked through the gate and back into the building, his world. Habi was in the office, preparing for another session with Palmer and the lawyer.

"How was lunch, Habi?

"As good as ever, sir. I see you didn't bother. Enjoy the sea air?"

"It helped."

Back down in the interview room Palmer looked dishevelled. His lawyer was small, slim, serious. Thick-rimmed glasses dominated a small face surrounded by black hair cut in a bob. A grey jacket over a white blouse matched grey trousers and black flat shoes.

"Superintendent Le Fanu. I'm Felicity Wilson. I represent Mr. Palmer, and we've already had a chat so we can start when you're ready."

Le Fanu introduced Habi who began the questions again. It had worked last time.

"Mr. Palmer. When we spoke last you admitted seeing the Rajah at your house the night he died, and keeping his revolver after he left. You say he reached your house around midnight or just after, and that he then left about one. You say you did not follow him and did not kill him. Do you stand by those statements?"

"Yes, I did not kill him."

"How did he travel to and from your house?" Le Fanu asked.

"Should my client know that?" the lawyer returned.

"Most likely," Habi said, "either by direct observation or from servants' reports."

"He travelled in his car," Palmer said, "with his driver. It was a large black vehicle."

"Where was the Rani?" Le Fanu asked.

"Relevance?" the lawyer commented.

"Obvious," Le Fanu retorted.

"She remained upstairs," Palmer said, oblivious to the exchanges. He looked beaten. "She did not want to see him, and I wanted to keep her safe. She was frightened. I had to keep him downstairs."

"Did you fight?" Habi was consulting his list of questions.

"No. As I said he'd had alcohol, was tired, and didn't look well."

"Did anyone follow him when he left?" Habi continued.

Palmer was startled. "Ah, followed him? How do you mean? Why would I follow him?"

Le Fanu was suddenly more alert. "Mr. Palmer, did your servant follow the Rajah? Did you give the servant your driver and car?"

Palmer looked at his lawyer, for the first time, Le Fanu noticed.

"Simple question, Mr. Palmer" Habi pressed.

The lawyer tried to deflect the question. "Even if he did, how is that relevant?"

"Really, Miss Wilkins, that's obvious. You're giving your client time to think. Mr. Palmer, could you answer the question, please."

"I, ah, do I have to?" He looked at his lawyer.

She nodded.

"Well, perhaps I did."

"Why?" Habi and Le Fanu asked simultaneously.

"I wanted to be sure he got home."

"Did he still have his sword?" Habi asked.

"I think so."

"You just wanted to see he got home, when he had a car and driver?" Le Fanu was sceptical.

"I didn't want him upsetting Charlotte anymore."

"She told me he was not upsetting her. She was bored which is why she turned to you for your special services." Le Fanu was scathing.

"Superintendent, please keep this professional." The lawyer looked less confident.

"It's personal as well as professional in this case," Habi said. "This man slept with the Rajah's wife, as he slept with many other wives. He didn't want the arrangement upset. He probably anticipated a financial benefit from the Rani, and was angry when it turned out her husband had money problems. There's a motive for murder, especially after the Rajah turns up at his house looking for the Rani."

Habi had pushed the right button again.

"That's not how it was!" Palmer shouted. The lawyer tried to stop him speaking but Palmer was in full flight. "I was annoyed he turned up, talking nonsense. He knew Charlotte came to see me. He should have stayed away. But no, he comes to my house complaining about his money problems."

"Why was that upsetting? It wasn't your problem," Le

Fanu asked.

"Because it upset Charlotte, and that upset me."

"Are you trying to say," Le Fanu continued, "that you care for the Rani? Given your record that's hard to believe."

"Superintendent," the lawyer interrupted, "your personal opinion is irrelevant here."

"It's relevant if this is part of his defence."

Palmer had not heard them. "It's true. I did really like her. And I hadn't expected that."

"Why send your servant after him?" Habi asked.

"To see he left and stopped worrying Charlotte, but I wish I hadn't."

"Why?

"Because he misinterpreted what I said in Tamil. I said make sure the Rajah got home. He thought I said take care of him."

Silence. The lawyer looked at her client, surprised.

"Does that mean," Habi said, "that your servant killed Pallampur?"

"Yes. When he came back and told me, I couldn't believe it. Because I took him in after his jail term, he would do anything to protect me. He thought the Rajah had upset me so he lost his temper. He lost control, really. That's why the Rajah was so, so terribly injured."

"Why not send your man away?" Le Fanu asked.

"I thought it would look too obvious."

"Where's the sword, then?"

"Down at the plantation."

"Why risk selling the gun?"

Palmer was leaning over the desk, drained. "I was going to give the servant all the money, so he could go away and start again somewhere."

"Even though he had committed murder." Le Fanu looked at the roof.

"He'll be charged with murder," Habi intervened. "And

you'll be charged as an accessory, at the least."

"One thing" Le Fanu asked, "does the Rani know?"

"No."

She might not react well to that news.

They finished the interview, Palmer was returned to the cells awaiting a formal charge, and his lawyer left.

Le Fanu and Habi shook hands. They were almost there.

Thirty-nine

James Westshire had travelled down from Ramsheed overnight, and looked more cheerful than last time.

"Westshire, thanks for coming, you're in better shape."

"Yes, things have clarified. Marjorie's happier. Some people in London explained things to her father and that made everything easier."

"Well, it looks better for you here as well. But we need to know exactly what happened in Ramsheed, and why you kept quiet. We know a lot more than we did, but it will help if you give us the full story."

Westshire's account was simple enough. The mineral sands company story was part of the much bigger one. Keen to improve the district's prospects, Westshire latched onto the first person who offered assistance. That was the Green Gang's local representative, but Westshire took two years to discover that. Until then, he thought the man a simple benefactor even though little development occurred. The Collector put that down to normal delays.

The local gang was so slick that Westshire remained unaware of the trade in girls in his district for some time. The District Super knew nothing, either. Special Branch performed badly on all counts. Whitney and the Governor had to repair that damage. It was a serious failure that ruined many Indian lives and even cost some. He remembered the young women enslaved in Hong Kong.

Westshire reproached himself for that failure, too. "I found out by chance. Couldn't believe what I heard. A man came to me with what I thought a wild story about his daughter having disappeared and someone else reporting she'd been shipped overseas. I thought it was a cover story for another runaway headed for Bombay or somewhere."

"How did you find out more?" Habi asked.

"I mentioned the story to someone at our club up there, a Frenchman who trades grain with China. He'd heard a rumour in some villages he dealt with about girls being taken across the water. I asked my so-called benefactor if he'd heard anything. That's when things became really difficult."

The local gang leader threatened Westshire. If the Collector approached Madras authorities, his family would be attacked. If he contacted London, they would be killed. The company papers were still in his name, and the gang threatened to make that public. His career was in jeopardy. Westshire had to keep quiet. To underline the point, the gang leader leaked the company information to the Board in Madras through a corrupt clerk. That saw Westshire hauled before Jamieson. It was a demonstration for Westshire of how bad things would be if he did not cooperate.

"Do you know," Le Fanu asked, "who wrote the internal report that Jamieson was so happy to use?"

"I do now. It was a friend of that junior in my office who passed on all the information initially. The friend works at the Board. They were in the same ICS intake and shared a house in Madras for a couple of years. The usual ICS politics."

"How much did you know about the gang itself, aside from this leader?" Habi asked.

"Very little, I dealt only with him. He said the gang was a large and ruthless one that came mainly from professional criminal elements in Bihar, recruited directly by the Green Gang. I hadn't heard of the Green Gang before this began."

"What did this leader look like?" Le Fanu asked.

Westshire gave a description.

"Sir," Habi said, "I think that fellow was among the dead. I'll check at the morgue." He picked up his papers and left.

"Westshire," Le Fanu continued, "did you ever think the Rajah of Pallampur was involved?"

"A couple of times. I'd met him because his estates were nearby, as you know, and I also met his people. I happened to see one of them talking to the gang leader in a coffee shop one day. A few months later, that same man came out of a bank carrying a satchel. He went straight to the same coffee shop where the gang leader was waiting. I put two and two together."

"The Rajah was a willing collaborator?"

"I doubt it. He was a good man, even if some Madras civilians thought he was a traitor for supporting Congress. He was a landlord, yes, but so are we. Like me, he wanted to improve things for his people, and thought Congress offered a chance to do what he couldn't see us providing. He was also like me because he was trapped into dealing with those people."

There was the problem, Le Fanu thought, too little too late from the British side. People like Jamieson spent too much time hounding subordinates like Westshire, and too little making things better for Indians.

"I assumed his murder was the result of his involvement with those criminals," Westshire continued. "There were times it seemed desperate measures were needed to break away from the gang. I thought the Rajah might actually have tried to resist and been killed as a result."

"So did we for a long time. Until today, in fact."

Le Fanu explained what had happened. "If we'd had the information we've only just received from Palmer and the Rani earlier, the gang and the trading in women might not have come to light for a long time yet, if at all."

Le Fanu reflected on what they now knew. The Rajah had been killed by a servant who thought he did what Palmer wanted. There was another communication failure in British India. Palmer was upset because he could see the cosy arrangement ending just as he realised Charlotte Lacey meant much more to him than he had intended. And the Rani was only with Palmer because her husband's money problems made him preoccupied. This tragedy, as usual, was the result of human failures. Le Fanu realised how fortunate he was to be back with Ro.

The gang connection and the trade in women might have gone undiscovered had the servant not murdered the Rajah. The secret services in Britain and in Delhi might have known, but Madras would never have become involved. Suffering out in those villages would have continued as more girls disappeared.

Without the connections provided by Caldicott and Barnes, he and Habi would have struggled to get information from London. Spies would have roamed Madras and Delhi unhindered. The Madras government would have remained wonderfully uninformed. Jamieson would have sacked Westshire. Taylor would have been left undisturbed having paid minor fines. Habi and Le Fanu would have laid a simple murder charge against the servant and not uncovered this international criminal conspiracy.

It was time to talk to Whitney. Le Fanu farewelled Westshire who announced he was being promoted to one of the wealthier Telugu districts. Whitney engineered that with a now in retreat Jamieson whose own reputation was damaged.

"I'm very pleased to hear that, Westshire, but do try to stay out of trouble."

"Perhaps you should take your own advice?" Westshire smiled back. "Your professional career is as challenged as mine. And I hear your personal life is interesting. Best of luck."

"Thank you. Perhaps we should keep in touch to compare notes?"

"Agreed."

Westshire was going to the Secretariat, so Le Fanu took him in the car. Along the way they discussed the case briefly, but the political prospects more. There were more demonstrations down on the sands, and the nationalist signs were back up on the college walls. They agreed that policies must change or the British exit from India would come sooner than anticipated, even if the diehards still thought that exit would never happen.

They passed through the checkpoints at Fort St George. There were now three to get in, and Le Fanu noticed there was even one to negotiate on the way back out. Security had strengthened since his last visit. Siege mentality was on the rise.

Sir Charles Whitney was waiting, immaculate as ever and surrounded by blue smoke.

"Chris, you've done it again. His Excellency wants to see you tomorrow and say thank you personally. He now knows much more than he did a few days ago, and is grateful. Delhi won't thank you, though, because Willingdon's now on a crusade. Come and sit down."

Whitney had organised a full meal rather than snacks, and Le Fanu realised it was again a long time since he'd eaten. He did the spread justice. Whitney joined in, eating the Indian food with his fingers, matching Le Fanu. The man became increasingly interesting.

They discussed possible ramifications of the case. Whitney thought the Rani would leave India, but that would complicate life for the Madras and Delhi governments. The estate would have to be finalised, and several authorities did not want her to benefit. Whitney thought she could not be prevented from gaining a share, but more insistent advisers reckoned she had disgraced the establishment and should suffer the consequences.

"Sir, that's ridiculous. Those energies should be devoted to dealing with the political issues pressuring us more each day. A vendetta is pointless."

"I know, Chris, but you also know what some of our people are like. Even I think we should be making concessions to Congress but Willingdon's digging in, and he has many supporters in the ranks and outside."

"Thank you for looking after Westshire, sir, he's a great district man."

Whitney lit another cigar. "Well, you would say that, Chris, wouldn't you? Birds of a feather, you two. Though he has a wife, which you don't. Time yet, I suppose?"

Le Fanu started another subject. "Sir, the more we've learned, the worse Special Branch looks. Something has to be done."

"I agree. Any ideas?"

"Sir, I'm wondering. Habi would be an excellent if controversial choice, but he doesn't want it because the post reports directly to the I-G. And I can't do it for the same and obvious reason, given past record."

"No solutions, then?"

"I have a wild thought. Caldicott's wondering what happens next for him. He's smashed up that elbow. He hasn't discussed it, but I think he's worried about his future with the unit as a result. His work on this case was excellent because he's an ex-spy himself. All the leads in London came from him and his contacts. He understands all this drama, and he's bright."

"Interesting thought, leave it with me."

They washed the last of the food down with coffee. By now it was seven.

"Getting late, Chris. Shouldn't you be getting along? You're still at the D'Angelis, I gather. Good thing, too. Don't waste the opportunity."

Le Fanu was still fathoming the Chief Secretary's words as he got into the car that then passed through the checkpoints and out onto the road. Half a dozen sari-clad and bare-footed women walked single file along the side of the road, enormous clay jars balanced on their heads. The last of the kites were hovering before roosting for the night. Street vendors were setting up, rows of kerosene lights stretched into the distance along the road and onto the beach. A brighter set of lights picked out a stage erected on the sands where a large crowd was already assembling. A local Congress leader was about to deliver a speech. Le Fanu wondered if any Special Branch officers were in the crowd. He saw police contingents gathering. They might control this immediate problem but the bigger one would remain.

The car turned towards headquarters, cut along past the cricket club and headed for the D'Angelis. As they passed the Chepauk ground, he wondered how Caldicott was faring.

Forty

Ro was waiting when he reached the hotel. He showered. They were late for dinner, again.

For this last evening he chose a restaurant along Mount Road, which they reached about eight thirty. It was an outdoor, local food venue he knew was good. He hoped, wrongly, they might relax without being noticed or approached.

Somehow, Chester Barnes had found the place as well. That was a surprise, because he knew little about local food, Krishna Rao's being his first experience. But it could have been worse. It might have been Jamieson. Well, that was unlikely, but someone like Jamieson.

Barnes greeted them. "LF, I hear you've unravelled the Pallampur murder. Is that so?"

"Yes. It was much more local, personal and accidental than we ever imagined." He gave Barnes the outline, promising more tomorrow. "Thanks to you, we stumbled on a lot more than a murder, so thank you. I'll give you as much as I can on that as well. Come and see me tomorrow afternoon."

"Thanks, LF. I'll leave you two to your evening, and go back to the office to write this story. See you tomorrow. Ro, it has been wonderful to meet you and I'm sure I'll see you again."

"Will I see him again, I wonder, Chris?" she asked, as Barnes walked away. Le Fanu hoped the answer was yes.

Their table was in the far corner of a garden. This was one of many things he liked about Madras, he realised, the chance to escape even in the heart of the city's European quarter. The food came soon after, full of the south Indian spices and flavours that now made Western food so boring for him.

They were subdued. The week had gone fast and this was the last night. He struggled for a conversation opener.

"Chris, it has been marvellous to see you again." She knew how to start the discussion. "I wasn't sure how good it would be. You were not encouraging over the past two years." He thought she was joking, but wasn't sure.

"I know and I'm sorry," he replied. "I'm especially sorry now because this week has been the best I can remember, even if I had to be off chasing criminals."

"That's what you do. You couldn't stop that for me." She was playful.

This was difficult for him. He had improved, but still found it awkward to discuss his feelings. He wished Hans Gross had written a manual on that as well as on criminology. Le Fanu would buy that.

"Ro, this week has taught me a lot, and I can say some things more easily, but not everything. I've been on my own a long time." He remembered Whitney's comment.

"Oh, I know that, Chris" she said, "I have low expectations of what you might allow yourself to say. Let me just say I've had a wonderful time, really enjoyed being with you, and if it was possible I'd love to do it again."

"Me, too, I just have to work out how to make that happen."

"We both have to, you know, if we're serious."

Le Fanu paid, and they went out to the waiting car. As they drove back the short distance to the D'Angelis, she slipped her hand into his, squeezed it.

"Something will work out, you know."

The driver pulled up at the front door where a footman

opened the door for Ro. Le Fanu went around to that side of the car, she took his arm and they walked up the steps, through the wide doors and into a crowded lobby. Several people recognised him, and called out congratulations on solving the murder. He spoke to some, but kept moving through the crowd.

A receptionist came from behind the desk, handed him a note and asked him to go to a small room off the lobby. He took Ro with him. They were led through corridors, and into a reception area outside a large oak door. The receptionist asked them to sit, knocked on the door, and left.

Sir Charles Whitney opened the door. "Good evening LF. Mrs McPhedren, I'm Sir Charles Whitney. We've not met but I've heard a lot about you. I'm delighted to welcome you here."

"Thank you very much, Sir Charles," she replied.

Le Fanu was struggling. This was the nearest thing possible to an official welcome, and for an Anglo-Indian. The world might never be the same. He doubted the Chief Secretary had come here just for that purpose, though.

"Sir Charles, thank you. Is there something else you need from me, though?"

"Of course, LF, but I could not pass up the chance to meet and welcome Mrs. McPhedren."

Ro smiled. "Sir Charles, this is an unexpected bonus for my trip to Madras. Chris has told me a lot about you, and it's all good. So it's a pleasure for me to meet you, too."

They sat at a small circular table with three chairs. A notepad and a pencil sat ready. The Chief Secretary had been there for a while. He lit up, and poured them each a glass of wine, a Riesling.

"LF, I've been thinking since you left this afternoon. You're a brilliant detective but there are some secrets we keep even from you. One is that the Inspector-General is taking leave, effective from now. You know his wife is ill and gone back? Well, before she left there was some talk he might accompany her, but that didn't happen. Now she's left, he feels he should have gone with her. So she's waiting in Colombo until he can join her, then they'll leave for England."

Le Fanu nodded. "I'm not surprised. He was despondent when I saw him last, and worried about his wife. I, well, I felt sorry for him."

"I know what you mean, and what that means. He tried to change but has not been on top of things. Which brings me to some points."

He pulled the pad towards him, switched between pages.

"Your idea about Caldicott's a good one. I discussed that with HE a couple of hours ago and he agrees. From next week, assuming he's back on deck, Caldicott will take over Special Branch and be responsible for getting it back on track. I thought you might like to tell him."

"I will, sir. He'll be shocked but pleased. And he'll do a good job for you."

"He won't be reporting to me. He'll still report to the I-G."

"But Jepson will be on leave."

"There'll obviously be an acting I-G. HE and I have discussed that, too, and we hope you'll take the post."

"Me?"

"Don't be disingenuous, Chris, you're the obvious choice and everyone knows that. There's no knowing when or if Jepson will return, and we need a strong person in there now, this is a critical time for us."

"You know I don't like the policies we're using at present?"

"Willingdon and I are prepared for that. We know there'll be tough exchanges, most of which we'll lose. We need this to work, Chris. I'm not sure even you know just how precarious things are currently."

"Sir, I'm really flattered, but what about the Unit?"

"We've thought about that. You'll be busy, but we thought

you might keep an active supervisory role, still be unit commander, as it were. But the day-to-day working would be handled by Habi as an Acting Head at Assistant Super level. We know he's good enough. It will upset a few people but we're prepared for that."

"That's a brilliant idea, sir. He'll be delighted, and very good. He deserves the chance and the promotion."

"Right, glad you agree. I'll be off, just wanted you to have all that but I've taken up too much of your time. Good night, LF, Mrs. McPhedren, again, delightful to meet you."

He left and they sat there, silent for a while.

"Chris, that's wonderful."

He took her hand, found some stairs nearby and went to her room. They slept, eventually.

The light flickered into the room around six in the morning. Her train left in three hours. She got up, showered, dressed, and began packing. Le Fanu showered and dressed. By then her bags were packed and breakfast delivered, bacon and eggs with coffee. She was seated, waiting for him to come and eat.

He stayed standing. "Ro, this is probably not the best place and my timing's poor, as always, but I think we should get married."

If you enjoyed reading **The Pallampur Predicament** why not check out **A Madras Miasma**, the first Superintendent Le Fanu Mystery, also published by Crime Wave Press.

A Madras Miasma – Brian Stoddart

Madras in the 1920s. The British are slowly losing the grip on the subcontinent. The end of the colonial enterprise is in sight and the city on India's east coast is teeming with intrigue. A grisly murder takes place against the backdrop of political tension and Superintendent Le Fanu, a man of impeccable investigative methods, is called in to find out who killed a respectable young British girl and dumped her in a canal, her veins clogged with morphine.

As Le Fanu, a man forced to keep his own personal relationship a secret for fear of scandal in the face British moral standards, begins to investigate, he quickly slips into a quagmire of Raj politics, rebellion and nefarious criminal activities that threaten not just to bury his case but the fearless detective himself.

The first Superintendent Le Fanu Adventure, A Madras Miasma, tells a classic tale of murder, corruption and intrigue with a sharp eye on British colonial politics and race relations. It is a story that, like its main protagonist, has its heart firmly in the right place.

Brian Stoddart is a writer, academic, blogger and commentator with forty years experience of Asia. He grew up in New Zealand, completed a PhD in Australia in the history of modern India, became a senior university executive in Australia and has lived and worked in India, Malaysia, Cambodia, Lao PDR, China, Indonesia and elsewhere. Brian Stoddart is also an acknowledged international authority on sport and culture, being a frequent keynote speaker at international conferences on issues like the governance and politics of Asian and other sport. In addition to working on aid and development projects dealing with higher education reform, he also lectures on passenger cruise ships. He has written or co-authored sixteen non-fiction works. His A House in Damascus: Before the Fall won gold and silver recognition at the 2012 eBook Lit Awards. The Pallampur Predicament is the second book in the Superintendent Le Fanu Mystery series . Dividing his time between Australia, New Zealand and elsewhere he reads crime fiction avidly, watches international affairs and sport, and collects Asian antiques.

Word-of-mouth is essential for any author to succeed.
If you enjoyed The Pallampur Predicament, please consider leaving a review on Amazon.
Even a couple of lines would make a difference and would be extremely appreciated.

Acknowledgements

Great thanks go first to Tom Vater and Hans Kemp of Crime Wave Press who have done such a wonderful job in producing this, the second Le Fanu. I owe them even more for having taken on A Madras Miasma, the first in the series when, these days, publication gets tougher. Their professionalism and enthusiasm have been encouraging and I enjoy working with them.

I owe even more to Madras, now known as Chennai, and its residents. After all these years I still enjoy and learn from the city. It is much changed from when I saw it, but much also remains.

Chennai has a wonderful heritage movement that produces excellent material. The indefatigable S. Muthiah has produced several works on the city that are "must" reads, while Sriram V's marvellous blog, "Madras Heritage and Carnatic Music" is a gold mine.

Some writer friends have given me great encouragement which I appreciate very much so thank you: Jeff Siger, Ruth Downie, Annemaria Alfieri, Quentin Bates, Tim Parks, Rob Darke, Stav Sherez, Helen Fitzgerald are among them.

While the Le Fanu novels are the work of fiction, it will be obvious that I have drawn on a deep background of study into south India and India more generally. All the work in the Tamil Nadu and other archives, all the reading of The Hindu and other newspapers, and all the discussions with other students of the subcontinent have had an influence here. There are a large number of those students who have helped in some way, whether they know it or not, but I won't list them all here. I do thank them all, though, warmly.

Some of the characters are historical ones, like Lord Willingdon, and like Arthur Galletti whose extraordinary life I attempted to capture in my biography of him, A People's Collector in the British Raj: Arthur Galletti. Some other characters have a basis in fact, but I have taken fictional license to better tell the contours of the stories.

A great number of friends have given me encouragement, people like Ruth Dunkin, Alan Cumming, Eva-Marie Nag, Lyndall Crisp, Simon Fraser, Mike and Marian Rose, Suvam Pal, Amitabh Mattoo, Sharmistha Guptoo, Boria Majumdar among others.

But none of this, or anything else I have been able to do could have happened without the love and support of Sandi, Kirsteen (Kitt) and Laura, because they have been enthusiastic supporters of every new career on which I have embarked in recent years. This is just another one, and their encouragement has made it possible.

49408114R00169

Made in the USA
Lexington, KY
04 February 2016